"How ... me alive ... ainst this guy?

Susan caught Mac's gaze and held it, whether he liked it or not. The last time she'd asked Mac a Big Question, he'd dodged it.

Her life rested again on his answer to her question. Did she dare trust him to be square with her this time?

Mac answered quietly. "We plan to guard you around the clock, not only until you testify, but until Ruala's captured, brought to trial and locked up for good."

His sapphire gaze bored into hers. Challenging her to believe him. But something else lurked in his intense expression. A promise—to keep her safe this time. An appeal—to give him another chance, to let him make up for Ruala outmaneuvering and outgunning him and nearly killing her last time. A plea—to trust him.

Could she do that? She'd trusted him once with her heart and he'd destroyed it. Could she trust Mac Conlon with her life this time around? She sighed in resignation. What choice did she have?

Dear Reader,

The weather's hot, and so are all six of this month's Silhouette Intimate Moments books. We have a real focus on miniseries this time around, starting with the last in Ruth Langan's DEVIL'S COVE quartet, *Retribution*. Mix a hero looking to heal his battered soul, a heroine who gives him a reason to smile again and a whole lot of danger, and you've got a recipe for irresistible reading.

Linda Turner's back—after *way* too long—with the first of her new miniseries, TURNING POINTS. A beautiful photographer who caught the wrong person in her lens has no choice but to ask the cops—make that *one particular cop*—for help, and now both her life and her heart are in danger of being lost. FAMILY SECRETS: THE NEXT GENERATION continues with Marie Ferrarella's *Immovable Objects,* featuring a heroine who walks the line between legal, illegal—and love. *Dangerous Deception* from Kylie Brant continues THE TREMAINE TRADITION of mixing suspense and romance—not to mention sensuality— in doses no reader will want to resist. And don't miss our stand-alone titles, either. Cindy Dees introduces you to *A Gentleman and A Soldier* in a military reunion romance that will have your heart pounding and your fingers turning the pages as fast as they can. Finally, welcome Mary Buckham, whose debut novel, *The Makeover Mission,* takes a plain Jane and turns her into a princess—literally. Problem is, this princess is in danger, and now so is Jane.

Enjoy them all—and come back next month for the best in romantic excitement, only from Silhouette Intimate Moments.

Yours,

Leslie J. Wainger
Executive Editor

Please address questions and book requests to:
Silhouette Reader Service
U.S.: 3010 Walden Ave., P.O. Box 1325, Buffalo, NY 14269
Canadian: P.O. Box 609, Fort Erie, Ont. L2A 5X3

A Gentleman and a Soldier

CINDY DEES

Silhouette®

INTIMATE MOMENTS™

Published by Silhouette Books

America's Publisher of Contemporary Romance

SILHOUETTE BOOKS

ISBN 0-373-27377-0

A GENTLEMAN AND A SOLDIER

Copyright © 2004 by Cynthia Dees

This edition published by arrangement with Harlequin Books S.A.

® and TM are trademarks of Harlequin Books S.A., used under license.
Trademarks indicated with ® are registered in the United States Patent
and Trademark Office, the Canadian Trade Marks Office and in other
countries.

Visit Silhouette Books at www.eHarlequin.com

Printed in U.S.A.

Books by Cindy Dees

Silhouette Intimate Moments

Behind Enemy Lines #1176
Line of Fire #1253
A Gentleman and a Soldier #1307

CINDY DEES

started flying airplanes, sitting in her dad's lap, when she was three, and she was the only kid in the neighborhood who got a pilot's license before she got a driver's license. After college, she fulfilled a lifelong dream and became a U.S. Air Force pilot. She flew everything from supersonic jets to C-5's, the world's largest cargo airplane. During her career, she got shot at, met her husband, flew in the Gulf War and amassed a lifetime supply of war stories. After she left flying to have a family, she was lucky enough to fulfill another lifelong dream—writing a book. Little did she imagine that it would win the RWA Golden Heart Contest and sell to Silhouette! She's thrilled to be able to share her dream with you. She'd love to hear what you think of her books. Write to her at www.cindydees.com or P.O. Box 210, Azle, TX 76098.

My warmest thanks to Lance Corporal Bryan Brady, 1st Combat Engineer Battalion, 1st Marine Division, United States Marine Corps, for his extensive and scary expertise in how to blow up absolutely anything. I rest easier knowing brave men and women like you keep watch over our country.

Chapter 1

Sonofa—

Mac Conlon slammed the wedding invitation down on his kitchen table in disgust. *Another* one of his bachelor buddies biting the dust. What in the hell had happened to Charlie Squad's long-standing death-before-marriage pact?

First Colonel Folly, and now Tex. What were they thinking? It wasn't like there was anything only a diamond ring could get from a woman. The proper amount of charm, properly applied, always yielded the same results. And without the life sentence to follow.

The invitation's fancy engraving leered up at him. "Captain Tex Monroe and Congresswoman Kimberly Stanton request the honor of your presence when they join in wedded matrimony…"

He swore under his breath. And caught sight of the liquor cabinet in the corner. *Aww, what the hell.* It wasn't every day a guy had to miss his best friend's wedding on account of a woman. He fished out a dusty bottle of whiskey and flopped in his leather recliner in front of the TV. The hell of it was that he actually wanted to go to the damn wedding.

But *Susan* would be there. Memories of her auburn hair, porcelain skin and laughing hazel eyes swirled around him. He could see them as if it was only yesterday that she'd gazed up at him while he'd lain with her in a room filled with candles. Her eyes were dark with passion that night. But after he'd dropped his bomb on her, he'd seen those eyes snap in outrage. Then fill with tears. Always those damned tears. His gut twisted.

No way would Tex's only sister miss her baby brother's wedding. And no way could he face the only woman he'd ever loved. Not after…

Damn. He chugged a fiery slug of forgetfulness straight from the whiskey bottle. He aimed the remote at the TV and flipped through the channels until he found a John Wayne flick. The Duke and Jack Daniel's would have to do for companionship tonight, since he made it a policy never to get stinking drunk alone. And he was about to tie on a big one.

Susan Monroe looked through the bulletproof window in front of her at the brightly lit concrete bunker on the other side. Empty. She announced crisply into her headset. "Test range is clear."

The firing range supervisor droned through several more checklist items.

Her turn again. She glanced down the list of testing parameters on her computer screen. An unbroken column of green. "Monitoring systems nominal," she announced.

A few more items and the checklist was complete. Her team was ready for the first live fire test of the RITA rifle. She exhaled a long, slow breath, but it didn't relieve her jitters. Her job, and a lot of other people's jobs, rode on the next hour's worth of work.

Building the highly classified sniper rifle was Fasco Inc.'s first government contract, and there'd been problems from day one. The company had to learn how to wade through stacks of government reports and forms. Their bid had been tightly budgeted, and they'd had trouble sticking to it. Fasco's promised production schedule had been a killer, too, and everyone in the company had worked long, hard hours to bring the weapon on line in time.

And today the rifle known as RITA, after its Roving Instant Target Acquisition system, was going to face its most critical test. In a few minutes a professional sniper would step onto the firing range and put Fasco's prototype production model through its paces.

If the sniper gave the go-ahead, her company would spend the next couple of years turning out dozens of the sophisticated rifles at a tidy profit. But if the sniper decided the weapon didn't perform up to Uncle Sam's specifications, Fasco risked losing the contract. There'd be massive red ink and layoffs at best, and at worst Fasco would go out of business altogether. *No pressure there.*

The range supervisor's voice sounded in her ear. "Send them in, Dr. Monroe."

She picked up the telephone on her desk and pushed the button that connected her to the armory vestibule just outside the firing range. Fasco's CEO picked up on the other end.

"We're ready to begin," she told her boss much more calmly than she felt.

A red light went on above the door in the firing range's far wall. The thick steel portal swung open. Several men stepped into the room. She recognized them as senior Fasco executives. All sucking up hard to the sniper, no doubt. Not that she blamed them.

And then she caught sight of the shooter. He was tall. A bit heavy. Light-brown hair. Prominent cheekbones in an otherwise smooth, round face. Kinda creepy looking. So bland her gaze just seemed to slide off him. He looked too soft to be holding the sixty-pound RITA rifle and, in fact, he rested it on its butt quickly after he stepped into the room.

She announced over the loudspeaker into the bunker, "We're ready whenever you are, Mr. Ford."

The shooter glanced up at her window and nodded.

And the world stood still.

Ohmigod. Those eyes!

She would never forget them as long as she lived. Glittering gold on blue over the barrel of his rifle. Just before he shot her in the knee and blew it to smithereens. She'd fallen out of her seat from the tearing force of the impact, which was the only reason his second shot only grazed her neck and didn't kill her.

Except this face wasn't right. Not angular or narrow enough for the man who'd shot her. And the hair wasn't black. This man's skin was too pale, not the nut brown of Ramon Ruala, the assassin who'd nearly killed her.

But those eyes...

How many men in the world could possibly have the same strange eye coloring, a ring of gold overlaid on icy, sky blue. The color was striking, fire and ice clashing in discord. And no two men could have exactly that same flat, deadly expression of penetrating malevolence that chilled her blood. It *had* to be the same guy.

But there was *no way* it was the same guy.

She watched in frozen horror as the man donned a clamshell headset and plastic shooting goggles someone handed him. He waved the Fasco executives out of the bunker. And hefted the rifle. Another glance up at her. She pushed her safety glasses higher on her nose as if they'd protect her identity from the killer in the room below. Dear God, let him not yank that rifle around and point it at her. The bulletproof glass before her was no match for the lethal power of the sniper rifle in his hands. Her knees shook and her gut turned to water. The same visceral terror of that night ten years ago roared through her. Every nerve in her body screamed for her to get up and run out of there right this second.

But somehow she managed to stay planted in her chair. She'd lost her mind. This was insane. Anybody could look at this poor man and see he wasn't the one who shot her a decade ago. This was some post-traumatic stress reaction that the guy's weird eye color had triggered. A flashback. Get a grip, for goodness' sake.

She stared at her computer monitor until it came back into focus and then broadcast into the bunker, "Let's start out with a few simple prone shots at a still target so you can sight in the rifle and get a feel for it."

The shooter nodded and lay down on a padded rubber mat to her left. Methodically, he set up a tripod stand, attached the barrel to the stand and lay down at a slight angle away from the weapon. He shifted to align himself with the weapon at exactly the right angle for every muscle in his body to relax when he fired.

His eye went down to the sight and his right hand came up along the trigger housing. His middle three fingers were folded down with only his thumb and pinkie finger extended. He rocked the two fingers back and forth rapidly against the side of the gun as he acquired the target downrange.

Lights exploded inside her head, sending shooting pain through her skull. She remembered like it was yesterday the way the sniper who'd shot her had done the *exact* same thing with his right hand mere seconds before he shot her.

Bang!

She about leaped out of her chair as the RITA rifle fired in the enclosed concrete bunker. Even through heavy layers of glass, the sound was painfully loud. There! He did that thing with his fingers again! He rocked his pinkie and thumb against the side of the rifle as he set up the next shot.

"Martin, come take a look at this," she said to the other computer scientist in the control room.

The former Marine Recon soldier loomed over her a second later. "What's up?" he asked.

"Watch this guy's right hand when he sets up a shot."

She and Martin watched intently. The sniper did the finger rocking thing again. "There. That!" she murmured tersely. "Is there any technical reason for a shooter to do something like that?"

"Nah. Nervous tic."

"Have you ever seen anything like it?" she inquired.

Martin frowned. "It's kinda weird, actually. You don't want to jar the rifle once you've acquired your target. The whole idea is to go perfectly still a couple seconds before you take the shot. A shooter tapping his weapon like that could jeopardize the shot if he weren't careful. Of course this dude's pegging the middle of the ten circle every time."

"Next sequence," a low, gravelly voice growled in her ear.

She jumped and looked up at the government sniper. He was staring at her impatiently through the window.

"Uh, of course. Let's start by adding wind into the calculations. We'll program a steady-state wind first, followed by random gusts," she replied. She hit the command sequence on her keyboard to start the wind machine in the bunker, and sat back while it ran.

The voice wasn't right. The man who'd ordered her death had a higher-pitched voice than that. Of course, vocal cords could be altered surgically and the sound of a voice changed. For that matter, an entire face could be changed surgically.

But those cursed eyes…

She couldn't take a chance. If it was the same guy and she didn't tell anyone of her suspicions, no telling how many people could get hurt or killed at his hands. But if it wasn't the same man—well then, she only risked pissing this guy off enough to flunk the RITA rifle and shut down her company. Lovely.

She agonized through the rain and smoke simulations, and still hadn't decided what to do when she set up the last and most difficult firing sequence. Moving targets. The RITA rifle's crowning glory was a computer brain that, once locked onto a target, tracked its movements and compensated for changes in firing conditions independent of any human inputs. The sniper started picking off moving targets like candy.

What were the odds that Ruala's showing up like this where she worked was chance? A violent criminal, whom she could put in jail permanently with her testimony? Who'd supposedly searched for her for years after their last encounter? Oh, no, he was here looking for her. Word on the street had it that Ruala's boss, crime lord Eduardo Ferrare, had personally ordered her killed. Fortunately, Ferrare's nemesis, Charlie Squad—a highly classified Air Force Special Forces team, whisked her away to a new life before Ruala or Ferrare could catch up with her. Charlie Squad. The very name sent a lingering shiver of excitement and agony through her.

She'd been working on a surveillance mission with the six-man squad when she lost her heart and nearly lost her life all those years ago. Surely her brother, Tex, a Charlie Squad member, would have told her if Ruala had picked up her trail again. Obviously the squad didn't know. No way would they have allowed the sniper to get this close to her.

The sniper's raspy voice caught her attention. "Give me random target movements."

She typed in the command sequence, her throat too tight to speak a response aloud. She had to call Charlie Squad. But the idea of inviting *him* back into her life positively set her teeth on edge. Mac Conlon. The one man she'd sworn she'd never, ever, not in a million years, lay eyes on again.

He was Charlie Squad's demolitions expert. An integral part of the team and part of the package if Charlie Squad came back into her life. Lord, she didn't want to make the call. But she had no choice.

She lurched as "Mr. Ford" abruptly jumped to his feet. He moved as light as a cat. She had to get out of here before he got another good look at her!

She snatched up her cane. Generally she didn't need it to walk, but spasms of remembered pain were shooting through her knee right now. She punched a code on the number pad beside the door to get out of the lab. The steel panel slid open. She walked forward and it shut behind her, locking her in a tiny, stainless-steel vestibule. A quick pass of her ID card through a magnetic card reader opened the outer door. Relieved to be out of that claustrophobic box, she moved out into the hallway.

The first order of business was to lay her hands on a copy of the video of Mr. Ford to show Charlie Squad. She made her way as fast as her artificial knee would go to the security office near the front of the Fasco building. A huge shape loomed directly in front of her. Her heart slammed into her throat before she recognized the giant as Shane Wilkins, head of Fasco's security. Apparently on his way out. She lurched and had to plant her cane quickly to regain her balance.

''You okay, Dr. Monroe?'' he asked, reaching out to steady her elbow.

''Not really. Got a minute?'' she asked with quiet urgency.

He looked sharply at her. Then stepped back for her to move fully inside and closed the office door behind them both. ''What's up?'' he asked.

She eyed the gray-haired man warily. He knew all about Ramon Ruala. When she applied for work at Fasco soon after the shooting, it had been conceivable that Ruala would come looking for her to finish her off. Wilkins had been alerted to keep an eye out for the guy. But as time had passed, the threat had diminished to nothing more than an unpleasant memory.

She glanced over at the bank of television monitors on the wall. ''Did you watch the test firing of the RITA rifle just now?''

He nodded. ''Looked like it went great.''

''Did you notice anything unusual about the sniper?'' she asked him cautiously.

''Mr. Ford? Good shooter. But then, a monkey would look good firing the RITA. Hell of a weapon.''

''That's not what I meant. Did he…remind you of anybody?''

Shane frowned. ''The guy in those marshmallow commercials who turns into one as he eats more and more of them?''

She grinned reluctantly. An apt analogy. ''Did you get a good look at his eyes?''

''Not on the monitor. He'd have to look right up at one of the cameras and then I'd have to zoom in to get a good look at them.''

''They're blue. With a gold ring in the middle.''

The security man frowned. And then comprehension broke across his face. ''Kinda like that Ruala fella?''

"Exactly like that Ruala fella," she answered tensely.

She took a deep breath and announced, "I think Mr. Ford is Ramon Ruala."

"That's crazy," Wilkins blurted. "They don't look anything alike. And after ten years?"

She looked the security man in the eye. "I know it is. But I'm telling you, they're the same person."

Wilkins spun in his chair and typed at light speed on his computer. The monitor directly in front of him flickered, and then video of the sniper walking into the building began to play. The security chief deftly followed Ruala's movements on video replays from the moment he entered the plant, jumping from camera to camera. And then footage of Ruala in the bunker came on the screen.

She leaned forward over Wilkins's shoulder and stabbed the monitor with her finger. "There. Watch what he does with his right hand."

Wilkins zoomed the picture in on the rifle, and Ruala's distinctive finger rocking came into focus.

"That's *exactly* what Ruala did right before he shot me," she declared.

Wilkins looked up at her. "You realize that if you're wrong about this, you could cost Fasco its contract for the RITA."

She nodded solemnly. Wilkins wasn't jumping out of his seat volunteering to go arrest Ford, and she couldn't blame him. They were talking about Fasco's survival, here. Over a hundred people's jobs. But they were also talking about her life.

Finally she broke the uncomfortable silence between them and said slowly, "Charlie Squad could tell us for sure if Ford is Ruala. I can make the inquiry unofficially. Quietly. But I'd need a copy of the video footage you've got of Ford to show the squad."

"Done," Wilkins answered in relief. He turned to his keyboard and began to type.

Ten minutes later he handed her a video cassette. She nodded her thanks to him and pushed to her feet using her cane. Her knee was killing her, but there was no earthly reason why it should be hurting like this.

"You be careful," Wilkins advised her. "If this guy is who you think he is, he's a dangerous sonaofa—'' He broke off. "Well, you know that already, don't you?"

She managed to force the corners of her mouth up into a parody of a smile. "Thanks."

Truth be told, she dreaded facing Mac Conlon almost more than Ramon Ruala. She stepped out of the security office, intent on getting to her car and thinking what in the world she was going to say to Mac if she saw him again. A group of men stepped out of a side hall directly in front of her and she looked up, startled. And stopped cold. Standing no more than five feet from her was the sniper. With several Fasco executives in tow.

His gaze went down to the videotape in her hand, then up to the placard beside the door she'd just stepped out of. And then to her face. Something flickered in that blue-gold gaze.

Terror washed over her like an icy bath. All she could do was stand there and stare back at him. Fear congealed in her throat into a sticky lump as Fasco's CEO stepped forward and gestured to her.

"This is Dr. Monroe, one of our defense systems analysts. She programmed the test firing sequence you went through today and ran it from the control booth."

The sniper nodded. "Nicely done." He held out a hand to her.

She stared down at it stupidly. She was supposed to shake hands with a man who might have tried to kill her? Fasco's CEO cleared his throat beside her. She shifted her cane to her left hand with the videotape and shot out her right hand belatedly. Awkwardly. His palm was hard. Painfully strong. Not at all in keeping with the rest of the man. She ought to say something. Congratulate him on how well he'd handled the RITA rifle. Any inane comment would do. But no matter how hard she tried, words wouldn't pass that glob of terror lodged in her throat.

Ruala disengaged his hand from hers. With a last glance down at the black plastic rectangle clutched in her hand, he stepped around her and allowed the CEO to herd him away from the geeky computer programmer with no social graces.

And then her knees started to shake like jelly. Right there in the middle of the hallway. Trembling until they were in real danger of collapsing. The walls began to close in, suffocating her. She had to get out of this place. Out of this building! A need to run away from the man behind her became so overpowering it was all she could do to walk to the front exit without breaking into a run.

Thankfully she had a spare car key on the ring of keys in her pocket that went with her computer, desk and filing cabinets at Fasco. Clutching the videotape convulsively, she paused impatiently for a retinal scan on the way out of the building. One last swipe of her magnetic ID card and she was logged out.

She all but ran outside, which was a trick with her knee threatening to lock up with every jarring step she took. The titanium and plastic joint was primarily designed with walking in mind. Light-headed with fear, she stumbled off the curb but righted herself awkwardly and lurched toward her car. Sweat beaded between her shoulder blades and rolled down her back maddeningly. Her neck tingled as if Ruala was staring right at it, choosing his shot behind her. Toying with her. Enjoying her terror. Doggedly, she headed for her car. *Please don't let him kill me. Please don't let him kill me*....

Almost there. Her light-headedness turned to outright dizziness. *Breathe, you idiot.* Passing out now would be incredibly stupid. A male voice called out her name behind her. Oh God. Not now. She looked over her shoulder and waved a hello at the biggest flirt in the whole company. He insisted on massaging her shoulders or, worse, hugging her every time he saw her, no matter how inappropriate it was. Please, not today! She just wanted to get in her car and get as far away from here as she could.

The flirt started to walk toward her. She called out something about being late for an appointment and, fumbling frantically, jammed her car key at the door lock. She missed the first time, her hands were shaking so bad. Finally a click and the door swung open. She banged her shin in her haste, but slid behind the wheel before Romeo could come over and put a half nelson on her. She locked her door for good measure.

It took three tries to get her key in the ignition, but praise the Lord, the engine turned over. Slowly, now. Carefully. It would do no good to kill herself in the process of running away from Ruala. She guided her car out of the parking lot and onto the main road. Profoundly relieved, she pointed her car toward home.

As the Fasco building grew small in her rearview mirror, she fished around in her purse and found her cell phone. Alternating looking at the road and her phone, she punched out a long series of numbers she'd memorized years ago in case of an emergency.

"Go ahead," said an anonymous male voice at the other end of the line.

"Is Colonel Folly available?" she asked.

"He's in the crisis room. Could be there for some time. If it's an emergency, I can get a message to him, though."

In his world, her dilemma probably didn't constitute a crisis. Besides, the idea was to check the sniper's identity without rocking the boat too hard. "When he gets a moment, could you ask him to call Tex Monroe's sister, Susan? Tell him I may have a problem and could use his help."

Susan jerked awake, her heart pounding like a row of Indian war drums. Silence lay heavily around her, as stifling as a thick wool blanket. She was just wired because Colonel Folly hadn't called back yet. *Come on. Call!* Her bedside clock said it was 2:00 a.m. The colonel certainly wouldn't contact her before tomorrow morning. She might as well just try to go back to sleep. Yeah, right.

Shadows wrapped around the room, clothing it in menace. She made out vague outlines of furniture, but the heavy blinds on her windows did their job well.

A scraping noise sounded. Not the slightest bit like a house squeak. It was more like…like a chair dragging across the floor. Downstairs.

Oh. My. God.

Somebody was down there. Certainty exploded across her brain. It had to be *Ramon Ruala.*

Her heart beat triple-time, racing like a jackrabbit running for its life. She looked around in the dark for a weapon. Nothing heavy and club-like in sight. Her cane was too light and whippy to do the job. What was she thinking? She couldn't attack a killer with a stick! She'd hide under her bed. Like *that* wasn't an obvious place for Ruala to check.

Call the police. She picked up the telephone on the nightstand beside her bed.

Silence.

Total silence. As in no dial tone.

Either it was the most ill-timed phone outage in history,

or the intruder had cut the line. And she was alone in the middle of five thousand acres of isolated ranch. Terror roared through her, leaving her shaking uncontrollably. She should've listened to everyone who'd told her she was crazy to live way out here by herself.

Her cell phone. It was in her purse. On the counter in her bathroom. She threw back the covers and swung her legs over the side of the bed, reaching for the ever-present cane by the nightstand and pushing herself upright. She paused, giving her bad knee a moment to adjust to bearing her weight. More than once she'd taken a spill by bounding thoughtlessly out of bed. She would think after a decade of living with her injury she'd remember it at some level of long-term memory. But her subconscious denial persisted.

She limped gingerly across her bedroom to the bathroom, easing around the spot in the floor that squeaked. She fished the cell phone out of her purse and punched out 911. An operator asked efficiently for the nature of the emergency and the address.

Susan whispered frantically, "My name's Susan Monroe. I live on the Flying M Ranch on County Line Road. There's an intruder in my house. Send the police!"

A brief pause, then, "They're on their way, ma'am. It'll take about fifteen minutes for them to get there. Do you have a bathroom with locks on its doors?"

"Yes. I'm there," Susan replied under her breath.

"Lock yourself in and sit tight."

"Got it," she replied. By the glow of the night-light by her sink, she caught a glimpse in the big mirror of the thick, ugly scar that trailed from the side of her neck down across her chest toward her heart. She still shuddered at how close she'd come to dying from that wound. The doctors said if the bullet had gone millimeters in either direction…

She felt that close to death again right now. If Ruala killed her tonight, what she knew about his new identity would die with her. She *had* to get in touch with someone before he found her! She dialed Charlie Squad headquarters for the second time that day.

"Go ahead," a male voice said in her ear.

She murmured tersely, "My name's Susan Monroe. I need to talk with Colonel Folly right away. It's an emergency this time."

"One moment, ma'am. I'll patch you through to him."

There was a squeak down the hall and she leaped to the second bathroom door that led out into the hallway. Her knee protested, sending a streak of white-hot fury up her thigh. Frantically she verified the lock was in place. And froze.

From directly on the other side of the door she heard a low rumble of Spanish. She lurched when a second male voice answered the first. Dear God. There were two men! Ruala had help. She plastered herself against the wall beside the door, too petrified to move a muscle.

A quiet slide of footsteps on carpet signaled that the men had moved on down the hallway. A distinctive creak sounded. The bedroom door at the far end of the hall. She'd bet they were going to do a room-by-room search of this floor, starting at the far end and working their way back toward the stairs. They'd discover the locked bathroom door in a few minutes, and then they'd find her.

Ruala wouldn't hesitate to kick down the door or shoot it out to get to her. He'd play hardball all the way. The 911 operator's advice to lock herself in might work with a regular robber but not with him.

She had to get out of here.

The spacious bathroom's walls closed in on her until it was no more than a tiny, airless cage. Its second-story window was too far above the ground for her to jump. It was out into the hallway and down the stairs, or else wait to be discovered. Gee, like that was a hard choice.

She heard voices in the background at the other end of the phone. A second male voice came on the line. He sounded like he'd just woken up. "This is Tom Folly. What's the problem, Susan?"

She whispered frantically, "Ramon Ruala has a new identity. I saw him today. He's going by the name David Ford and came to Fasco to test fire a rifle, but I think he was looking for me. I have videotape of him…"

Another door squeaked open. That was right next door! She had to get going. "Sorry, got to go. He's in the next room," she whispered.

The colonel barked, "Get out of there. Run away. Hide if you can't run. Don't worry about getting lost. We can track down your cell phone signal. Keep the line open…"

Those were the last words she heard as she stuffed the cell phone, still connected to Charlie Squad headquarters, in the pocket of her cotton pajamas. She pressed her ear to the door and didn't hear anything but blood rushing in her ears.

She took a deep breath, cracked open the door and peeked out into the dark hallway. It was still and silent. She could do this. Just a few steps to the stairs and then down and outside. Away from the house. Away from Ruala. To the welcome darkness of the night. Her shoulder blades tickled as imaginary bullets slammed into them, exploding her lungs and tearing out her heart.

She pushed the grisly image away, but her heart beat so hard it hurt. Something bumped next door, and she bolted out into the hallway. Of course in her panic she forgot her cane. But it wasn't as if she was going back for the stupid thing.

She moved down the hall as gracefully as her bad knee would allow. She dared not run for it. Her leg collapsed every time she tried that. She hop-skipped as quickly and quietly as she could away from Ruala and toward the front stairs.

She almost made it. But then the fringe on the hall rug caught her right big toe. She pitched forward awkwardly. Her left leg swung out in front of her to stop the fall, but her bad knee jammed. Instead of cushioning her stumble, the stiff leg became a pivot point. She spun half-around on it and then fell backward, her arms flailing. Into space.

Oh God. *The stairs.*

Chapter 2

Mac cracked one eye open infinitesimally and groaned in agony. Satan's own fires shot through his skull. To hell with sobriety. He lifted the whiskey bottle to examine its contents. Empty. Damn. Even drinking himself senseless hadn't helped. Susan Monroe's innocent, wounded eyes still haunted his dreams.

He'd gotten drunk on Jack Daniel's that night, too. After he ripped out her heart and stomped all over it and then watched her nearly die at the hands of Ferrare's personal assassin, Ramon Ruala. Now, Ferrare was a man he'd love to get his hands on. An international crime boss who dabbled in everything from stolen art to terrorism. Charlie Squad had been after the bastard for over a decade.

Mac gripped the neck of the liquor bottle convulsively. God, he'd been a fool. Why had he followed Folly's orders, anyway? His boss told him she'd be safer somewhere else. And so, like a good little toy soldier, he'd followed orders to the best of his ability and run her off.

He could've at least gone easy on her when he drove her away from the op. But no. The op was about to get messy and they needed her gone. Hell, he needed her gone. He was so head-over-heels in love with her he could hardly see straight. The thought of her in danger damn near made him freeze up. And he couldn't afford to do that when they surrounded Ferrare and took him out. He'd been beyond gung ho to follow Folly's order to drive her away that night.

Of course, he could've just told her the truth and asked her to leave for her own safety. But that had seemed too easy. Not likely to work. He'd been too damn inexperienced back then to realize that sometimes the easy way works best.

Oh no. He'd played the security game straight and told her nothing of the classified plan to ambush Ferrare. And what did she do instead of running away from him like she was supposed to? Plucky, heroic, save-the-world Susan bolted right into the middle of the damn sting. Nearly got herself killed. It was a miracle she lived through that fiasco.

He'd never forget the sight of Ramon Ruala walking right up to the driver's side window of the surveillance van she'd commandeered and looking in at Susan, then lifting that rifle and blasting at her from point-blank range. He'd never forget Susan covered in blood and moaning in pain as he pulled her out of that van. He'd lost it completely. Had to be dragged away from her himself.

He snorted in disgust. Dutiful soldier and damn fool that he was, he'd done such a good job of breaking Suzie's heart and wrecking her life that night he couldn't ever go back to her, no matter how low on his belly he crawled.

Just his luck. No more whiskey left to drown the ache in his heart. To drown himself. Thankfully, the liquor already in his system spun him away toward oblivion again.

This time. But one of these days he wasn't going to win the fight to beat it all back. God help him when he lost.

Some hours later Mac jerked awake, swearing. His skull pounded like little men with jackhammers were hard at work in there, doing their best to crack his head open. What in tarnation was that noise? Something high-pitched caterwauled incessantly in the background.

Damn! It was his cell phone. His *work* cell phone. He staggered to his feet and stumbled into the kitchen, following the source of the earsplitting noise.

"Yeah," he growled into the receiver.

"Colonel Folly, here. Get into base, ASAP. The secure briefing room. We've got a situation."

Aww, hell. He felt like death warmed over. He cleared his throat. "Right, sir. I'm on my way."

He squinted at the clock on the stove—4:30 a.m. Why did the world always have to go to hell in a hand basket in the middle of the damn night? He tipped a jar of instant coffee over his mouth and poured the dry granules down his throat. He chased it down with a quart of water and headed for the closet and a uniform.

Mac made it to Charlie Squad headquarters in under a half hour, but he was still the last to arrive. A handful of aspirin and more coffee, in liquid form this time, had knocked back his hangover to manageable proportions. But he still felt like roadkill.

His boss, Colonel Folly, nodded at him when he entered the room. "Close the door, Mac. Everybody's here, now."

Mac pushed the heavy hatch into its soundproof casing. A green light went on over the door frame, indicating the room was completely sealed and being bombarded with radio and electromagnetic waves to prevent eavesdropping.

He took a seat at the conference table beside Dutch, one of his fellow squad members. Howdy and Doc, two of the team's other members, sat across from him.

A bulky rifle lay on the long table in front of his boss. Mac recognized the weapon as the prototype of a high-tech sniper rifle Charlie Squad had acted as the sniper consultants for as it was designed.

Was Charlie Squad finally going to be allowed to take the RITA rifle and its Roving Instant Target Acquisition system into the field to try it out? Tex Monroe, Charlie Squad's absent member tonight, had gotten a chance to play around with the weapon in a South American jungle a few months back. Reported that it worked like a charm. He leaned forward intently. The adrenaline rush of picking up a new assignment hit him, and he reveled in the light, hungry feeling tingling through his gut.

Colonel Folly spoke without referring to the file sitting on the table beside the rifle. "This is classified at level Tango One, gentlemen."

The tingling in Mac's extremities became a storm of anticipation. That was the highest classification they dealt with. This mission was going to be a big one.

The colonel continued. "You know the drill. Don't reveal anything you hear in this room to anyone for any reason. No notes, no conversations among yourselves..."

Mac and the other men nodded impatiently.

Without further ado, the colonel started his briefing. "A couple hours ago, our command post received a call over one of the red phones." The colonel pushed a button on the audio-video console beside the table. "Here's part of the call."

Mac listened as a clearly terrified woman whispered into the phone. Something about the timbre of her voice rang a bell, but he couldn't put his finger on it before the tape continued. Like everyone else in the briefing room, he jolted when she murmured the name Ramon Ruala. He'd made it his personal mission to find and kill that bastard someday, but he had yet to make good on that silent promise to Susan.

He blinked when a series of heavy thuds abruptly came across the tape. It sounded like the woman had fallen down. Hard. Maybe down a flight of stairs. Then the sound of rushing footsteps and two men shouting in Spanish. The woman screamed.

Then a sharp crack of flesh on flesh. The woman cried out. Mac half rose out of his chair along with every other guy at the table. They were in a cold, violent business, but that didn't mean they listened easily to a woman getting hit.

Another slap.

Mac's fists clenched. Every protective impulse in his body screamed to do something to save this woman. He sagged in relief as the sound of police sirens became audible. A single gunshot rang out. And then footsteps pounded as if the attackers were fleeing the scene.

Colonel Folly pushed the stop button. His voice was grim. ''The woman dodged as the shot was fired and was only grazed by the bullet. Paramedics treated her at the scene. She wasn't seriously injured.''

Mac felt sick to his stomach. He could slit a guy's throat without the slightest twinge of discomfort, but listening to a woman get hit and shot at like that was almost more than he could stand. He frowned. As unpleasant as it had been, why would a house robbery and assault launch a Tango One mission? There was something familiar about that woman's whisper…. The sick feeling in his gut intensified.

The colonel spoke. ''She's convinced her assailant is Ramon Ruala, surgically altered and operating under a new identity.''

Mac frowned. He felt another even bigger bombshell coming.

On cue, the colonel dropped the other shoe. ''I've run

the name she gave me and had a preliminary forensic comparison made between photographs of this David Ford guy and Ramon Ruala. The plastic surgeon I spoke to believes they could be the same man.''

Holy sh— Mac leaned forward aggressively. "How did this woman recognize Ruala? Since when does he leave anybody alive who recognizes him? We better move fast before he comes back to her house to finish off the job. Damn, I want to get my hands on that bastard.''

Colonel Folly answered, ''I think you're the best person to talk to her. See if this lead is legit.''

"Put me on the next plane," Mac declared.

"Before you get on that plane, here's the woman you'll be speaking to.'' The colonel dimmed the lights with a switch under the edge of the table, and a picture flashed on the screen behind him.

Mac jolted as if fifty thousand volts of electricity had just shot through his chair. Bloody *hell*. Susan Monroe.

Ramon Ruala had attacked Susan again? In a flash, his blood boiled and a vein pounded in the side of his neck. Sonofa… He was going to *kill* the bastard for laying a hand on her! A surge of protectiveness raged through him. His need to keep Susan safe overrode every logical, reasonable bone in his body. He ought to beg off of this mission, ought to leave well enough alone and stay away from her. They hadn't seen each other in ten years, and he should leave it that way. But then the sound of that gunshot cracking echoed through his head. The room went red before his eyes.

Blood rages got people killed. The name of the game was to stay calm and detached. To keep your brain engaged at all costs.

The litany from his training rolled through his head, gradually forcing back the crimson haze. Not far back, but far enough for him to breathe. Far enough for him to snarl, ''Ruala's going to *pay* for touching her.''

Colonel Folly watched him intently. Sympathetically, even. He asked quietly, "And why's that?"

Mac caught the hint. The colonel wouldn't take kindly to him letting his emotions get the best of him. Might not even allow him to go help Susan if he didn't pull his stuff together in the next, oh, millisecond. He spoke with forced calm. "Besides the fact that she's Tex's sister, you know damn good and well that she and I were close." He added belatedly, "Sir."

"How do you feel about her now?" the colonel pressed.

Anger flashed through Mac. He understood why the colonel had to ask the question, but that didn't mean he had to like dredging up the answer. He shrugged with fake relaxation. "I haven't seen or spoken to her in ten years. It's ancient history." He ignored the voice in the back of his head calling him a goddamned liar.

Colonel Folly gave him a long, considering look. "History has a way of coming back to haunt you. Maybe it's time you made your peace with her."

Mac suppressed a mental snort. Haunting him? That was putting it mildly. But make peace with her? Folly didn't know what he was asking. And if he explained it to his boss, there was no way the colonel would let him work on this op. And *no way* was he getting left behind if Suzie Monroe was in trouble. Wild horses couldn't keep him away from this mission. "I can handle it. I want in on this one. I *want* Ruala."

The colonel stared at him for upward of a minute. Heavy silence stretched out between them. Maybe the colonel *did* know what he was asking. Finally Folly spoke. "I think I'd rather send Dutch to talk to Susan and watch her videotape."

Mac retorted, "Dutch wouldn't know Ruala if the bastard punched him in the nose."

It was an exaggeration, of course. Every member of the

team had studied the assassin thoroughly and would recognize him without trouble. But Mac knew everything there was to know about the guy. Every gesture, every nuance of expression, the way he walked, talked. He'd committed to memory every visual image, moving or still, ever made of Ramon Ruala.

Colonel Folly replied, "I don't need any kissy-face reunions here. I need a focused, competent professional to protect Susan Monroe until we nail Ruala's happy ass."

Mac rocked back onto the rear legs of his chair, violently displeased with the idea of Dutch going in his place. If anyone was going to save Susan Monroe, it should be him. "I can be objective about this," he insisted.

Colonel Folly still frowned at him.

Mac spoke as calmly as he could. "Susan's going to be traumatized as hell by Ruala's reappearance. She knows me. She'll work better with me than with some scary stranger who shows up on her doorstep."

Dutch protested. "I'm not scary."

Mac grinned. "Sorry, man. I keep forgetting you're the Easter Bunny." Jim Dutcher was six foot five of sheer Nordic brawn. With his short, brush-cut hair and square jaw, he looked liked a cyber-soldier from a future century.

Everyone around the table grinned.

Mac's immediate urge was to push his case even harder for going. It was a Tango One mission. He was the one who wanted Ramon Ruala the most. Susan Monroe had been hurt and was in need of saving. He bit back the arguments rushing to his lips. Colonel Folly would make him sit this one out for sure if he acted desperate.

But as the silence stretched out, Mac couldn't hold his tongue anymore. "Look. It's been a long time. Susan and I have both changed a lot. She'll barely remember me."

Susan sighed her relief when, as dark fell the next evening, the last policeman finally left. She was lucky she'd managed to talk the sheriff, Bill Franks, out of taking her into protective custody. Thankfully he'd had a crush on her since the sixth grade and gave in when she pleaded trauma and a desperate desire to stay in her own home and sleep in her own bed.

He'd wanted to keep a cop inside her house, but the idea of a strange man in her home, even if he wore a police uniform, freaked her out. Bill had agreed, reluctantly, to post a cruiser at the end of her driveway and put a pair of roving foot cops on patrol around her house. Apparently, Colonel Folly had asked him to guard her around the clock until his men arrived.

Charlie Squad here. In her house. The thought sent whispers of excitement and terror down her spine. The most thrilling time in her entire life had been helping them out with a dangerous surveillance mission against Eduardo Ferrare ten years ago. Right up to the part where Mac inexplicably turned on her and, in her ignorance and anguish, she stumbled into a sting operation and escaped death by a hair.

The silence of the vast ranch slowly wrapped itself around her, not nearly as comforting as usual. Exhausted, but too frightened of what awaited in her dreams to go to bed, she headed for the back of the house. Echoes whispered off the vaulted ceiling of the great room as she passed through it. Something creaked and she jumped nervously.

Mostly by feel, she made her way into the kitchen. She made a cup of hot chocolate from scratch on the stove and poured herself a big mug of the creamy drink. She sipped at it until it went cold and a skin formed on its surface. Finally, with no enthusiasm but with no reason to delay any longer, she headed for bed.

She'd just started up the stairs when a loud noise made her jump. The front doorbell. Her heart slammed against her ribs until she remembered the police outside. They'd probably forgotten something. She flicked on the porch light and peered through the peephole. Four elongated figures stood there. They didn't look like cops. Although she did see a uniformed officer standing behind them at the bottom of the front steps. Whoever they were, they'd passed muster with him. Leaving the chain on the door, she eased it open a few inches.

"What can I do for you?" she asked suspiciously.

One of the men answered back, "We're from Charlie Squad. We've come to protect you until Ruala's arrested."

She fumbled to unlatch the chain and threw the door open. A tall, blond Viking stood on the far left. An Omar Sharif look-alike stood beside him. The third guy was fair in coloring and lean of build, and the fourth guy...

She started.

It couldn't be.

She blinked and looked again.

It was.

She stepped forward, drew back her clenched fist and let fly with it as hard as she could.

Chapter 3

"Well, Mac," the Viking said dryly, "I'd say the lady remembers you."

Susan reeled back, appalled by what she'd just done. How did he *do* that to her? One second she was a calm, rational, logical human being. Then Mac Conlon showed up, and the next second she was a certifiable psychotic. One glimpse of the face that had haunted her heart for the past decade and instinct took over. She'd slugged him before she even knew her arm was moving.

What in the blue blazes was he doing here? Why couldn't he have just stayed in Washington, D.C., and let the other guys protect her? If he'd had the good grace to stay away from her for the past ten years, why did he have to go and change his mind tonight?

Pain radiated outward from her knuckles. Seething, she reached for inner serenity. Heck, right now she'd settle for reasonably calm. Yoga mantras flitted through her head. She focused on her breathing. She imagined floating on a tranquil ocean. She even counted to ten. Nothing worked.

Mac Conlon. She'd been passionately in love with him practically from the first moment she met him, and he'd remained firmly, stubbornly lodged in her heart ever since. She'd tried everything to get over him, and damn him, nothing had worked.

She schooled her voice to calm. "Come in, gentlemen." She stepped back to allow them inside. A momentary brush of panic stroked her spine as the men piled into her house. It would be okay. These were the good guys. They wouldn't hurt her. But, oh, did Mac have the capacity to if she didn't guard her heart!

To fill the awkward silence she asked, "Are you guys hungry?"

Their relieved smiles were answer enough. She led them into the huge kitchen that dominated the back of the house. She made a batch of sandwiches and carried them to the table.

Déjà vu broadsided her. Ten years ago she'd sat around a table with a couple of these same men, planning surveillance on Ferrare with the new digital audio analysis program that had earned her a Ph.D. She'd been fresh out of college, and so excited she could bust at the prospect of working with a totally cool Special Forces team. Tonight the adrenaline rush was still there, albeit tempered by the pain of the abrasion under her ear and an aching knee to remind her of her naiveté all those years ago.

Mac's eye was red and starting to swell. A pang of remorse shot through her. She filled two plastic bags with ice and wrapped them in dish towels. She gave one to him and kept the other for her hand as she sat down at the table.

"Thanks," he murmured.

She didn't deign to reply. She dragged her attention to the Viking, who was talking to her.

"In case you don't remember us, I'm Dutch. This is Doc." He gestured at Omar Sharif. "And this is Howdy."

He pointed at the fair fellow. "I gather you're familiar with Mac."

She glanced over at the man in question. Mac lounged in his seat, his crossed arms displaying breathtaking muscles, his piercing blue gaze taking in everything. Lord, he was still as gorgeous as ever.

Memories of long nights spent working with him in a cramped surveillance van came rushing back. The air had been so electric between them it was a wonder the listening equipment had still worked. Just sitting in the same room with him now made breathing difficult.

Dutch continued imperturbably. "What can you tell us about Ruala?"

"A guy calling himself David Ford showed up at the Fasco plant yesterday to test fire a rifle we're building. I believe he's Ramon Ruala, surgically altered to look different. I've got some videotape of the guy, if you'd like to look at it. I can't think of anybody else more likely to recognize Ruala than Charlie Squad."

Mac interjected, "Can we look at it right away, Suzie?"

Her insides twisted as he spoke. His mellow voice sent sexy little shivers down her spine. Nobody else before or since him had ever called her Suzie. Old memories and feelings flooded her, catching her off guard. For an instant she was that young woman all over again, dreaming about a guy who was way out of her league and who, miraculously, returned her interest. She struggled to think past the onslaught of images flashing through her head.

Mac's blue-velvet eyes gazed into hers with all the hypnotic intensity she remembered. And yet there was a dangerous edge to them—to him—that she didn't remember. Even his voice held a hint of violence. "Where's the tape?" he prodded politely. "Can I get it for you?"

That's right. Save the cripple from having to walk anywhere. "I'll get it," she snapped. "I have a VCR in the living room you can watch it on." She nodded and pushed herself up painfully from the table. Her knee was swollen like a cantaloupe after last night's fall. Mac's hand materialized on her elbow and he whisked the chair out from behind her, steadying her until she planted her cane firmly on the floor. She glared at him until his strong, warm hand fell away.

Her cane scorched her palm as she made her way out of the kitchen. She felt Mac's gaze lock on the hideous thing. Humiliation smoldered like a hot coal in her gut. The last time he'd seen her walk she'd been lithe and graceful, an athletic and whole person.

The sound of her cane's rubber tip thudding rhythmically on the stairs was obscene in her ears. Tears burned her eyelids before she made it to the second floor. She stopped in the hallway upstairs, out of sight of Mac, and sagged against the wall. She dashed the back of her hand across her eyes. Damn him! Why had he come back and opened up all these old wounds? Why couldn't he have left well enough alone? She bit back the sob rattling in her chest. She would *not* cry in front of Mac Conlon.

She took a deep breath and made her way to her bedroom. She opened the desk drawer in the corner and pocketed the videotape she'd stuck there after the police came.

Mac was waiting at the foot of the stairs for her. As she brushed past him, she couldn't help sucking in a sharp breath at the familiar scent of his cologne. Memory washed over her of their unforgettable nights together. His gaze snapped to hers, blue fire flickering hotly in his eyes. *He remembered, too.*

She loaded the tape and hit the play button. Mac pulled up a chair and sat down directly in front of the TV. He leaned forward intently and stared at the images fixedly for several minutes. And then they got to the part where Ruala fired the RITA rifle for the first time and did that finger rocking thing. Susan jumped as Mac abruptly muttered a foul curse under his breath. Apparently he agreed with her assessment. Not that she'd doubted it for a second.

Mac pulled out a cell phone and dialed a number. The conversation was short. "Mac here, sir. Yup, it's him. No doubt about it. Roger. Right away."

He closed the phone and tucked it back in his pocket. "Colonel Folly wants this tape in Washington ASAP. He also wants a signed statement from you about how you got the tape and how you recognized Ruala. Doc and Howdy will fly the tape and the paperwork back to him, and Dutch and I will stay here and keep an eye on you until the bastard is arrested and off the street."

Susan looked hard at him. "You mean, until you know Ruala can't come here again and try to kill me."

If four faces could possibly have gone more stone-like, she didn't think she'd ever seen them. She announced, "Don't even *think* about holding out on me. I handed you this guy on a silver platter. Heck, I'm the one he shot in the first place and came after last night. Surely I deserve straight answers, here."

Mac flinched. She *hated* the sympathy that flashed across his face. But then, she'd had ten long years to get touchy about pity. She rubbed her knee out of reflex.

"Why aren't you guys just sticking me in protective custody?"

Mac sighed heavily. "There have been some problems with witnesses against this guy in Federal custody."

"Problems?" she asked sharply.

"Yeah. They died," he said shortly.

It was one thing to know that kind of thing happened, but it was another thing entirely to hear it stated as fact. By an expert who knew what he was talking about. She gulped.

Mac continued. "Charlie Squad has no authority to hold

witnesses. We'd have to turn you over to the Federal justice system. And we can't take a chance on Ruala or Ferrare getting to you."

She asked soberly, "Is Ruala still working for Eduardo Ferrare?"

"Yeah. As far as we know." Mac's turbulent gaze locked with hers. *Not a happy camper.*

So, it took a threat to her life to smoke Mac Conlon out of whatever hole he'd been hiding in all these years, did it? Abruptly, she was furious at him for never coming back. For never fighting to fix their relationship. Never mind that he'd been a complete jackass, or that she'd sent him away from her bed with orders never to darken her doorstep again. What she couldn't forgive was that he never even tried. For ten years she'd been relieved that he had the decency not to bug her, and now she was mad about it? Lord, she was a mess.

Susan asked, "So what are you going to do with me?"

Grim looks passed all around the table.

Mac answered for all of them, "We're going to find someplace way isolated to hide you until we catch up with Ruala."

He made apprehending an infamous assassin sound easy. "And just how do you plan to catch up with him?" she asked.

He looked her square in the eye. "Ruala broke in here last night looking to kill you. He's got to keep trying until he succeeds. Neither he nor Ferrare can afford to let you testify against them. If we stick close to you, I expect he'll come to us."

And what did that make her? Bait? No, thank you very much. She had no desire to be the minnow the barracudas fought over. Worse, it would mean Mac living with her for days or even weeks, until Ruala showed up again.

"But I don't want you with me, Mac." Drat. Her voice

wobbled as if she was some scared little girl. She'd be damned if she'd show weakness in front of him!

He looked exasperated. "Susan, this isn't open for discussion. We're here on an official mission. I'm under orders to keep you safe until Ruala is apprehended."

She studiously ignored the little flicker of joy deep in her gut that he couldn't leave. "You'd come here and impose yourself on my life? You, of all people?"

Mac sent her a warning look. From the brash, fun-loving guy ten years ago, she would have ignored such a thing. But this man had an air about him that suggested she wouldn't like it if he picked up the gauntlet she'd just thrown down. Tough. She wasn't letting Mac Conlon intimidate her.

"We've got to stop this guy. Do you have any better ideas on how to find him and neutralize him?" Mac ground out.

She stared at him in impotent anger. It wasn't as if she had any choice in the matter. And that was what rubbed her fur the wrong way the most.

He leaned forward, glaring at her. "You give me the name of someone else whom Ruala knows has fingered him, and who Ruala's likely to try to kill in the next couple days, and I'll get out of your hair."

The other men shifted, looking uncomfortable. Omar Sharif—Doc—spoke for the first time. "Ma'am, you've had a tough experience and we don't want to make matters any worse. We really are trying to help you."

Mac stared at her, his mouth tight and his gaze troubled. This meeting wasn't easy for him, either. And she'd called them, after all. She sighed. "Fine. You can stay."

But an hour later, as she signed a detailed affidavit at the kitchen table and passed it over to Howdy, she wasn't so sure about what she'd gotten herself into. Days or even weeks of sitting across the kitchen table from Mac like this?

Living in intimate proximity to the one man who made her heart pound just by looking at him?

She asked Mac, "Now that I've turned this tape and my statement over to Uncle Sam, is there any chance I can step away from this whole mess from a legal standpoint?"

He frowned. "Not by a long shot. You'll have to testify against Ruala in person."

Her heart sank. That's what she'd been afraid of.

"Look, Susan. To my knowledge, you're the only person still alive today who has both seen Ruala at close range and been shot by him. Your testimony is going to be important to the government's case. You can also testify against Eduardo Ferrare. You know what was on the surveillance tapes of Ferrare that were destroyed in the van the night you and the van got shot up."

She didn't like the sound of that at all. "I *really* don't want to stand up in plain sight of these guys and testify against them. You and I both know they'll find a way to take me out."

Mac leaned forward. "Suzie, even if you back out now, they know you fingered them. The only reason you're alive right now is because the police got here when they did. You've got nothing to lose by testifying. If you can help Uncle Sam put Ruala away once and for all, then and only then will you be safe."

"What about Ferrare?" she asked.

Mac smiled without humor, the expression of a wolf on the scent of prey. "Ferrare's got issues of his own to deal with at the moment. We're hot on his heels. Believe me. You're not his biggest problem right now."

She looked around at the other members of the team for confirmation, and they all nodded grimly at her. Lord, what a choice. Hide and be hunted forever by a murderer, or agree to testify and be hunted even more aggressively until Ruala landed behind bars.

"How do you plan to keep me alive until I can testify against this guy?"

She caught Mac's gaze and held it, whether he liked it or not. The last time she asked Mac a big question, he'd dodged it. Failed to tell her that the reason she'd been pulled from the Ferrare case was because Charlie Squad was about to spring an armed ambush on their target and it would be too dangerous for her to be there. Instead, he'd left her with the impression that he was walking away from the case, and so should she. She'd argued that it was career suicide. That it was a disservice to the nation. That the two of them were on the verge of breaking the case wide open, and if he'd just stick with it another day or two, they'd get the wiretap evidence they needed to put away Ferrare. But her pleas had fallen on inexplicably deaf ears.

She'd been outraged. So furious and hurt she'd taken the surveillance van out by herself to listen in on the meeting she knew had to happen any second between Ferrare and the Gavronese rebels who wanted his financial backing in overthrowing their country's government. And she'd driven smack-dab into the middle of the shoot-out between Ferrare's men—led by Ruala—and Charlie Squad.

She looked up at the man she'd loved and hated enough to die for that night. His proximity tonight hit her like a high-velocity slug. He'd filled out in all the right places since she'd last seen him, and his cobalt eyes were more breathtaking than ever. His gaze shot right through her, leaving her weak and wanting. She gathered her scattered thoughts and tried to slow her breathing.

And now her life rested again on his answer to her question. Did she dare trust him to be square with her this time? To tell her the true risks of testifying against Ruala? Would he pull his punches with her again?

Mac answered quietly. "We plan to guard you around

the clock not only until you testify, but until Ruala's captured, brought to trial and locked up for good.''

His sapphire gaze bored into hers. Challenging her to believe him. But something else lurked in his intense expression. A promise—to keep her safe this time. An appeal—to give him another chance, to let him make up for Ruala out-maneuvering and outgunning him and nearly killing her. A plea—to trust him.

Could she do that? She'd trusted him once with her heart and he'd destroyed it. Could she trust Mac Conlon with her life this time around? She sighed in resignation. What choice did she have? "So what do we do first?"

All the men at the table exhaled in relief.

Mac answered briskly. "The first order of business is to get you out of here and tuck you away somewhere safe until you can testify. The next order of business is to bring in a female operative and set her up to look like you. Then we find and arrest Ruala."

She lifted a skeptical brow. "No offense, but he's no dummy. He knows exactly what I look like. And he's managed to avoid you guys for ten years. What's so different now?"

Waves of frustration rolled off of Mac's broad shoulders, and he stared at her in tense silence. Uh-huh, just what she thought. No answer to that one.

She leaned forward. "I'll tell you what's different. You've got something Ruala will risk walking into your trap to nail, even if he knows there's a trap waiting for him."

Mac's dark brows drew together in a heavy frown. He saw where she was going with this, and he didn't like it. Tough. She was going there whether he liked it or not. "And what might this irresistible bait be?" he asked ominously.

"Me. The real me. Not some ringer."

Mac all but threw himself backward in his chair. "No way. Not a chance!" he declared forcefully.

"Look, Mac," she argued. "I'll admit I'm scared to death. But I'll be scared until this guy's put away, whether I'm sitting in a bunker staring at the walls or I'm out here helping you catch him. If you don't use me for bait, it could take you guys months or even years to track down Ruala. He'll head for the nearest plastic surgeon, completely change his appearance, invent a new life for himself on the other side of the world and you'll be back to square one. You don't have any choice but to use me to draw him out. Besides, this is my life we're talking about, here. If I can help with this mission, I want to do it. I'd rather take action against Ruala than sit back and wait for him to take action against me."

Mac glared at her. Nope, he didn't like the idea of using her as bait at all. Problem was, she was right and he knew it.

She stated matter of factly, "You know you need me. And I promise I won't get in the way."

"That's what you said the last time," he bit out.

She stared him down. "I didn't have all the facts when I got in that van and drove it into the middle of your op."

He exhaled in frustration. "I'm not here to dredge up old arguments. I'm here to save your life, dammit."

"That's right. *My* life. I'd say that gives me the right to participate in saving it."

"Things have changed, Suzie. You've changed. This op will be much more…physical than the last time."

She said aloud the words he left unspoken. "And I'm a cripple now."

She blinked at the irritated, narrow-eyed look that comment earned her. His demeanor had a harder edge than she remembered. Like he'd seen a lot of the world since they'd last met.

"Crippled or not," he replied with thin patience, "it would be extremely dangerous for you to help us apprehend Ruala."

"Dangerous to whom?" she challenged. "To me or to you?"

His gaze snapped to hers. "I'm not trying to avoid being with you," he ground out. "I'm trying to do the right thing, here."

"Good," she snapped back. "Then stop being an ass and agree that you need my help to bring Ruala in."

He reached up with one hand and pinched the bridge of his nose. She recognized the gesture. A sure sign he was hanging on to his temper by a thread.

"Are you willing to bet your life on this op?" he challenged.

She never could refuse a dare. "Of course I am. Besides, my life is already on the line."

He stared hard at her, measuring the truth of her words. She stared back, throwing down a silent dare of her own. She swore she saw the tiniest moment of pride in her flash through his eyes. Eventually, reluctantly, he nodded. His gaze slid away. "All right. Fine. We use you as bait to land Ruala."

Chapter 4

Mac woke up to a throbbing pain in his left eye, but not enough to explain his sudden lurch to consciousness. He listened intently. The night was thick and dark and silent around him. But then he heard a thump downstairs and Susan's melodic voice yelping in pain.

Surely Ruala wasn't back...

Not this soon...

But it could be...

Sh— He grabbed the pistol from under his pillow, leaped out of bed and tore down the stairs. He stormed into the kitchen in a running crouch, the pistol held low and ready in front of him.

One target. Civilian female. Quick scan. No other targets.

He straightened slowly, his heart pounding like a jackhammer. He tucked the gun into the waistband of the gym shorts he'd worn to bed as a concession to being a guest in Susan's house. He scowled as she hopped around on her right foot, simultaneously holding her left foot and glaring at one of the long, heavy benches that lined the enormous kitchen table.

"Are you all right?" he asked curtly.

Her glare shifted its aim to him. "I'll live," she answered from between gritted teeth.

He leaned against the edge of the kitchen table, glaring back at her. "Geez, Suz, I thought Ruala was in the house. Don't yell like that around guys trained like we are. You're liable to get yourself shot." Damn. His heart was beating a mile a minute.

He continued, "If you're going to help us, you can't pull any more stunts like this. We're in full-blown commando mode on this op."

She observed dryly, "Yes, I recall that aspect of working with you guys. No sudden moves, hands in plain sight at all times, no sneaking up quietly behind one of you."

"You forgot the one about following all orders we give you," he added.

"I didn't forget it," she said lightly.

He gave her a narrow look. Her tone of voice definitely promised rebellion. He stepped closer, invading her personal space and intentionally looming over her. "We're about to step on the toes of one of the most sadistic bastards ever deposited on this planet. You'll do what I say, when I say it, no questions asked."

"Or else what?" she challenged.

He shrugged. "Or else you'll die." God, it was hard to say that and sound casual about it.

That shut her up. He rarely resorted to such scare tactics, but she needed to be set back on her heels. It was all well and good for her to bully her way into this op, but it was another thing altogether for her to actually function as part of the team. Intimidating her wouldn't help her opinion of him as a human being much, but it wasn't as if her opinion of him could go a lot lower.

''Let me have a look at your toes,'' he said to distract her. ''I have a little first-aid training.''

Silently she sat down and held out her foot. She must really be in pain because she offered it to him without protesting, and she had a contrary streak almost as wide as his.

He knelt down and reached for her foot. Shock slammed into him as he got a good look at her mangled knee for the first time. Missing was the smooth bump of a kneecap. In its place was a puckered scar as wide as his finger, extending the entire length of the front of the joint. Acid burned in his gut at the sight of what Ruala's bullet had done to her. He'd *kill* the bastard someday. But in the meantime, he had a hard question to ask.

''How much mobility do you have with your artificial knee joint?''

She answered woodenly, ''I can walk normally, and do light exercise after a fashion. I can go up and down stairs, squat if I'm careful, and even ride a horse. But the joint is not designed for running or quick changes of direction.''

He nodded, his throat tight. She'd loved to dance and had been a 10K runner before Ruala wrecked her knee. He ought to say something to her about that night. Apologize for making love to her and then turning on her. For following orders and being a macho jerk. For hurting her so badly he couldn't face her anymore. God, what had he cost them both? The one decent thing about it all was that he'd rather have the woman he loved alive and hating his guts than dead and gone forever.

He glanced up. Her face was averted. Was that a shimmer of tears in her eyes? Aww, hell. Now what was he supposed to say?

He looked away carefully from her knee. Her foot was slender and beautifully shaped. Like the rest of her. He'd forgotten how good she smelled. She still wore the same fragrance, something clean, almost green smelling. Abruptly, he recalled the silky slide of her auburn hair across his skin, her mouth under his, the taste of her—

Damn, where had that explosion of memory come from? Better not let his thoughts go *there*. He cleared his throat. "You didn't break any toes. They should feel okay in a day or two. Why don't you try to get some sleep? It's late."

He resisted an errant impulse to let his fingers linger on her foot, to massage her arch with the heel of his hand. He didn't need a second black eye to match the first one.

She pushed to her feet as if she was antsy to get away from him. Eyes narrowed, he watched her walk gingerly out of the kitchen. Her curves were more mature now. *Sexier than ever, dammit.* To think he could have been with this woman for the long haul. Could have come home to her every night. Laughed and fought with her. Made love with her for the last decade.

He followed her silently down the hallway and up the stairs. Without saying good-night, or even looking back at him, she stepped into her room. He waited outside her door until he heard the lock turn. His mouth curled sardonically as he headed on down the hall to the next bedroom. *Who'd have thunk getting locked out of one woman's bedroom could make a guy feel so lousy?* He'd made "There Are Always More Fish in the Sea" his motto for women for the last decade. And the theory hadn't let him down yet. Until that damned lock snicked shut in his face.

If she'd shown the slightest pleasure at seeing him again—a smile, even a spark of interest—he'd have been all over picking up where they left off. But all she'd been when he showed up on her porch was mad. Wet-cat, spittin' mad. Damn.

He'd been an idiot to come on this mission. Susan Monroe was a troubled ghost from his past. One he should have known better than to try to appease. Or to exorcise.

* * *

She smiled when her lover came to her, slipping ghost-like into her bed and into her arms. His form was dark and powerful, his kisses sweet and hot enough to drug her into insensibility. She pictured his physique as her hands felt him in the darkness. He was all flat planes and hard bulges, too complex to memorize in every detail.

Ahh, but she'd like to try. Maybe later, when his mouth and hands weren't driving her out of her mind, when she could think again. Breathe again. The ecstasy built, and he beckoned her toward a pleasure so intense it was almost painful. She surged upward with him, reaching for more, and yet more, of him...

A jangling bell yanked her out of her dream.

Susan smacked her alarm clock into silence and sagged back on the mattress, breathing hard.

Years ago she'd given up trying to rid herself of Mac's appearances in her dreams. She figured it was her subconscious's sick sense of humor. For some inexplicable reason the one man who'd walked away from her was the one her dreaming mind most craved. A psychologist would probably have lots to say about that. She'd given up on fighting it long ago.

It was especially irritating to have such a vivid dream of Mac when she had to go downstairs and face him in the flesh this morning. Susan sprawled on her back while she mustered the willpower to turn her thoughts to something besides Mac Conlon. It didn't work.

Reluctantly she forced herself to get out of bed and spent several minutes carefully loosening up her knee. It still wasn't recovered from her twisting fall down the stairs two nights ago. It was swollen and stiff, and pain shot through it as she carefully worked through its stretching regimen.

She looked at her neck in the mirror as she got dressed. A long scratch marred her flesh where the bullet had grazed

A Gentleman and a Soldier

her, but it felt better this morning. It was a far cry from the other bullet scar on her neck. She pulled on a polo shirt along with jeans and a pair of hot-pink cowboy boots. She steeled herself not to blush horribly when she saw Mac, and headed downstairs.

By the time she painstakingly reached the first floor, the scent of freshly brewed coffee tickled her nose. That was definitely French toast she smelled, too. She walked off the worst of her morning limp in the long hallway leading to the kitchen and managed to stroll into the room casually.

All four of her house guests looked chipper and well rested, even Mac who'd been awake in the wee hours of the night. She scowled at them all over the steaming cup of coffee Howdy passed to her. It just wasn't fair that men got out of bed in the morning looking so good.

She watched in awe as they consumed an enormous breakfast and then cleaned up after it. Even performing a mundane chore like washing the dishes, they functioned as a well-honed military unit. The last dish went into the dishwasher and Mac turned to Susan. He wore a pair of faded jeans and a black T-shirt this morning. The denim looked painted on to his long, muscular legs, and the black cotton shirt stretched across rippling muscles that beggared the mind. Remnants of her steamy dream floated across her mind's eye. She looked away from him hastily.

But then Mac sat down beside her, placing himself directly in her line of sight. "Ready to talk business?" he asked.

She looked him in the eye. And barely managed not to melt into those mesmerizing oceans of blue. Get it together! "Uhh, sure. What's the plan for today?"

"To get you out of here and onto a battlefield of our choosing."

A battlefield? She didn't like the sound of that. "And just where is this battlefield going to be?"

The certainty in Mac's eyes wavered a bit before he replied obliquely, "We know a few things about Ramon Ruala. First, we know he's an urban operator all the way. Hates leaving behind his creature comforts and does *not* like operating in field conditions."

Dutch leaned forward and added, "Second, he doesn't look to be in especially good physical condition in your videotape. He smoked a couple times in the tape, too, so he probably doesn't have the greatest stamina if he's a heavy smoker."

Mac picked up the line of reasoning. "Then there's the matter of your mobility. You can ride horses. We can use that to our advantage. Ruala probably doesn't expect that. It'll level the playing field, as it were."

Smart thinking. That way, her only physical limitation would be the strength and stamina of her horse, instead of her own puny physical capabilities.

"Won't Ruala climb in a Jeep and follow us?"

"We had a look at the terrain maps we brought with us. There's some really rough country at the back end of your next door neighbors' property that wheeled vehicles can't handle. Plus, we ought to have a good head start on him and be able to reach it before he can catch up with us."

That made sense. The panic tickling the edges of her consciousness subsided a little.

Mac continued. "The plan is for the three of us to hide out until Doc and Howdy get back from delivering your affidavit with an arrest warrant for Ruala. Then the three of us will ride back in, join Doc and Howdy, and we'll all set up our trap for Ruala."

"Arrest. Right," she mumbled.

Mac shrugged. "We have to play by the rules. But if Ruala gives us an excuse, we'll splatter him all over west Texas." He paused. Asked cautiously, "Is riding around the ranch for a couple days going to be too much for your...for you?'' he finished lamely.

Thank God his eyes didn't flicker sympathetically. The tough, brave facade she was doing her best to maintain would've cracked for sure. ''I can ride all of you guys into the ground,'' she retorted. ''But we could go a whole lot farther a whole lot faster if we just got in a car and drove away from here.''

Mac shook his head. ''Then we'd be operating on Ruala's playing field. We want him on our turf. And that means pulling him out into the wilds where there are no roads, no hotels, no phones.''

Camping, in other words. She sighed.

Mac leaned down, his palms flat on the table in front of her. He loomed close enough for her to notice he smelled like soap and something else masculine and wonderful that she couldn't place. He murmured, ''With some jobs, the easy way isn't always the best way.''

She leaned away from his towering closeness, hoping he wouldn't notice. He did. He flashed her a grin that declared her a coward. Drat.

He tossed a smile at her. Her stomach turned to molten lava and formed a puddle somewhere near her feet.

He straightened abruptly, releasing her from the byplay between them. She sagged on the bench. Damn him.

Mac smiled at her, but the expression didn't reach his eyes. ''Time to go.'' He led her out to the main horse barn, where Frank Riverra was waiting for them. She made introductions all around. He owned the spread next door and took care of Susan's ranch along with his own for a percentage of the profits from this place. It was his land they'd be riding on.

She gaped when Frank nodded at Mac and said, ''I took care of the arrangements for the ranch hands like you asked. The guys said to thank you.''

Susan rounded on Mac. He'd been talking to her foreman behind her back? "What arrangements?" she asked darkly.

Mac answered casually, "I put your employees on paid vacation for a couple of weeks. All expenses covered by Uncle Sam, of course."

"And who's going to clean my barn and unload hay and paint fences and—"

"We will." Mac gestured at Dutch.

The two men grinned at her like total greenhorns. They didn't have a clue what it took to operate a ranch like this. She scowled. She was tempted to let them find out the hard way. Except she didn't want the livestock to suffer.

"I thought you guys didn't know anything about ranching."

"Frank says he can show us what to do."

She glared at Mac. "This is *my* home. *My* employees. You had no right!"

Mac's gentle gaze almost did it. She almost allowed herself to get lost in those china blue depths, to forget about everything else and open herself up to him. It was such hard work being strong all the time. The gut-wrenching terror of the last couple days was finally catching up with her, and her facade started to crack. Her worries and fears crowded forward, jostling for her attention. She did her best not to give in to it all, but she was just too tired to be brave anymore. A tear rolled down her cheek.

Mac brushed away the droplet with his thumb. "You've had a rough couple days, kiddo. But we'll fix it. I promise."

She fought an overwhelming urge to collapse onto his shoulder and borrow a little of his strength while she bawled her eyes out. This was the side of Mac that had beguiled her, had kept her waiting for him all these years. Whoa. All *what* years? That was Mac Conlon's shoulder. She would swallow broken glass before she'd show any weakness to him. She took a deep breath and stiffened her spine.

Mac stepped back immediately and assumed a professional tone of voice. "If, in fact, one of your hands could be bought off by Ruala, we just made the job of infiltrating your ranch a lot harder for the bastard." His gaze took on a reproachful air. "Besides, we don't want your employees getting caught in the crossfire. We sent your men away for their safety."

The air left her sails in a rush. "Oh." Here she was being all tense and grouchy while he was looking out for her people. Her eyes burned. Great. She must have contracted a severe case of weepy hormones overnight. She turned away fast—she was *not* going to cry in front of Mac.

She made her way to the next barn over, speaking briskly over her shoulder to mask her wildly surging emotions. "We keep camping gear in here. You guys figure out what you want to take, and Frank will help you pack it on the horses."

She left Mac and Dutch rummaging around the storeroom and went back to the horse barn to collect herself. A little gray Arab mare named Moofah munched on her sweet feed as Susan entered her stall, but she took a moment to greet Susan with a friendly snuffle.

What if Ruala was en route to her ranch this very minute to kill her? A noise behind her made her jump, and she spun around.

"Easy, Suz," Mac murmured.

"You startled me," she mumbled, rubbing the mare's neck.

"Sorry," he replied. Gently Mac reached out and brushed a strand of hair back from her face. Her senses tumbled at the sweet familiarity of his touch. She remembered how good it had been between them in the beginning.

Their romantic relationship had been as natural as breathing and as powerful as a hurricane rolling in off the open ocean.

Mac's voice was regretful. "I wish I could tell you this will all just go away, but it won't. Not until we take out this guy. I swear, though, we'll give you your life back."

She stared into the clear blue depths of his eyes. For a moment his gaze was warm and open, and she felt the old connection between them. Just as it had been before. Before he showed up at her apartment that night and blew her world apart. Before she acted blindly and blew his op apart…

Mac snapped closed the shutters to his soul once more. He took a step back to a more impersonal distance. "I came to tell you we're ready to go."

"So soon?" she replied, surprised.

One corner of his mouth turned up in what might pass for a smile. "We're not raw recruits who take all day to pack. Besides, we brought our own gear. We just supplemented our usual equipment with a few extras from your supplies for you."

Would he and Charlie Squad really be able to catch Ruala and return her life to normal?

Mac gestured toward the door of the stall. "After you."

Except how was anything ever going to be normal again, now that Mac had come back into her life? As much as she'd hated him for the pain he'd caused her, as many times as she'd vowed she never wanted to see him again, his return forced her to acknowledge a stark fact: she might have moved beyond him, but she'd never gotten over him.

Stunned by the revelation, she followed him numbly back to the waiting cluster of horses.

Frank finished tying down the last pack and announced, "All ready." Worry darkened his eyes and made the wrinkles etching his face look deeper than usual this morning.

She gave him a grateful hug. "Thanks, Frank. Don't worry about this mess. Everything will turn out fine."

He nodded, but the expression in his eyes told her he didn't buy that any more than she did. Maybe if she repeated it to herself a couple hundred times she'd start to believe it.

She moved around to the right side—usually the wrong side to mount on a horse, but necessary with her bad left knee—and climbed awkwardly onto her favorite mare, Malika. She was a long-legged, chestnut Arab with velvet gaits, the endurance of a marathon runner and a heart as big as the desert she was bred for.

Susan settled into the saddle and moved her knee with reasonable ease. She grinned as she watched the big, bad, Special Forces soldiers attempt to climb into their own saddles. Clearly they had basic horsemanship training, but born to the saddle they were not. Legs, elbows, stirrups and reins went every which way, and the horses jigged, alarmed by the theatrics. Frank met her gaze briefly, humor dancing in his eyes. They looked away from each other quickly lest they laugh aloud.

Mac caught her expression and grinned, complaining from his big bay gelding, "How do you make this thing go?"

Susan grinned back. "The crucial question when you're astride twelve hundred pounds of horse is, 'How do I make it stop?'"

He flexed his feet in his stirrups. "Now that you mention it, I don't see any brake pedals," he groused.

Susan led Mac and Dutch to a paddock and gave them a quick refresher on starting, stopping and turning her horses based on how they were trained. She was surprised by how fast they caught on. But then, she supposed the men chosen for Special Forces were pretty quick studies.

Of course, it didn't hurt that Frank had mounted them on the two most unflappable horses in her stable, either.

Within ten minutes or so, Frank pronounced them ready to go. Susan shook her head. They were the most motley cavalry types she'd ever seen. Fortunately, she trusted her wonderfully trained Arabians to keep both men out of trouble. Frank opened the paddock gate and let them out into one of the pastures that made up her ranch. They'd reach Frank's land around lunchtime. She rode up to join Mac and Dutch. "How long do you expect us to be out there?"

Mac scanned the horizon. "Three days, maybe."

Three days with Mac Conlon in the wilds of West Texas? Her stomach flip-flopped. She clamped down on the unwelcome sensation. She was not even going to *contemplate* falling again for Mac Conlon. Wordlessly she turned her horse and pointed the mare's nose toward the mountains on the horizon. She looped the packhorse's reins around her saddle horn, waited until Dutch's and Mac's horses fell in behind, then she clucked to Malika. They headed out.

It wasn't as bad as she expected. It was worse. Mac and Dutch acted like Ruala was lurking behind every outcropping of rock. Before the day was half over, their paranoia had rubbed off on her. The rugged landscape ceased to be beautiful and peaceful, a place that restored her soul. Instead it became an unfamiliar and threatening wilderness. She jumped at every little thing and rode along in a constant state of nervous agitation. Malika picked up on her jumpiness, too, and was a handful to manage.

She felt exposed and vulnerable, with only Mac and Dutch standing between her and disaster. She didn't like the idea of needing Mac one little bit. But then a twig would snap, her heart would slam into her throat and she was reluctantly glad for his solid presence beside her.

They stopped for the night in a small valley. Mac and Dutch set up camp while she took care of the horses. Her knee ached, but she'd be darned if she'd admit that to Mac. The extreme normalcy of the scene belied the tension in all of them. Beneath their calm exteriors, Mac and Dutch must be wired, because their horses were nervous wrecks as she unsaddled and hobbled them. Eventually she managed to calm all the animals with a good brushing. If only her nerves could be quieted so easily.

She finished grooming the last horse and joined Mac and Dutch by the already merrily crackling fire. Her tent was set up, her sleeping bag spread inside it, her pack of gear sitting beside the tent's front flap. She commented, "You guys are really good at this camping stuff."

Mac shrugged. "We do it for a living. We'd better be good at it."

"I mean it. You'd make Boy Scouts green with envy."

Both men laughed at that. Dutch remarked, "Hey, maybe they'd give me a merit badge for my one hundredth kill."

Susan blinked. Was he serious? She couldn't tell from his casual tone of voice.

"Nah," Mac retorted. "If you really want to rack up the merit badges, you have to blow up stuff like I do."

Susan shuddered and asked, "How can you be so casual about something like that?"

Mac replied, "It's just a job. Analyzing weapons systems is your job. Covert ops is mine."

Disturbed, Susan got up and walked a lap around the camp, trying to stave off the stiffness that was setting into her knee. Finally she returned to the fire and sat down, rubbing the joint absently. Mac had changed. Gone was the careless young man who worked hard and played harder. In his place was this serious, focused professional, talking casually about killing people. The younger man had been so much simpler to deal with. This man was too complicated, with too many new sides to his personality, too much darkness where there once had been light.

Dutch ate a quick bite and slipped off into the encroaching blackness of night. Susan looked up from her supper as he left and realized she was completely alone with Mac. "Where's Dutch off to?" she asked nervously.

"Patrolling," was Mac's brief reply.

"What does that mean?"

He glanced up at her. "He's having a look around, setting up a perimeter and standing guard."

She looked around the little camp, abruptly uncomfortable with the idea of being alone with Mac. "How long will he be gone?"

His mouth turned up in a sardonic smile, but there was little humor in his voice. "Long enough for you to take a chunk out of my hide if you want."

Susan was taken aback. The guy she remembered didn't have this hard edge. She studied Mac as he sat on a rock, staring intently into the fire, his thoughts a million miles away.

He'd grown up.

He'd been tall when she knew him before, but now he'd filled out. Muscles rippled across his shoulders and neck, and his biceps bulged in a supremely male display of power. His waist was flat and hard beneath his cotton shirt, and his jeans hugged muscular thighs. His face was leaner, no longer round with the boyish charm of youth. Now his features spoke of maturity and self-assurance, of a man in his prime. In all these years, she'd never dreamed Mac Conlon could possibly get one bit sexier than the guy she'd known. But he had. In spades. And she was sitting with him under a starry sky beside a quietly hissing fire.

Oh, boy.

She rubbed her arms to chase away a sudden chill.

Mac looked up and without speaking reached into his bulky, nylon backpack. He pulled out a black sweatshirt and tossed it to her. The night air was nippy. She shrugged into the garment, keenly aware of its soft, fleecy lining against her bare arms. She inhaled slowly, savoring the scent of him clinging to the cloth.

She recalled another night like this, another bright, starlit sky. They'd sat in the back of his pickup truck and talked into the wee hours of the morning. When they'd gotten ready to leave, he'd kissed her for the first time. She still remembered the surprise of his warm mouth against hers, his arms tight around her, his breath as uneven as hers. They'd been young and awkward and eager, but somehow they'd managed to get it right. She'd never forget the sweetness and poignancy of that first kiss.

"Suzie? Susan!"

She looked up, startled.

Mac was squatting in front of her. "Are you all right? You made a noise like maybe you were in pain. Is it your knee?"

"I'm fine. So's my knee." When he didn't back off, she added, "Honest."

He frowned. "Are you sure? I know the last couple days have been pretty hard on you. Some people don't handle being in danger real well. If you're going to crack up on me, I need to know now."

Confusion swirled through her. She was supposed to despise him for breaking her heart. But this flash of the old Mac, as perceptive and considerate as ever, reminded her why she'd fallen head-over-heels for him in the first place. If two days in his presence had her this flustered, how was she going to handle a week? A month? *Years,* a voice whispered in her mind.

She needed him to go away. She wanted him to stay. He continued to watch her with that meltingly warm gaze of his that always did her in.

"I'm worried about you, Suzie."

"I'll be okay. I just want it to be over."

His mouth turned down. "Yeah, I know. So I can get out of your life once and for all. I'm sorry about showing up here like this. I should've talked my boss out of sending me. My mistake."

Coming here was a mistake for him? Somehow that idea hurt almost worse than seeing him again.

Why did she care if he didn't want to deal with an ex-girlfriend who refused to sit in a bunker and knit while he went out and saved the world? She obviously hadn't meant much to him back then, since he'd walked out and never, not once, looked back. And now she was just someone he was trying to avoid.

Fine. If he was over her, then she was definitely over him. If he could put aside the past to do this mission, then she would do the same right back at him. "Look, Mac. You do your job, and I'll do mine. This will all be over soon, and then we can both get on with our lives."

He stood up, towering over her, his expression completely, frighteningly, blank. She was struck suddenly by how imposing a man he'd become.

His voice was flat. "I'll go relieve Dutch. Get some sleep if you can, Susan. It'll be a long day tomorrow."

So. She was Susan, now, was she? Pain cut through her. Why did everything he said suddenly hurt? He'd only used her real name, for goodness' sake. Except he'd always called her Suzie. The rest of the world looked at her and saw the intelligent, self-contained computer programmer, Susan Monroe. Only Mac, always Mac, had seen the outdoorsy, fun-loving girl named Suzie, who just wanted to be loved.

She watched, her heart breaking, as Mac's silhouette retreated into the darkness beyond the firelight. Her mind flashed back to another dark night. Another view of his unyielding back retreating into the darkness. *Out of her bed and out of her life.*

She'd called him to tell him she'd decoded a critical piece of garbled surveillance tape. A phone call by Eduardo Ferrare setting up a meeting with the Gavronese rebels. In it, Ferrare confirmed a meeting time of midnight that night. It was the piece of information they'd been waiting for. She'd been so excited to tell Mac, so proud of the digital audio enhancement program she'd developed and how well it worked.

Mac had come over to her apartment. She'd just assumed it was to pick her up to help with the surveillance of the big meeting. He'd kissed her wildly, passionately, and they'd ended up in bed. Mac had never made love to her like that before, almost as if he was desperate to capture a lasting memory of her and to leave one with her forever. Like an idiot, she'd put it down to pre-mission jitters.

But then he'd gotten up, gotten dressed and paced her bedroom like a caged tiger. And like a tiger, he'd bared his claws without warning and shredded her heart. Told her the relationship was over. That she was too emotionally involved with him and that he didn't need some teeny-bopper groupie hanging around his neck. But he didn't stop there. He told her she wasn't needed on the op anymore. He knew how to operate her computer program and she was getting in the way of the mission. She was nothing more than an amateur computer geek, a wannabe of the worst kind. Case in point, her getting all excited about a snippet of meaningless audio.

She'd argued. Tried to convince him that tonight was the big night. He'd rolled his eyes and told her she had no idea what she was talking about. She'd been infuriated when he refused to listen to her. She'd pushed as hard as she could to get him to take action. And all he did was tell her scornfully that he didn't find women who wanted to have cajones like men attractive. He accused her of endangering the team with her wild conclusions and said she'd blow the mission if they didn't dump her. And then he'd turned and walked out of her life.

Like he'd done just now. A shadow blending into the dark until nothing remained but the night sounds and the wall of black beyond the campfire.

In a few moments Dutch appeared in almost as ghost-like a fashion. The tall Viking—she'd always think of him like that—stretched out on his bedroll and fell asleep in a matter of seconds. Maybe it was a Special Forces trick to go to sleep instantly like that. She sighed, wide awake.

As she sat there, mesmerized by the dying flames, Mac's scent rose from his sweatshirt, and she hugged the baggy garment close. It was comforting to know he was out there in the dark somewhere, protecting her from unseen dangers. Wait a minute. Comforting? Mac? The man who'd mortally wounded her heart with his careless cruelty?

Oh, she was in danger, all right. But tonight it wasn't from Ramon Ruala.

Chapter 5

Even though his gut yelled at him to run like hell, Mac forced himself to walk away from the campfire and Susan. For all the years he'd run from facing her, now that he was here he couldn't turn his back on her. Wouldn't. He had to make amends to Susan. It was now or never. And if he chose never, he'd fall off that razor's edge he'd walked for so long and end up destroying himself for good.

But how in the hell was he supposed to make things right between them if she wouldn't let him past her defenses? She was freezing him out with a cold shoulder made of dry ice.

He put his body on autopilot, going through the familiar motions of perimeter surveillance by rote. Crouching down in the long grass, he eased to the top of the next ridge line. He scanned the area, unseeing, through his field glasses.

The gentle movement of the grass on the dark plain reminded him of Suzie's auburn hair, flowing around him as they made love. The twinkle of the stars reminded him of the way her eyes used to light up whenever she'd look at him. The wide-open spaces of this country even reminded him of her free spirit when they first met.

How was he supposed to do his job if he was all tied up in knots thinking about her? He needed to concentrate here.

He was a professional.

He was on a Tango One mission.

He'd promised Colonel Folly he could handle this.

He'd *lied*.

Damn. He could still do this job. The trick would be to stay objective. He'd catalogue the changes he'd noted in her so far, analyze options for helping heal her heart.

Her girlish slenderness had transformed into a willowy, womanly form. She was more beautiful than ever. Her youthful good looks had matured into the kind of ageless beauty that would shine when she was sixty-five. Of course, he'd have to convince her of that. She'd gotten damned self-conscious since he last saw her. Frankly, he thought the slight limp and the scar on her neck lent her character. But then, he was used to hanging out with beat-up soldiers whose scars were viewed as trophies.

She was more guarded, more defensive than he remembered. It might even be fair to say she'd become a shade reclusive. God help him, was she ashamed to go out in public? Clearly he'd have to fix that one. A weariness of spirit hung over her sometimes, now. As if she'd done a lot of hurting over the years. Both the physical kind and the emotional kind that wilts a person's soul.

The good news was she wasn't quite dried up inside yet. No woman who rode around in a pair of hot-pink cowboy boots had gone totally dead. Those boots had had him thinking dirty thoughts all day.

He slipped on a pair of night-vision goggles and scanned the area for infrared targets. The outlines of a couple of distant coyotes popped into view.

God, he'd missed her. His whole world had revolved around her once upon a time. He'd been so sure she was The One. His soul mate. He'd flung himself headfirst into loving her and hadn't looked down or looked back. Hell, he still blew off dating other women because they weren't her....

Abruptly Mac froze, his train of thought snapped. His attention riveted on the landscape in front of him. Something had moved. Something that didn't belong there. The hairs on the back of his neck stood up, and every sense went on full alert. Very slowly he scanned the horizon. And sucked in a sharp breath. *There was a person out there.* He magnified the zoom on his NVGs and made out one man. He was dressed in dark clothing and carried a standard pair of civilian night-vision goggles. They didn't look like heat seekers, which was good, or the guy would have already seen the column of hot air rising from their fire beyond the next ridge.

The guy was maybe a quarter mile away, moving from right to left across Mac's field of vision. He wasn't bothering to move stealthily, so he probably didn't know Mac was out here. It also meant he hadn't spotted their camp yet. Mac reached for his throat mike out of habit, and realized he wasn't wired. Sloppy. A mistake they couldn't afford. He couldn't warn Dutch to hit the dirt with Suzie. He cursed under his breath. Had Ruala picked up their trail already? Dammit! They needed one more day to get to the rough terrain where the horses gave them the advantage. How had Ruala mobilized so blasted fast? The guy must be outrageously motivated to find and neutralize Susan. Chagrin filled him. It wasn't often Charlie Squad underestimated an opponent or got caught flat-footed.

He slithered backward until he was below the ridge line and then he took off running, low and silent, toward Dutch and Suzie. By paralleling the guy's course, Mac could get to the camp first—if he hustled.

He hustled, all right. He busted his butt, in fact, and was panting when he burst into the circle of firelight. Dutch was on his feet before Mac even skidded to a halt.

"What's up?" Dutch asked shortly, as he tossed on a bulky ammo belt and picked up his rifle.

"One man, dark clothes, night-vision goggles, a holstered pistol, looks to be scouting. Approaching from the northwest, estimated time of arrival, two minutes. No time to pack up and ride out of here before he arrives."

"Ruala?" Dutch bit out.

"No. Too short. A flunkie."

Dutch glanced around their camp. "No time to bug out. Do we take him down?"

Mac ignored Susan's gasp. He thought fast. "If we take him down and he doesn't report back in, more men will follow. I hoofed it back here and didn't locate his base camp to see how much backup he's got."

"Options?" Dutch asked, smearing black grease hastily on his face.

"Diversion. Suzie and I will be a guy and his girl out for a tryst. We'll give him a show and distract him while you get into position to track him. Drop him if he threatens Susan."

"You got it," Dutch said grimly, pulling the black dew rag from around his throat up and over his light hair. "Get wired. I'll call when I can." Although he was a big man, Dutch slipped away in catlike silence.

Mac hurried to Suzie's side. She was already bundling up Dutch's bedroll and stuffing it in her tent. He hefted Dutch's saddle and tossed it inside as well. It would be hard to explain two humans toting three saddles.

She looked up at him, her eyes wide with fright. "Is it him?" she asked breathlessly. "Ruala?"

"One of his men probably. Unless you can think of anyone else who'd be sneaking around out here in dark clothing using night-vision equipment."

"How did he find us so fast?"

His gut roiled ominously. He'd like to know that one, too. This was *not* good. He looked up into Suzie's worried gaze and managed to shrug nonchalantly. "It's no big deal. Dutch and I have it covered."

She shuddered. "So what do we do now?"

Mac knelt down and rummaged in his bag, coming up with a handful of gear. He tossed one of the saddle blankets over his black nylon Special Forces pack and checked his watch. Their two-minute head start was over. From here on out, he had to assume they were being watched.

"Come sit beside me, hon." He sat down casually on the broad rock beside the fire.

She did as she was told. He saw her hands shaking as she moved toward him. It wasn't supposed to happen this way. Ruala was supposed to come in from the south, the bastard.

"Now what?" she whispered.

"Smile, darlin', you're on *Candid Camera*," he said lightly. He rummaged with one hand in his pile of supplies and came up with two spare radio antennae and a plastic bag. "Let's roast some marshmallows," he announced brightly.

"You're kidding."

He smiled grimly at the shocked expression on her face. *Come on, baby. Play along.* If the slightest thing went wrong, a single inadvertent twitch, people could die tonight. "I found them in the kitchen this morning when I made the French toast. I threw them in because I thought you might need a little stress relief at some point."

"Good call," she mumbled back.

"We need to look like we're enjoying ourselves," he

murmured aloud. He raised his voice. "You do like marsh-mallows, don't you, sweetheart?"

"Uhh, yes." She answered in a similar volume. She poked a marshmallow onto the long, thin rod he handed her and held it out toward the fire. "Do you like yours brown and puffy or black and burned?"

He replied lazily, "I like mine soft and sweet on the inside, and I don't care about the outside."

She looked up sharply at him.

"Smile for the audience," he directed under his breath.

She pasted on a grin and mumbled, "Can you see him, Mac?"

"Nope, but he won't show himself if he knows what's good for him. If I had to guess, he's on his belly crawling up that ridge across from us."

"I'm scared. What am I supposed to do if he attacks?"

He answered reassuringly, "Keep your voice low but don't whisper. That way it won't carry as far. If I tell you to get down at any point, throw yourself backward off this rock as fast as you can and stay down behind it. Okay?"

"Okay," she murmured.

He raised his voice. "Now aren't you glad we came out here? No parents or brothers to chaperone us for once." He added under his breath, "Do you know anything about using a gun?"

She laughed low and sexy. Despite his tension, Mac's gut coiled a little tighter at the sound. "I don't know, darling," she teased loudly.

He assumed she was answering that she didn't know how to use a gun. Damn. He put one arm around her, pulling her close by his side. She went as stiff as a board under his touch. She felt as if she might break into a million pieces any second. Her tension had to be visible to the watcher. He reached under her hair to massage the nape of her neck. "Relax, sweetheart. We've got all night."

She threw him an apologetic look. "You're right. I'm sorry."

He popped a roasted marshmallow into his mouth and murmured around the sticky lump of sugar, "You're doing great." He continued sotto voce, "There's a beeper in my pack. If something happens to me and Dutch, hit the square button on the end of it. It's a panic button, and Uncle Sam will show up shortly to rescue you."

She nodded as she poked another marshmallow on her makeshift stick. "Next one's for you, honey bunny," she added in a normal speaking voice.

"As long as you feed it to me," he replied playfully. He murmured, "Honey bunny? Jeez, I hope Dutch didn't hear that."

She grinned and popped a wad of goo into his mouth. Mac slogged through the marshmallow until he could mumble, "I've got to get my throat radio on. I need your help."

"Uhh, okay. What do I do?"

"I'm going to roll us on top of the horse blanket. Reach underneath it, grab the wad of wires you'll feel, and stuff it under the front of my shirt."

He didn't give her time to tense up over how this maneuver was going to work. He just wrapped his arms around her and lay back, pulling her down on top of him. She felt good, stretched out across him. Correction. She felt great. Her body was slim and lissome against his, and she squirmed against him, protesting playfully, until he nearly moaned at the sensation.

He didn't have to act when he groaned aloud, "You feel so good, baby. Even better than I remembered."

Her eyes were pools of black, her pupils dilated in shock, when she propped herself up on his chest and stared down at him. He saw it in her eyes, too. Recognition that something was still there between them. Something hot and electric and sexual. Her hand slipped around his rib cage and under his back. He lifted infinitesimally to help her search beneath him.

"Got it," she mumbled. "Don't call me baby," she added loudly.

"Why not, pumpkin?" he crooned. His voice dropped. "Now slip it between us and under my shirt."

She pasted on a teasing smile and made a production of slipping her hands under his shirt. He growled in response and quickly reversed their positions. Susan looked startled as he towered above her.

"Your knee okay?" he bit out, low.

"Yeah," she murmured back.

"I'm going to kiss you now, Suzie, and while we're doing that, I need you to run the round necklace-shaped thing up my shirt to my neck."

Her jaw dropped, no doubt in outrage at the idea of Mac Conlon kissing her again after all these years. But their lives hung on making this look good. They had to convince the guy on the ridge that this was real. He prayed she'd play along. If she blew their cover now, while he was lying on the ground, in the open, with his arms around her and his weapon a full arm's length away, he was dead meat. And so was she.

Mac had never been so tense about kissing a woman, not even the first time he'd kissed Susan, all those years ago. But then, this was the first time that doing it wrong might get him killed. Please God, let Dutch not fail to cover their backs.

"I'm sorry, Suzie," he murmured. Surprised, he realized he actually meant his apology. And then his mouth closed on hers.

He'd forgotten.

How could he ever have forgotten the berries-and-cream taste of her, the way she arched up into him, kissing him with her whole body, the little sound she made in the back of her throat when she was aroused. Her lips were warm and soft beneath his. They opened eagerly, beckoning him forward. He deepened the kiss, tasting marshmallow and Suzie. Her body molded to his, cushioning and cradling him in a perfect fit. Her hand crept up his chest, exploring the muscled contours there. Suddenly he was glad for all those grueling hours of exercise. Her fingers traced upward, taking his blood pressure higher, as well, his heart pumping harder and faster as her hand roamed across his skin.

Aw, hell. Dutch, my back's all yours. And then the last remnants of rational thought drifted away like ashes on the wind, leaving only hot desire burning in his gut. He wanted her. All of her. Right here. Right now.

The cool circlet of the throat mike touched his neck, and he abruptly remembered what they were supposed to be doing. He rolled off the rock they'd been lying on, holding Suzie close. He absorbed the impact with the hard ground into his own body. She lurched against him, surprised.

"Tickle me, honey," he murmured.

"You hate being tickled," she murmured back.

He smiled seductively. "Just do it."

He gritted his teeth as she complied, and he promptly wrestled her onto her back, carefully pinning her beneath him. He hoped he wasn't hurting her knee. Their mock struggle brought them too close to the fire, so he sat up, dragging her beside him to a safer distance.

"What was all that about?" she asked under her breath.

"It covered me hooking up my mike and inserting my ear piece."

"You did all that while you were tickling me and practically hog-tying me?"

He flashed her a genuine smile. "I'm a man of many talents."

"Either that or you've got eight hands," she retorted.

He chuckled, pulling her casually against his side. ''I wish, baby.''

He sincerely hoped this act was working. Unfortunately, a single kiss wasn't likely to hold their scout's interest for very long. They were going to have to up the ante. Mac turned toward Suzie, shielding her from what he estimated to be the view of the watcher. The last thing he needed was for the scout to positively ID Susan Monroe and start shooting at her. Although with her hair messed up like that and her cheeks flushed the way they were, he doubted many people would recognize cool, sophisticated Susan Monroe right now. Who'd have guessed such heat lurked in her?

Suzie had grown up. She was tough, gutsy and the hottest number this side of the Rio Grande. He most definitely wanted to get to know this woman. At the moment he wanted inside her pants as bad as he wanted inside her heart. He clenched his teeth. *The mission, dammit, the mission.* Control came, but precariously. He closed his eyes briefly, shoving back his guilt and the pain of her anger at him. He pushed away his sudden urge to overpower her physically and emotionally until she yielded to him once more. This was all an act. It was only an act. Yeah, right.

Susan gasped when Mac's arms closed around her in an inescapable bear hug of steel. It felt good to be held—really held—by someone. Her world was so lonely and sterile she'd almost forgotten what human contact felt like.

But Mac had slipped right past her defenses. He'd brushed her self-protective prickliness aside and gone straight for her. It was exciting and frightening all at once. She leaned into his embrace, meeting his body with her own, cushioning his hard angles and edges with her yielding softness. Her breath stuck in her throat at the sensation. It would have been perfect except for the expression of acute pain that flickered across his face. Helpless frustration washed over her. Why did she have to be so bloody attracted to a man who obviously wanted nothing to do with her? But here she was, hoping he'd kiss her again. Hoping he'd do a lot more than that, in fact.

She was an idiot. She was neurotic and insecure to throw herself at a man who'd walked away, no run away, ten years ago and never looked back.

She was in heaven. Never had a man's arms felt so safe and strong around her. Never had a man so completely surrounded her, sheltering her and protecting her like this. Never had another man made her insides melt into a shapeless lump of white-hot desire. She burrowed against Mac's heat. He went as rigid as rock. It was like snuggling up to a granite boulder. He was so tense he all but vibrated. Was that good or bad? Did he want her and was he trying to hide it, or did her closeness just make him horribly uncomfortable? Should she pull away or snuggle even closer? In an agony of indecision, she did neither.

"How dangerous is the guy watching us?" she whispered into Mac's shoulder.

"He's not. As long as we don't do anything to arouse his suspicions, he's not going to try to shoot us."

Susan lurched. "He'd *kill* us?" she squeaked.

"Shh," Mac warned. "He's not going to kill anybody. Dutch will take him out long before he gets off a shot at us. You're a nonexpendable resource."

"Gee, that's comforting."

Mac chuckled, the sound a low vibration in her ear as she snuggled against him. "It should be. If the mission is to keep you alive and get the bad guys, then that's what we'll do, come hell or high water. We never fail."

"Never?"

"Never. Charlie Squad's the best, Suz. You're completely safe right now."

Somehow she believed him. There was a confident ring to his words that proclaimed their truth. She laid her head in the hollow of Mac's shoulder, beneath his ear. She couldn't count how many times she'd rested her head in this exact spot before. It gave her a powerful sense of déjà vu to be doing it again.

"So now what do we do?" she asked.

Mac opened his mouth to answer, but instead, Dutch unwittingly answered her question. Susan's ear was close enough to Mac's earpiece that she also heard Dutch's words. "Pick up the action, Mac. This guy's getting antsy."

Mac casually reached up to rub his throat, activating his mike while he was at it. "Roger."

She looked up at Mac, and he met her gaze squarely. Apology shone in his lovely eyes. It hurt like a hot poker in her heart. She didn't want him to be sorry he had to kiss her, darn it! But kiss her he did.

Her thoughts spun away like dandelion fluff as he swept her into his arms, transporting her to a place where nothing existed but the two of them. His kiss started sweetly, testing around the edges of her restraint, coaxing her to come with him further into his magical world. She had no will to resist him. Her hands slid up and into his thick, glossy hair, pulling him closer to her. Her breasts felt full and tight against his chest, her uneven breathing rubbing their peaks against him with tantalizing results.

His arm closed around her waist, pulling her higher against him, and his free hand speared into her hair, massaging her scalp and urging her ever closer. She groaned when he tore his mouth away from hers, only to sigh in ecstasy when his lips closed upon the soft spot just below her ear. His fingers twined in her hair, tugging gently, and she gladly offered him her neck to feast upon.

He accepted her wanton invitation. Her eyes closed, and she felt nothing but the fire of his mouth blazing upon her skin and an answering fire roaring inside of her. The two flames twisted and wrestled like lovers, their pagan dance entwining them in a single inferno that consumed her entirely.

Oh no, her scar. Her hands flew up to cover it, but he intercepted them. He kissed his way across the damaged flesh as if it was perfectly normal. He must be a good actor if he could act completely unaffected by the ugly scar. The thought was cold water on the flames within her.

But his kisses continued, heating her flesh anew, sending the fires inside her flaring even higher. She craved the touch of Mac's hands on her nearly as much as she craved the feel of him beneath her own fingers. She reached for his shirt, but his hands stopped hers.

The wire. She mustn't reveal the wire.

He rolled over, partially covering her with his body. *Protecting her from the shooter.*

"I don't want to crush you, baby," he murmured.

"Do I act like I'm in pain?" she murmured back.

A low, growling chuckle was his only reply before he covered her even more fully. His elbows supported his weight on either side of her head, and she reached up, looping her fingers around his massive biceps. She reveled in his hardness, in the size of him, in the way their bodies fit together.

"More, Mac," she gasped. "I want more."

He lowered his head, kissing her hungrily, and she returned his kisses just as voraciously. If she could consume him entirely, make him a part of herself and herself a part of him, she'd do it. This was a man she could lose herself in completely and revel in the experience.

Whoa. Time out. This was *Mac*.

The thought repeated itself in her head, a gentle sigh in the face of the wildfire between them. Yes. This was Mac, indeed. Her first love and, truth be told, her only real love.

Dutch's voice came across Mac's earpiece, startling Susan out of her sensual reverie. "The scout is moving away. I'm following him back to his camp."

"Don't be too long, Dutch," Mac replied in a completely businesslike tone. "I'll have us ready to move out by the time you get back."

Susan went limp with disbelief beneath him. How could Mac talk so calmly after what they'd just been doing? She was panting like a dog on a hot summer day, and he was as cool as a cucumber. Had that sizzling embrace meant nothing to him? Had all that been an act after all? Had he just been doing his job?

She wriggled beneath him, and he rolled aside immediately. She sat up indignantly while she gathered her tattered emotional defenses. She stood up awkwardly, momentarily taller than Mac as he leaned back against the boulder, gazing at her expressionlessly. She glared down at him and let her humiliation and rage build to a smashing crescendo. It was better than sobbing like a little girl.

She snarled at him, "Don't you get any ideas from what we just did, Mac Conlon. I was saving my neck and nothing more. You stay away from me. Got it?"

One dark eyebrow rose sardonically. "Got it."

Chapter 6

Susan's temper wasn't soothed one bit when Mac stood up and towered over her. "Go pack your things so I can take down the tent."

"Is that an order?" she challenged.

He shot a level stare at her. "Yes, it is."

Ooh! She balled her fists. How could one man make her so mad so fast?

And then he leaned close and murmured into her ear. His voice sent sexy shivers racing up and down her spine. "Just so you know. You may have been acting in order to save your neck, but I wasn't."

He *wasn't acting* during that hot embrace? Her jaw sagged in shock.

It eventually dawned on her that she was just standing there staring at him like a complete idiot. She lurched into motion awkwardly, stuffing things randomly into saddle-bags. Her thoughts whirled wildly. Why had he told her that? Was he actually attracted to her? A hunk like him? To a scarred, crippled wreck like her?

Susan forcibly calmed herself as she approached the horses. She didn't need four skittish Arabs on her hands right now. She led the animals into the firelight and directed Mac while he loaded the packhorse. She tied down the load herself and set about saddling the riding horses. As she bent to lift the heavy western saddle onto her mare, Mac's hands pushed hers aside. He hoisted the saddle easily and set it gently on the animal's back. Susan cinched the girth just enough to hold the saddle in place. Mac helped her saddle his horse and Dutch's, as well. A quick tightening of the cinches, and they could be on their way.

"Now what?" she asked.

Mac answered calmly, "Now we wait for Dutch to come back."

"How long will that be?"

He shrugged. "No telling. Could be a few minutes, could be several hours. We can keep the fire going until he returns, or we can wait it out in the dark."

The idea of sitting in the middle of a huge wilderness in pitch-blackness with a bunch of thugs out to kill her nearby didn't sound at all appealing. It was bad enough having to be with Mac after that shockingly steamy kiss. Her insides were one giant, painfully tight knot. Surely she'd misread what he'd meant when he said he wasn't acting. She wasn't the beautiful, desirable girl she'd once been. Men didn't find her attractive anymore. "I'd prefer a fire," she managed to choke out.

Mac's only response was to toss a couple more sticks on the cinders. He sat down beside the fire and stretched out his legs. What was he doing? Bad guys were lurking just over the next hill! "Aren't you going to stand guard or something?" she asked incredulously.

"Dutch has things under control. He'll call if he needs help."

How could Mac be so bloody relaxed? There was an

armed killer out there, somewhere beyond the ring of fire-light. She plunked herself down in a huff on the opposite side of the fire. After a couple minutes it dawned on her that Mac was sitting serenely by the fire, peacefulness fairly radiating from him. What was up with that? Patience never had been his strong suit. Since when had he embraced this Zen ideal of calm?

"Mac?"

"Hmm?"

"What are you doing?"

He looked across the fire at her with a perplexed expression. "Come again?"

"I know you. You're not this laid-back. What are you doing?"

"Ahh. I'm listening."

Susan stilled, straining to hear what he did. There were a few crickets, and the grass rustled in a light breeze, but that was it. "I don't hear anything unusual," she ventured.

Mac nodded. "Exactly. There's a certain rhythm to the night sounds. You can hear it if you try. If anybody approaches, I may not hear them, but I will hear a change in the rhythm out there." He gestured beyond the circle of firelight.

"Oh." She stared at the fire for a minute. "What are we going to do when Dutch gets back?"

"We're going to ride as fast and as far as your horses can go tonight and put some distance between ourselves and Ruala before dawn."

She frowned. "It can be risky to ride at night. The good news is the horses have had several hours of rest and a decent meal. So stamina's no problem for us."

Mac raised an amused brow. "Glad to hear it."

She blushed and scowled. Leave it to Mac not to let her off the hook gracefully for her poor word choice.

He spoke seriously. "We stand a decent chance of getting away safely if your horses are as good as you say they are.''

''What do you mean, a decent chance of getting away? I thought you said I wasn't in danger!''

His voice was tight. ''You weren't from a single scout. I can't promise the same if Ruala and an entire gang of his thugs jump us. Once Dutch finds out what we're up against, I'll make a more accurate threat assessment for you.''

Susan swallowed hard. His words were spoken with precision, but the Zen act only went so far. She knew him too well to be fooled. Underneath his bravado, he was worried. Great.

Mac settled back into his intense listening. Susan shifted around, trying to ease the throbbing ache in her knee. After a few minutes Mac stood up and went to the packhorse. He opened one of the saddlebags and pulled out a blanket. As he walked toward her she couldn't help noticing the long, muscular shape of his legs. Their lines, so powerful and perfect, were so unlike her owned ruined limb.

Mac handed her the blanket. ''Why don't you catch a nap? It's going to be a long night.''

Her fear had kept her alert so far. But now that he mentioned it, a sudden wave of exhaustion slammed into her. ''You'll be able to stay awake by yourself?'' she asked him.

He grinned. ''During Hell Week we stayed awake for more or less the whole week. Losing one night's sleep won't bother me.''

Susan shook her head. She'd forgotten for a minute that she was camping with a veritable superhero. She took the blanket and wrapped herself in it, tucking her arm under her head for a pillow. She did her best to get comfortable on the hard ground but failed miserably. How cowboys slept like this for months on end was beyond her.

* * *

She jolted awake some time later when Mac's hand touched her shoulder.

He murmured, "Dutch just radioed me. He's on his way."

Susan roused herself. The air had gotten colder while she was asleep, and it was an extreme effort to force herself out of the blanket's warm cocoon. Shivering, she fetched a jacket out of her saddlebag and packed away the blanket. By the time she tightened the horses' girths and slipped on their bridles she felt awake.

Mac had just extinguished the fire when Dutch's voice came out of the dark, startling Susan terribly. The horse beside her shied, too, and she soothed the animal while she listened to Dutch's low voice report what he'd found.

"It's him, all right. Ruala. He may look like that Ford character, but the way he moves, the way he talks—there's no mistaking the bastard."

It felt as if someone had just dumped a bucket of ice water over her head.

Dutch continued, "There are six men. They have two vehicles—an SUV and a small, four-wheel-drive, all-terrain vehicle. They're armed and generally well equipped, but their gear's not state-of-the-art. We have an edge over them in that regard. They didn't post a guard, so the scout didn't get a good enough look at Susan to ID her. But, I did hear Ruala say he'd pick you two up in the morning and check you out."

Mac interjected, "Then I suggest we be long gone by then."

Dutch nodded. "Agreed."

Susan piped up. "We can be halfway back to the ranch by sunrise if we push the horses hard."

Mac shook his head. "Our plan is sound. If Ruala's traveling by motorized vehicle, he'd overtake us long before we got back to the ranch. We need to let the horses and the terrain give us a tactical advantage.''

Susan gulped. ''What are we going to do, then?''

Mac answered soothingly, ''First, we're not going to panic. Dutch and I are trained to handle situations a lot worse than this, so I want you to relax. We *will* keep you safe. Okay?''

She took a deep breath. ''Okay.''

Mac asked, ''How long do you think it'll take us to reach the heavy arroyos, Suzie?''

She thought fast. ''The really rough terrain is still a good three or four hour ride from here.''

The three of them mounted up in silence and headed out. Susan felt her horse's confusion at this night ride, but the loyal mare dutifully forged onward. Even though she'd gotten a couple hours of rest, the hour before dawn was painful for Susan. Her whole body demanded sleep. She struggled to keep her eyes open and her body upright in the hard saddle. How did Mac go without sleep so casually? Finally the sun began to peek above the horizon. Although the light roused her to a more alert state, it also brought the perils of daylight and good visibility with it. Renewed fear brought Susan the rest of the way to full consciousness.

She looked around and realized they had reached the beginnings of gully country. The land rose more sharply now toward the head of a huge valley. There were more undulations and rock outcroppings in the terrain than before, and boulders marred the horizon. Mac took the lead, and she noticed he used the contours of the land, following the ridge lines, but staying below them.

Malika was tired, and Susan began keeping an eye out for somewhere to stop and let the horses get a drink. They rode for another fifteen minutes or so before she spotted what she was looking for. ''Guys,'' she called out quietly, ''we need to water the horses, and there's a spring over there.'' She pointed to a cluster of cottonwood trees announcing the presence of water.

Mac veered his horse toward where she pointed.

It felt heavenly to slide out of the saddle, even if her feet did burn with a thousand needles of pain when she first stood on them. Her knee felt more like someone was jabbing knives into it. Big, sharp butcher knives.

While the horses drank, Mac and Dutch put their heads together, and Susan went behind a boulder to relieve herself. When she returned, they gestured her to join them.

"How are the horses holding up?" Mac asked.

"They're tired, but they can go for another hour or two. Once it warms up significantly, they'll need shade and rest."

Dutch spread out the map for her. "Our GPS coordinates place us here. Does that jibe with where you think we are?"

"Yeah, looks spot-on. We have to go this last bit, and then we should hit the big, nasty canyons."

Dutch asked, "How long will it take us to get there?"

Susan cast back in her memory for what the terrain looked like ahead. It got steeper and rockier, and the footing for the horses deteriorated, too.

"If we're cautious and don't want to risk hurting the horses, I'd say an hour. If we have to hurry, I'd guess half that long. But the horses will be done if we go that fast."

Mac nodded. "Good enough. Let's get to it, then."

They'd been riding for about twenty minutes when Mac said quietly to Dutch. "Here they come."

Susan looked back over her shoulder and gasped. A puff of dust was just visible on the horizon behind them.

Dutch gazed through some sort of gadget that looked like a sawed-off telescope. "Three miles," he announced.

Mac replied calmly, "Visibility's pretty good out here. I'd have guessed they were closer than that."

"How can you guys talk so damned placidly about

this?'' Susan demanded. ''Can't you at least sound a little bit worried?''

Mac actually laughed at her. ''But we're not worried.''

''And why not?''

''Because we have enough firepower in our packs to obliterate those men without leaving enough bits to tell how many bodies there were, let alone identify them.''

Dutch commented, ''I'd hate to land Susan in the middle of a firefight, though. You remember what it was like when Colonel Folly's wife got caught in a war zone with us.''

Mac rolled his eyes. ''No kidding. I thought we were goners on that one.''

Susan simply could not believe it. They were reminiscing about old missions when killers were closing in on them. Fast!

She was slightly mollified when, about ten minutes later, Dutch looked through his field glass again and said, ''We need to pick up the pace if we want to reach the rough country first.''

Susan nodded and urged her mare forward. The gallant horse responded by breaking into a careful trot. ''Let me take the lead, guys. This mare is the most trail savvy of the horses we've got. She'll find the best footing for the other horses.''

Dutch and Mac reined aside for her to go ahead of them. Susan gripped the reins lightly, staying out of Malika's way so the mare could pick a path.

The horizon began to break up heavily in front of them. Crags and crevices became frequent, and the red, rocky soil shifted more and more into rough sandstone outcroppings.

The puff of dust behind them had become two distinct clouds of dust. She could even make out the dark spot of the larger vehicle. Dutch calmly announced the range as just over a mile.

Susan's heart pounded, and her breath came too fast. Her

shoulder blades itched. She *hated* being chased like a defenseless rabbit.

Her mind kept straying to thoughts of what Ruala would do if he caught her, Mac and Dutch. She could only guess at how ruthless he would be. As Ruala and his henchmen closed in, terror choked her.

Mac commented, "The good news is, they're about to start hitting some terrain troubles. The stuff we've been moving through should slow them down significantly."

Susan's panic abated. A little. "Why's he coming after us so hard?" she asked.

Mac answered grimly. "He can't take a chance that the woman his man saw last night is actually you. You can positively ID him, but he can positively ID you, too. And none of his other men can. He's got to lay eyeballs on you personally."

Mac left unsaid the part where Ruala would kill her the moment he knew for sure who she was. Her life depended on a narrow gap of terrain that was shrinking by the minute.

All four horses were beginning to labor in their breathing. It was time to slow them down and give them a blow. But it wasn't as if they had any choice about pushing onward. She spoke encouragingly to her mare and prayed she wasn't causing the horse any lasting damage.

The next few minutes were an interminable nightmare. The vehicles behind them did, in fact, stop gaining ground. But they had to push the horses to their limits to stay ahead.

Finally Susan's mare stepped through a narrow opening bounded by sheer walls of stone that reached some twenty feet up into the air. Susan had to lift her legs high to squeeze through the opening. She'd bet Dutch and Mac had to raise their legs practically over their horses' necks to squeeze through it.

She looked back in time to see the packhorse get stuck.

Oh God. And then the little mare tugged her way through the pass.

Susan reined her mare to a halt. Malika stopped instantly, her head hanging low, breathing hard. "There. That ought to slow that jerk down a bit. No way will a car fit through that crevice."

Mac grinned. "You did good, Suzie. We made it."

She grinned back. "Thanks."

Dutch interrupted. "When you two are done gushing at each other, we still need to put some distance between us and Ruala. He'll find a way around this gap eventually, and a couple of his men will keep chasing us on foot in the meantime. I expect they'll be ticked off enough to shoot at us when they find us."

Susan groaned mentally. Dutch was right, but it was killing her to keep asking her courageous horse for more.

Mac seemed to understand her agony. "Just a little bit, farther, Suz, and then we'll let these horses rest as long as they want to. Lord knows they've earned it." He reached down to pat the neck of his own exhausted mount.

Reluctantly she picked up the reins. At least Malika had gotten a few seconds to catch her breath.

The sound of an engine drifted to them on the breeze. Susan jumped. She urged her mare onward, praying the horses had enough strength left to climb into some truly hostile terrain. The horses seemed to pick up on their riders' urgency and had one burst of energy left. They scrambled and scrabbled, goat-like, into and through several steep, rocky gullies.

Finally Dutch called out quietly, "That ought to do it, Susan."

She sagged in her saddle and brought her stumbling horse to a halt. Thank goodness. She slid to the ground, her legs as limp as noodles. Her left leg collapsed, but she'd expected it and was hanging on to the saddle when it went.

She turned around and was startled to find Mac hovering right behind her.

"You okay?" he murmured.

She nodded, too tired to tell him to stop worrying about her.

"You've got grit, babe," he said with quiet pride.

A warm feeling flooded her as Mac turned to Dutch and said, "I'll take the first watch. You two take care of the horses."

Susan watched Mac scramble off into the rocks, back the way they'd come, amazed at his reserves of energy. She couldn't help but notice the lethal-looking rifle he carried with him. It had a large telescopic sight and an ungainly, curved clip protruding from its underside.

She shuddered and turned to the horses. Dutch was already stripping off the saddles. She used a towel to wipe off the worst of the lather and sweat from the animals' heaving sides.

"We need to get them water if we can," Susan told the blond man.

He nodded. "That may have to wait a little while, but as soon as one of us can get away safely to scout around a bit, I'll see what we can do."

"Thanks, Dutch." Susan added, "By the way, where did you get that nickname?"

"My last name is Dutcher, and I suppose my coloring had something to do with it."

His rugged good looks *were* distinctly Nordic. But she preferred Mac's startling coloring—the sable hair, fair skin, and sapphire eyes of the black Irish. She cast a look around. Forbidding looking walls of stone surrounded them on all sides. "What's next?" she asked.

"We set up camp and get some rest."

"Ruala won't come looking for us?"

Dutch grinned. "Nah. He doesn't know what to make of us right now. He's gonna sit and think about it for a while."

"If you say so," she responded dubiously.

He gave her a kind look. "We've been in this business a long time. We know how this guy thinks. That's why we're better than he is. We're inside his head and he doesn't even know it."

Dutch was right. He and Mac knew what they were doing. She let go of the tension across the back of her neck.

He spoke behind her. "I hate to ask for your help, but in these rocks, it'll be tricky to set up your tent by myself."

"As soon as I'm done with the horses, I'm all yours."

Dutch threw her a broad grin. "Don't let Mac hear you say that, eh? I'd hate to have to kill him."

Susan looked over her shoulder at Dutch, surprised. "I beg your pardon?"

"Mac's a little, uh, proprietary, where you're concerned."

Susan glared at Dutch over the back of the packhorse. "Despite what you may have seen last night, Mac Conlon's got no hold on me, whatsoever. Anything we had between us was over a long time ago, and I wouldn't trust him now any farther than I could throw him."

Dutch said earnestly, "My job last night was to watch the scout, and that's what I did. Whatever happened between you and Mac, I didn't see a thing."

Susan was more relieved than she'd expected. What had happened between her and Mac had been so…raw. So personal. It was bad enough knowing a total stranger had witnessed it, but it had been even worse thinking that Dutch might've seen it, too.

She set down her mare's hoof, which she'd been checking for stones and bruises, and straightened slowly. "I'm sorry I snapped at you."

"No problem. It was a rough night."

Susan was impressed when Dutch rigged her tent cleverly between two large boulders, tarp-like, at least doubling the amount of space under cover that way. She eyed its shady interior longingly and didn't hesitate when Dutch suggested she get some shut-eye. She crawled inside and stretched out on top of her sleeping bag, so happy to be horizontal she didn't care that the ground was hard and uneven beneath her. Her last thought before she went unconscious was that this was how cowboys managed to sleep on the ground. They were too exhausted to care.

Sometime later, her bed got comfortable all of a sudden, and a pillow materialized under her head. She snuggled into it, moaned her contentment and settled back into oblivion.

Chapter 7

Of its own volition, Mac's hand wandered to Susan's hair, stroking it gently as she sprawled half on top of him, dead to the world. What in the hell was he going to do about her? He shouldn't even think about her in that way, let alone have feelings for her. He was on a mission, for God's sake.

His impulse to play amateur psychologist was huge. Every time she called herself crippled or told him what she couldn't do, it set his teeth on edge. One of the first lessons of special ops was to think positive. Concentrate on what assets you have and what you can do with them. But it wasn't as if Susan was going to listen to him anytime soon. She could hardly stand to be in the same state with him. Unless… He turned the idea over in his head. It might just work—a little reverse psychology to get Susan defending her abilities. It was worth a try. If that killer kiss last night hadn't knocked the negative attitude out of her, not much else was likely to work.

One step at a time. First he had to gain her trust. Then he could show her how valuable a person she was. And then he could move on to the real challenge—gaining her forgiveness.

At least she was speaking to him now. It was an improvement over the past ten years of stony silence. He'd asked Tex once if she ever mentioned him, and her brother hadn't hesitated in answering, "Never."

He could only hope she wasn't so far gone that he couldn't rescue her from the lonely, unhappy world she'd locked herself away in. Whether or not Susan wanted to admit it, there was definitely something simmering between them that still had to be dealt with. Something spicy and wild. Ten years ago their relationship had been sensational. But last night…that kiss had been in another class altogether. Hot. Racy. Unlike anything that had ever passed between them. He wanted to know more about this new Susan. A lot more.

But not here. Not now. They were in the middle of a dangerous situation, and he needed to make decisions with his head, not his libido.

Despite his assurances to her, this mission had a couple of serious problems. In the first place, they were undermanned. Tex was on a well-earned vacation with his fiancée, Colonel Folly had wrecked his leg and was out of the game for good, and it would be a couple more days before Doc and Howdy got back from Washington.

In the second place, Ruala was a highly dangerous opponent no matter what the environment, unpredictable and smart.

Protective worry for her surged in his gut. He *would* keep her safe. At all costs. And that was their third problem. The surest and fastest way to send a mission straight to hell was to inject personal feelings into the mix. They were distracting, caused undisciplined behaviors and were a general pain in the butt.

The way the other guys on the squad were standing back from Susan bothered him. Like he'd staked out his territory with her. He supposed Dutch could've made out with Susan instead of him while *he* tracked the scout…

Mac's thoughts derailed abruptly. Damn. The very thought of Dutch doing with Susan what he'd done last night had just shot his heart rate up thirty points and sent a rush of hot, adolescent rage to his face.

He froze beneath her sleeping form. He was in trouble here.

Susan murmured sleepily, her hand wandering across his chest, her mouth nuzzling the base of his neck like a kitten seeking food. Her thigh rode higher, rubbing him in places that didn't need to be rubbed just now. He gritted his teeth and tried to think of cold, painful things. It didn't help.

"Take it easy, honey," he murmured into her hair. "You're killing me, here."

Her reaction was violent. She lurched upright, awakening with a squawk of outrage. "How dare you let me do that!"

"How dare I…?" he spluttered.

"Yes! How dare you!"

He glared at her, matching her outrage. "How is it I'm to blame because you were crawling all over me in your sleep?"

She glared back at him. "You just are."

"Hey. I'm out here putting my neck on the line to save your cute behind. A little gratitude wouldn't hurt."

"Gratitude? Why you arrogant…oaf! Why don't you just go home?"

The insult bit a lot deeper than he wanted to let on. She'd been the one with the stellar future before her as a brilliant computer scientist. He'd been just a slogging soldier. Except now they were on his turf. This was his world, his area of expertise.

"An oaf, am I? Who found the scout last night? Who laid the false trail away from our camp to buy us time this morning?" He couldn't shout, but he did lean forward until he was nose to nose with her. "Who spent the last three hours doing a perimeter check of this whole godforsaken corner of Texas so you could have a peaceful nap? And who spent a solid hour hauling water so your damn horses could have a drink?"

That made her blink. "They're already watered?"

"Yeah," he grumbled.

"Darn it, Mac Conlon! Just when I was sure I hated your guts, why did you have to go and do something thoughtful like that?"

He stared down at her, shocked. "Thoughtful? I was just doing my job. We need the horses, so I took care of the asset."

"It was still kind of you to take care of them so quickly," Susan declared.

He added slowly, "Do you have any idea how many people I've killed in the last decade?"

"No, and I don't want to know. Thank you for watering my horses."

"You're welcome," he mumbled. Kind? Him? Not hardly. Mac couldn't remember the last time he'd met a woman who was completely unimpressed by his work. Yet here was Susan, tickled pink he'd watered her horses so quickly and totally disinterested in the number of people he'd killed. He couldn't say that about most of the women he met. There was a certain security to his ego in knowing that his profession made him irresistible to enough chicks that he'd never have to worry about getting sex.

But what about being loved? The question crept insidiously into his consciousness and stuck there. He tried to shake it off, but it wouldn't go away. What did he care about love? It was a weak emotion meant for women. Another thought wormed its way inside his head. *Susan had loved him once. And it had been wonderful.*

Dammit! He wasn't going down that path again. Love had been great right up until the part where his whole life and hers had come crashing down upon his head. Would that damned night never end? Its horror stretched on and on in front of him, swallowing his whole life in that one, black moment.

All he had to do was close his eyes to hear the shots ringing out below him. A high-powered rifle. Ripping into the thin metal skin of the surveillance van like Godzilla's claws. He could still feel the gut-wrenching nausea of realizing Susan was caught inside a tin-can death trap with bullets ricocheting around in it like pinballs. He'd never run so fast in his life. He had one lousy pistol on him. Nine shots. But by God, he'd knicked Ruala. Made the bastard take cover and then run before police arrived. More important, he'd backed Ruala off of taking any more shots at Susan.

He'd been out of his mind with terror when he literally tore open the van's ruined door with his bare hands. He'd *never* forget the sight of Susan crumpled on the floor inside, lying in a huge pool of her own blood. He'd died inside. Right there on the spot. Until she took a single rattling breath. It was the longest couple of seconds of his life until she drew the next one. And then the paramedics had shoved him aside and hauled her away to the nearest hospital.

He still felt guilty as hell for not anticipating that she'd take the van and try to do the surveillance on Ferrare's meeting by herself. He should've seen it coming. She'd been too smart to buy his line that Charlie Squad was just walking away from the mission. She was too confident, too focused on nailing Ferrare to walk away herself. He'd underestimated her. And the rest was history.

"Could you please step outside?" Susan's voice intruded upon Mac's bleak thoughts. He blinked as a tent came back into focus overhead.

"It's my turn to sleep," he protested. That probably didn't make any sense to her. He tried again. "I'm supposed to be asleep right now. I'm taking the first watch tonight." He didn't add that he hadn't slept at all last night and wouldn't sleep tonight, either. He could go sixty hours without sleep if he had to, but it was no fun, and he'd rather skip the stimulant pills.

"You can sleep as soon as I've changed my clothes and freshened up. I'm wearing half the dirt in Texas right now."

He supposed cranky was better than that long-suffering-victim mode of hers. Rather than burn any more time arguing with her, he just crawled out of the tent. He passed in a jug of water for her and stood up, surveying their position.

Susan eventually appeared beside him. "Go take your precious nap. I'm going to check on the horses."

"Gee, thanks," he said dryly. It was probably just as well that she was being antagonistic. It made objectivity where she was concerned a whole lot easier to achieve.

Susan headed for the horses, a little farther up the valley. The task of brushing them usually was soothing to her, but today her thoughts kept going around in circles. She was supposed to hate Mac. But she kept remembering how good it used to be between them. Kept wanting to crawl all over him. Kept wishing he found her as attractive as she did him. But that was a dead-end road. She couldn't get rid of the scars or the limp. Except when he'd put his arms around her and kissed her into oblivion last night, her imperfections suddenly hadn't seemed nearly as important.

The horses' coats glistened, and still she'd come up with no profound revelations. Frustrated, she headed back toward camp. A movement up the hill caught her eye. It was Dutch, stretched out on the ground, peering over the ridge through a pair of binoculars. She picked her way up to his position.

"See anything interesting?" she murmured.

He passed her the binoculars. "Look for yourself."

She put the lenses to her eyes and another camp leaped into view. Ruala and another man stood by a truck, smoking. She recoiled sharply. "They're so close!" she gasped, startled.

"They're about a quarter mile away," Dutch replied.

"What's keeping them from just walking right into our camp?" she asked.

Dutch grinned over his shoulder at her. "Besides the fact that we'd blow their heads off if they tried it?"

She gestured at Ruala and his men. "They don't know that."

"They don't know we wouldn't do it, either. They're being cautious. Ruala's suspicious of us, but he's not willing to chance a confrontation until he knows more about us."

"And how will he learn more about us?"

Dutch shrugged. "He'll try to draw us out, test us. We'll no doubt play some cat and mouse games with him tonight."

"You sound like you're looking forward to that."

He grinned wolfishly at her. "I am."

Susan shuddered. She didn't like being a mouse one bit. Especially with a deadly cat like Ruala camped over the next hill.

"Can I bring you anything, Dutch?"

"Nah, I'm fine. But you could…"

"What?"

"Never mind. It's none of my business."

"What were you going to say?" she prompted. "It was about Mac, wasn't it?"

"Yeah," he answered reluctantly. "Back off a little, okay? He hasn't slept much since the colonel told us you were in trouble. He didn't get any sleep last night, and he's going to be up all night tonight."

She hadn't realized…and she'd been snippy to him about taking a nap, too. Sheesh. She owed him an apology.

"Thanks for telling me, Dutch. I'll leave him alone."

"No problem." The Viking trained his binoculars on his quarry once more.

She puttered around the camp, fidgeting really, trying to keep her mind off cats and mice until Mac woke up. He emerged from the tent just as the sun touched the western horizon.

Susan held out a canteen. "Water?"

He took the canteen and tipped it up. The tanned column of his throat caught her attention, its corded muscles contracting each time he swallowed. Lord, he oozed sex appeal.

He handed the canteen back to her. "Thanks."

He sounded distant. Impersonal. Panic tickled her ribs. "Look, Mac. I shouldn't have snapped at you earlier. I appreciate you putting your neck on the line for me."

He looked hard at her but didn't say anything.

She swallowed her pride and added, "I'm sorry."

He nodded briefly, acknowledging her apology. Shoot. Why did he have to go all strong and silent on her now, when she was laying her guts out to him? "Truce?" she asked.

He considered her grimly for a moment. Then his dimples flashed in that devastating grin of his. "Truce."

Relief poured over her. She watched Mac sit down on a boulder and rip open a brown plastic pouch he'd dug out of his pack. He pulled out something that looked marginally like food.

"What's that?" Susan asked dubiously.

"Supper," he replied with obviously false enthusiasm. "Want an MRE of your own? It's a 'meal ready to eat.' Seventeen hundred calories of prepackaged swill, but it'll keep you going."

"Aren't you at least going to add water to that…stuff?"

He grinned. "We reserve that for gourmet occasions. I suppose this qualifies." He pulled out another pouch and prepared it, adding water and squishing it around in the plastic pouch. In a cheesy Italian accent, he said, "For your dining pleasure, I geeva to you zee beefa ravioli."

Susan grinned. "Dehydrated ravioli, huh? Sounds yummy."

They ate in companionable silence. It felt shockingly familiar. Once upon a time they'd been so attuned to each other that words weren't necessary to share their thoughts. An insidious warmth seeped through her as the moment drew out. She ventured a glance up at Mac, and he was looking at her, a curious expression in his eyes. She'd almost describe it as affection, if that weren't the farthest thing from what he must feel for her. She looked away, but the warmth persisted.

When they finished eating, Mac gathered the food packaging and stowed it in a saddlebag. He sat down on his rock once more. "Talk to me about the horses, Suz."

Susan blinked. Just like that, the charming man she used to know and love was replaced by this hard, businesslike warrior. She replied, "They're tired but not hurt. As long as they get plenty of water and rest, they'll be fine. Right now, they're grazing some grass I found."

"When will they be ready to go again?" he asked.

"It depends on what you mean by going. They could move tonight if they had to, but I wouldn't do more than walk them."

Mac shook his head. "When we move again, we'll go hard, like we did this morning. How long until they can do that?"

Susan flinched. They were going to have to do that to her lovely Arabs again? "They'll need at least twenty-four hours of solid rest before they give another maximum effort."

Mac nodded. A frown of intense concentration wrinkled his brow. She'd never doubted that Mac was highly intelligent, and it was gratifying to see him apply his formidable intellect to the work. She only wished their lives didn't depend on it.

He spoke abruptly. "Dutch has the right idea. We'll mess around with these guys tonight. Ruala should back off by daylight tomorrow. We'll rest through the day, and then leave tomorrow night."

"Please tell me we'll be heading back to the ranch," she said.

"Yes, we will. Okay, now for our next problem."

When he didn't continue, Susan asked, "And that is…"

"You."

"Me? And here I was trying so hard not to be a pain in the neck."

"It's not that," Mac answered, grinning reluctantly. "Dutch is tied up doing surveillance on our visitors. I need to go set up a few traps in the hills, but I don't want to leave you alone in camp. If Ruala moves on us, Dutch might not be able to get back here fast enough from his current position to pull you out."

"So take me with you." It seemed like a perfectly simple solution to her. Except Mac tended to treat her like some porcelain doll in constant need of protecting.

He looked hard at her. His gaze strayed down to her leg. "I dunno…"

She winced as liquid shame pooled in her gut. "I try not to let it stop me from doing much," she said quietly. She would *not* beg. And she would *not* argue. Not with a killer waiting for her just over that hill.

He gave her a long, assessing look and then finally nodded slowly. "Okay, then. You'll go with me."

Wonderment wiped her brain blank. He'd said yes? He was letting her go with him to do his work? "Great!" she said brightly to cover her utter amazement. "It'll be fun. I've always wanted to know how to lay a booby trap."

He scowled. "This isn't fun and games. People will die tonight if anyone gets stupid. You could die."

She met his worried gaze head on. "I know, Mac."

He looked away first. And sighed. "Why don't you go check the horses while I get my bag of tricks and radio Dutch."

She was annoyed he wouldn't let her carry any of the gear until she lifted his pack by one of the shoulder straps a few minutes later. It weighed a ton. "Good grief! What's in this thing? Bricks?"

Mac crouched in front of her, surveying a small pile of rocks by the side of a natural path in the rocks. Without looking over his shoulder, he replied absently, "Explosives. Detonators. Wire, batteries, pliers, timers, det cord…"

Susan gulped. She watched, fascinated, as Mac fished around in his pouch by feel with one hand. He came up with a gob of gray putty. He rolled it into a cone shape and wedged it carefully between the rocks. He poked a blasting cap into the putty and ran an olive-green, gossamer-thin wire across the path about twelve inches off the ground. He secured the far end of it on the other side of the trail.

"What is this going to do?" Susan asked.

"I've put just enough of a directional charge in there to make those rocks roll down into the path. They'll knock down whoever trips this wire and make a lot of noise."

"What if an animal hits the trap?"

Mac grinned over his shoulder. "Never fear, Miss Greenpeace. There's too much fresh scent of humans here for many critters to be wandering around this valley tonight. They'll stay well away from the area."

In a matter of minutes it became clear to her that Mac was a veritable artist at his work. None of his traps were lethal in scope, and they were all set up to look like natural occurrences. A branch snapping in someone's face, a cactus popping up under foot, rocks sliding down in the path. All of it sure to annoy and hinder whoever encountered it, however.

As hard as she wished for the light not to fade, the heavens went from twilight gray to dark blue to black, and the first stars began to shine. The vast emptiness of the void above sent shivers down her spine. "Isn't it about time we headed back to camp?" Susan asked nervously.

"We're not going back to camp," Mac answered as he balanced a rock on top of a log that was set to roll down a hillside.

"We're not?"

"Certainly not. It's the first place the thugs will go. Besides, while you were checking the horses, I trapped the bejeezus out of the whole place."

"Where are we spending the night, then?" She felt stupid for asking, but her mind wasn't coming up with any mental images of where they were going to sleep. Or at least hide.

"Out here." Mac gestured around him.

She'd been afraid he'd say that. "It'll get cold," she protested weakly.

He grinned at her. "Cold is when you spend six hours swimming in fifty-degree ocean water to a beach landing."

"That's practically ice water!"

"Keep your voice down," he admonished. "Yeah, it's cold."

"You guys are nuts!" she mumbled.

He chuckled. "So I've been told. I had a little extra room in my pack, so I tossed in a blanket for later. We'll be plenty warm."

One blanket. Singular. That they'd share. Susan gulped at the memory of what had happened between them last night. Would there be a repeat tonight? Her heart beat faster.

"The fun should begin soon," Mac commented, interrupting her train of thoughts. "I want you to wear this radio, Suzie."

She looked at the jumbled wires he held out to her. "How do you put it on?" she asked around the tightness in her throat.

Would he run his hands up under her shirt like she had his when she helped him don a microphone? Shivers of anticipation raced across her skin, and her cheeks felt hot all of a sudden.

He stepped so close she felt the warmth radiating from his body. One of his hands eased under the edge of her shirt and settled on her waist. His fingers slid up her torso, counting ribs and threading cool wire across her skin. His palm slid around to the front, and continued upward into the warm valley between her breasts. His touch was hot, exquisitely gentle.

"I'm sorry, honey," he murmured.

She wasn't. Oh, no. Not at all. His fingers traced higher, approaching the hollow above her collarbone. And then his other hand traced her shoulder to the neck of her T-shirt, sliding across her throat in a dangerous, delicate caress. His fingers scooped down into her shirt, meeting his other hand. The heat of them scalded her skin and sent her heart racing.

His fingers encircled her neck as he guided the throat mike into place. He reached under her hair to her nape. His thumb ran once from her hairline down to the base of her neck, sending wild sensations cavorting across her skin.

Then his nimble fingers attached the Velcro closure, and threaded the earpiece into her right ear. His fingertips ran around the sensitive shell of her ear, then trailed down her neck as if reluctant to retreat.

His voice was a bare whisper of sound. "You activate your mike by pushing the button here." His fingers entwined with hers, guiding her fingertip to a flattish button at the base of her neck. His palm cupped her hand, swallowing her flesh in his heat and carefully restrained strength.

"Or you can go hot mike, where everything you say gets transmitted automatically," he murmured, his mouth close enough to her temple for her to feel the warm humidity of his breath.

Her skin felt hot to the touch, her pulse beat rapidly under her fingertips where he held them against her neck. Blood rushed through her ears, made louder by the earpiece she now wore. Or maybe that sound was her breath rushing in and out of her suddenly constricted lungs.

"You slide this button forward to go hot." He guided her fingers to her ear, showing her a tiny switch.

How wrong he was. All she had to do to go hot was think about him. She was imagining him running his fingers all over her body in just the same way he was doing to her ear right now. Her breath rasped loudly as he slid the little switch forward. She was huffing like a racehorse.

Mac looked down sharply at her. "Are you okay?"

How in the heck was she supposed to answer that? Of course she wasn't okay! "Uh, yeah, sure. It just makes me a little…nervous…being out here in the dark with Ruala and his men out there somewhere.''

Mac slid the hot switch to the off position, and the sounds of her racing breath went away.

"Don't worry about Ruala and his men," he murmured. "Dutch is keeping an eye on them. He'll let us know when they start moving. Until then, there's nothing to worry about.''

Nothing except keeping herself from leaping on top of Mac and tearing all his clothes off.

"Relax, sweetheart," he murmured. "There'll be plenty of reasons to get nervous later.''

The promise in his voice was thick and hot and made her insides melt. One blanket, huh? Oh, boy.

"Come on, Suzie. Let's go find a spot to watch our handiwork.''

"Uh, right.'' She followed him on wobbly legs as he picked his way up a steep hillside. Whenever the terrain got rough, he stopped and put a hand under her elbow. Little did he know that when he touched her like that, he put her in grave jeopardy of her legs collapsing right out from under her. At one point they stopped before a wide patch of loose shale and gravel.

"Suzie, when you walk across this stuff, set your feet down slowly. Test the gravel roll under your foot by moving it side to side before you put your full weight down. Can you do that?''

She nodded, watching closely as he took a few steps.

He started across the treacherous terrain, and she followed, very slowly. It wouldn't have been so bad if there weren't a sheer drop to her right, maybe ten feet away. Worse, she realized with dismay that the patch of gravel sloped gently toward the cliff. If she slipped the wrong way, she could slide right over the edge. She risked a peek into the abyss. And froze.

The gully fell away into blackness. She could see a good fifty feet down the opposite cliff face before it was lost in the dark.

"Suzie," came Mac's voice very calmly. "I need you to take another couple steps."

She turned back toward his shadowed form, which loomed ahead of her on the far side of the pale patch of shale flakes. She put her right foot down and took a step. And then her left. She began to feel light-headed and realized she was holding her breath. She stopped to breathe for a second.

"Just a little bit farther, honey," Mac coaxed.

She reached out with her left foot and moved it side to side the way he'd shown her. There was an ominous little wobble beneath the ball of her foot, but she was too terrified to stop moving. She was going to keep going until she reached Mac.

She put her weight on the foot, and it shot out from under her. Her knee collapsed and there wasn't a chance she could stop herself from going down.

A scream escaped her as she fell. She crashed onto her left side, sliding feetfirst toward the beckoning ravine. She picked up speed as she scrambled for a toehold or a handhold. Anything to stop her from going over that cliff!

And then her left arm was all but yanked out of its socket. Her death slide was halted abruptly. Her feet were hanging in midair.

"I've got you," Mac grunted.

She looked up, and saw him sitting on his behind, his heels dug into the gravel, both powerful hands wrapped around her wrist in a painful grip.

"Don't move a muscle, Susan. Let me do all the work. Got it?"

"Yeah," she panted.

"Okay, here we go." He wiggled his heels into the

gravel and pushed backward gently. She moved maybe an inch. But it was an inch away from the edge of the cliff. Gradually he eased them higher, away from the ravine. It took several minutes, and Susan was sure her arm was being torn off before Mac gave a final heave.

He let go of her, and she realized she was lying on solid rock once more. And then his arms went around her as he gathered her into a fierce hug. ''God, that was close, Suzie.''

Way too close. He'd saved her life. ''Thanks,'' she whispered.

One of his hands pressed her head suffocatingly tight against his shoulder. He murmured into her hair, ''What would I have done if I'd lost you?''

Susan froze. She pushed away from his chest far enough to look up at him in the scant moonlight. ''Would it really have mattered to you that much?''

He stared back at her, his eyes dark, unfathomable pools within the black night around them. He looked at her for a long time before he finally answered.

''Yeah, it would have mattered.''

Chapter 8

Susan froze. She stared hard at the midnight shadows cloaking his face, trying to make out something, anything, of his expression.

Yeah, it would have mattered. His voice hadn't given away a thing. Did he mean it would matter to him personally if something happened to her, or did he mean it mattered in general because she'd been classified as nonexpendable? Did she dare believe he was saying he still had feelings for her?

Her mind tumbled, disoriented. Did she return those feelings for him? Should she allow herself to feel anything at all for him until she knew for certain what he'd meant? But how was she supposed to figure that out?

"Mac, we need to talk..."

He cut her off abruptly. "Not now."

"Why not?"

"Didn't you just hear Dutch?" he asked impatiently.

"No," she answered, confused.

His hand touched the side of her head, and she jumped. His fingers traced her ear quickly. "Ahh. You knocked your earpiece out in your fall." Quickly he replaced the small device.

"Come on, Suzie. We've got to get out of here. Dutch called a minute ago. Ruala's getting ready to come out and play. Probably heard you scream."

"Sorry about that—" she started.

"Don't worry. You did a pretty fair imitation of a mountain lion," he retorted gruffly.

He helped her to her feet. Her left side felt mauled and her knee was already beginning to swell, but fear of continuing the treacherous ascent drowned out her aches and pains. She'd nearly died, and the dangerous stuff hadn't even started yet.

"Mac, I'm scared. Tell me this path gets easier."

"This path gets easier."

"Don't humor me, dammit!"

"Keep your voice down," he murmured sharply. "Sound travels forever in terrain like this. I'll go first. Grab on to my belt and don't let go. You'll be fine. I promise."

He turned his back to her, waiting for her to do as he said. She could seriously do without making like a mountain goat anymore tonight, but if she had to do it, hanging on to his belt was better than nothing. His black silk turtleneck shirt was soft against the back of her hand. The hard, vertical bulges of his back muscles flexed as he took a step. And another. It was mesmerizing.

"You okay back there?" he asked after a minute of climbing.

"I guess so." Please let him think that breathless sound in her voice was fear, or maybe exertion. She'd die if he realized how disconcerted she was at the mere touch of him.

His mellow voice caressed her. "Tell me if I'm going too fast."

"Okay," she panted.

"Promise?"

"Yes, already," she grumbled at him. "Thanks for your concern, but I can still walk, you know."

"Yeah, I noticed." Humor infused his voice. "You've still got that sexy cat walk that used to drive me crazy."

She tripped over her own feet and barely managed not to fall on her face. She righted herself hastily. *He thought her walk was sexy?* Her entire brain tripped over the concept.

They worked their way steadily higher. Dutch gave them occasional progress reports on Ruala and his men as they moved out of their own camp and toward the valley.

Listening to a play-by-play description of armed killers stalking her nearly undid Susan. Dutch's terse descriptions conjured images she could do without. Six men. All armed. Semiautomatic weapons. Radios. Headsets. Night-vision goggles.

These guys were the pros Howdy had predicted they'd be. Hunters. And she was their prey. Oh, Lord. Her hands shook, and her knees actually trembled. It made walking that much harder than usual. She had to concentrate on every step she took. Were it not for her death grip on Mac's belt, she'd have fallen down a half-dozen times already.

The path opened out into a level, rock-strewn summit.

"Stay low," Mac commanded.

Awkwardly, she tried to mimic his crouching stance as he eased forward. She couldn't do it. Her knee locked up on every step and it was agony to forcibly flex it each time. She panted. "I'm really sorry, Mac, but I can't crouch and walk. Isn't there something else we could do?"

"We could crawl," was his dry reply.

That sounded even worse.

"We're almost there, Suz. Just a few more seconds. Try bending over at the waist but walking with your legs straight."

She tried it, and the clumsy posture worked. Barely. She gritted her teeth and leaned on his belt, letting him pull more of her weight as her strength drained away. It didn't seem to slow him down at all.

Her forehead bumped into something firm yet resilient. Startled, she looked up. Oh, dear. She'd just plastered her face against Mac's rear end. He whirled around to stare at her. Thank goodness it was pitch-black out, or he'd be seeing possibly the worst blush of her life. Horribly embarrassed, she mumbled, "Uh, sorry."

He grinned. "No apologies required."

Desperate to distract him, she looked around. Waist-high boulders littered the summit. "Now what?" she asked.

"Well, either you let me plant my face in your behind now, or we go set up our surveillance."

"Say *what?*" It was Dutch's voice over her earpiece.

She closed her eyes, mortified.

Mac chuckled. "Nothing, Dutch. We're at look-out point two and setting up. We'll be in place in sixty seconds."

Susan whispered to Mac, "Could you *please* go off hot mike if you're going to say things like that?"

A bit of moonlight peeked through a wisp of cloud and illuminated his wide grin. "I'll try to contain myself."

She looked through the infrared binoculars he passed her, and the hill jumped out at her in lime-green relief. Plants and rocks were clearly visible, and nearly white blobs moved here and there. She guessed they were mostly jackrabbits, but the indistinct outlines were hard to identify.

She took a sharp breath when Mac stretched out on the ground beside her, his body pressed full-length against hers. His warmth seeped through her clothing. The more aware she became of him, the more details registered. Like how his flexed bicep was large in comparison to her slender arm. Like how his hip bone was hard against hers. And how his thigh rubbed against hers with shocking intimacy. She counted his breaths as his ribs moved against hers.

She lowered her binoculars and turned her head. Was his earlobe still ticklish? Her mouth was only a few inches from the part in question. It would be so easy just to lean forward and nibble it.

He looked aside from his own field glasses, and his gaze met and captured hers. Her thoughts must have been mirrored in her eyes, because he mouthed, "Damn, Susan."

"Kiss me, Mac," she murmured in a moment of sheer insanity.

His eyes widened and he leaned toward her. "Oh, man, I…" He pulled away slightly. "Honey, I'm working."

Oh man, he *what?* She'd kill to hear the rest of that sentence.

"There's nobody here yet, Mac. Just one little peck?"

His voice was tight. "It's my responsibility to keep you safe. I need to focus on my job right now." A pause. "Besides, when have we ever managed just a little peck between us?"

Were it not for the rippling muscles in his jaw, she might have believed he was as calm as he sounded. But as it was, he radiated tension like a tiger waiting to spring on its prey.

She didn't push him. After all, he was right. Silence fell between them as he scanned the valley below, apparently engrossed in his surveillance. Except his tension didn't go away. She still felt it vibrating powerfully through his body. The ground was hard and rocky, and she shifted, trying to get comfortable. Her knee was really going to make her pay tomorrow, but for the time being, it was bearable.

What had possessed her to ask him to kiss her? Was she that ready to fall back in love with him again? She hardly knew Mac Conlon anymore. Every now and then she caught glimpses of the engaging, charming guy he used to be. And then the dangerous, disciplined soldier would take his place. She had no business chasing after this man.

He moved against her, to get a better view of the valley or maybe to ease a cramp. His muscular thigh pressed even closer, his hip grinding against hers in a way that made her think wicked thoughts. Her pulse shot through the roof, and her gaze slipped back to his earlobe. A sensual haze coiled around her until it all but suffocated her. She was uncomfortably warm. A heavy languor wrapped around her limbs, and her body craved the weight of his pressing down upon her and into her. She watched avidly as he closed his eyes and swallowed hard.

"Suzie," he murmured. "Cut it out."

"Cut what out?" she asked as innocently as she could muster.

She was surprised when, instead of answering her, he reached for his throat. "Dutch, current position on the targets?"

"Sneaking loudly toward our base camp. They're about five feet from the first perimeter trap."

A cracking noise drifted up the valley, followed by a gentle rumble.

The Viking's deep voice came again. "Correction. They just found the first perimeter trap."

"How'd it go?" Mac asked.

Dutch chuckled. "Have you ever seen six macho guys lying in a heap trying not to touch anything embarrassing while they untangle themselves?"

Mac grinned. "Outstanding. Let me know when they head this way."

"Roger," Dutch murmured.

Mac released the button. Susan rolled onto her back as Mac raised himself up on his elbow and stared down at her grimly. "Suzie, you're playing with fire. I'm not a kid anymore. Don't tease me unless you're sure you can deal with the consequences.''

The threat in his words was tangible. If she baited him, she'd better be prepared to follow through. Was she? Was she ready to get involved with this version of Mac? There were so many reasons to say no. But the only answer that came to her was a yes from deep down in her soul.

He didn't give her any more time to consider her answer. His mouth swooped down upon hers like a night-flying hawk pouncing on its prey. He surrounded her like the darkness, a blanket of hot and cold, rough and smooth, strong and gentle. His leg slid across hers, trapping her on her back. His arms were like the hawk's wings, spread wide in a protective tent around his prey.

And his mouth. It was hot and restless upon hers. And then it slid to her cheeks, her eyelids, lower to her neck. He fed upon her flesh greedily, testing and tasting. He shifted slightly, and one of his hands was under her shirt, sliding higher.

She lurched, and he rolled instantly on top of her, pinning her immobile. ''Careful, honey,'' he murmured, his voice dark silk. ''I've told you before not to move too suddenly around someone like me. Don't you remember?''

Jittery, yet enthralled, she gazed into his eyes, which burned hot and hungry as she nodded.

Beneath his predatory gaze, she panted with the thrill and vulnerability of being so exposed. She reveled in the desire that devoured Mac's gaze. And then he all but devoured her.

All thought ceased as her world became a tangle of hot kisses, cold ground, the roughness of his beard stubble, and the silky softness of his mouth upon hers.

Half out of her mind with wanting more of him, she reached between them, seeking to remove the fabric keeping her from ultimate fulfillment.

Mac groaned, grabbing her wrist, and she looked up. His face was drawn with pain and pleasure so intense, it looked as if he was completely lost in a private hell somewhere between the two extremes. "Later, Suzie," he mumbled, breathing heavily.

"Look sharp, Mac. Four hostiles headed right at you. They got sick of messing around with your traps. The other two are scouting a spot where they can keep a lookout on the camp."

Mac spit out a curse with more disgust than Susan had ever imagined could be packed into one word. He rolled away and lay on his back, his arm flung across his eyes. She was gratified to see that he was breathing as raggedly as she was.

"Susan," he murmured. "We've got to go. I'm sorry..."

Not half as sorry as she was. She sighed, supremely frustrated. "I suppose we'd better get to it, then."

He laughed shortly. "I'm not sure I can walk." But despite his words, he rolled onto his stomach and pushed himself to his feet with quick power.

She sat up more slowly. The sexual haze hanging in the air around them cleared slowly. What was it about him that drove her completely beyond the edge of sanity? She couldn't get enough of a man she ought to want nothing to do with.

Except this was Mac. Her Mac. The only man she'd ever loved and the only one who'd ever loved her. For all the world, it appeared that he felt at least some of the same feelings for her that he had a decade ago. The thought fairly made her head spin. Her body tingled from head to toe, and she felt more alive than she had in years. It was like coming out of a long sleep.

Mac moved close enough behind her to murmur into her

ear without using the mike, "How's your knee holding up?"

"It'll be fine as long as we don't jog for any long distances." She turned around to face him. He was so close she could almost count his eyelashes. "Shouldn't we be going?" she murmured.

He looked down at her for a long moment, his expression turbulent. What was he thinking? He nodded to her and turned to lead the way deeper into the canyon.

They'd been on the move for fifteen or twenty minutes when Mac suddenly crouched down in front of her. He gestured sharply with his hand for her to do the same. Sticking her left leg out to the side and squatting on her right heel, she was able to get down as low as Mac. She tried to breathe quietly, but they'd been moving uphill for a while, and she was huffing.

And then she heard it. Rocks sliding under feet.

Close.

Really close.

A rush of adrenaline screamed through her body, and it was all she could do not to leap up and run the other direction as fast as she could. Mac eased down onto his hands and knees, and she did the same, her whole body trembling. Rocks were sharp beneath her palms, but the pain had no meaning. Someone out to *kill* her was only a few yards away!

Mac crept to their left, off the faint trail and behind some scrubby bushes. She followed suit, dragging her useless left leg behind her. Top speed for her was painstakingly slow. Every second passed in an agony of anticipation. If only she didn't already know what it felt like to have a bullet tear into her, destroying flesh and bones and stealing life.

Mac barely breathed into her ear. "Lie down and cover yourself with this. Stay here. I'll be back soon." He pressed something that felt like a folded bed sheet into her hands.

Chagrin gnawed at her. She couldn't keep up and he was forced to leave her here. No doubt he was going to go be a decoy or do something equally dangerous to draw Ruala away from the cripple.

If Mac got hurt, or worse, it would be all her fault. The euphoria of a couple hours spent on a real mission with Mac faded, leaving behind only the bitter gall of her disability.

She pulled on the corners of the blanket and it slithered open soundlessly. It was a dull, gray-black color. Mac tugged it over her whole body, leaving only the tiniest slit for her to see through. He eased away from her, crawling parallel to the path in the direction they'd just come from until she could hardly see him anymore. She waited, her heart pounding, for Ruala and his men to draw near. And then she glanced down the trail in the direction Mac had gone. She stared in horror as he moved into the path behind the thugs, clearly visible in the bright moonlight.

Dear God, let the bad guys not be looking that way.

Mac fiddled briefly with something about the size of a brick, and then he melted back off the path into the shadows. Susan released her breath slowly. It was hot under the cover. She fingered it, and it felt like a cross between plastic and satin.

She jerked as it lifted away from her suddenly. Her heart all but stopped beating in the shock of discovery. She sagged as Mac slid in beside her, under the cover. He gestured her to be silent. She didn't think she could speak if she had to. Her heart clogged her throat completely. He plastered himself against her, and his arms settled protectively around her. And then she heard feet sliding on rock. The bad guys were very near their position. Mac's arm tightened, pressing her down into the dirt, half beneath him.

The footsteps drew even with her head and stopped. She guessed the men were maybe ten feet away.

A gravelly voice spoke in accented English. *Ruala.* "They've got to be here somewhere. Can't you see them with that gizmo?"

Another male voice answered, irritated. "I can't see what's not there to be seen."

Ruala growled, "When I find these three, I'm gonna hurt them bad before I kill them for causing us so much trouble."

Susan gulped. The footsteps moved back down the trail toward Mac's latest handiwork.

A few seconds later Mac's weight eased off her. He gestured to her again. He wanted her to go with him now? But what if Ruala saw them? Why couldn't they just lie here under their magic blanket of invisibility? He gestured again, more insistently. She supposed she ought to get moving. He'd probably sling her over his shoulder and drag her up the hill if she didn't go of her own volition. She gathered what nerves she had left and pulled back the blanket.

She ventured a quick look over her shoulder. Good Lord. The bad guys' backs were in plain sight heading down the trail.

Mac tugged on her arm, and she turned back to him. Worry for her was plainly etched on his face. There was no doubt about it. He genuinely cared for her. But did she dare let him? Time froze, suspended like a dewdrop on the end of a leaf. He blinked once, in slow motion, as she stared at him. She'd reached a crossroads and she must choose a path.

His hand moved as slowly as the creeping of a glacier toward her cheek. His fingertips touched her face lightly, promising her everything she'd ever need from life. The dewdrop moment in time trembled and fell away.

"Come on, baby," he breathed. "I've got to get you out of here."

She couldn't do it. She couldn't harden her heart against Mac any longer.

As fast as she could go on one leg and two hands, she crawled up the hill behind him. He stopped behind a boulder near the top of the hill and sat down, his back leaning against the rock. Susan mimicked his action, grateful for the rest.

He murmured, "We'll stay here until those jerks get to my trap. I didn't have time to set a trip wire, so I've got to blow it manually. When I do that, we'll roll over the top of this ridge, and hump it fast down the other side. Can you do that?"

"I'll make a lot of noise."

"There's going to be a lot of noise. I set up a bunch of shale to come down. It'll rain rock for a couple minutes."

Susan nodded.

"I'm going to stay behind to watch our backs. Just head straight down that hill. There are a lot of big rocks casting dark shadows on the way down. Stick to those as best you can. I'll meet you at the bottom. Okay?"

"Okay."

He eased around the side of the rock, gazing through his night-vision goggles. Without looking away, he passed Susan the other night-vision glasses from his pack. Using the gadget, she peeked around her side of the boulder.

Four white silhouettes moved down the hillside. They were getting close to where Mac had crawled out into the path.

Mac murmured, "Would you like to do the honors?"

"Uh, sure."

He pressed a small remote control into her hand. "When I say so, push the red button."

Her palm went slick with sweat, and her finger trembled on the button. Each step the four men took brought them closer. Then closer still.

Finally Mac hissed, "Now."

She mashed the button, then jumped as rock abruptly cascaded down the hillside. She was just turning away to head over the ridge like Mac had said to, when she heard him let loose a profanity. She froze. Had she screwed it up? "What happened? What's wrong?" she asked frantically.

He nodded back behind them. "Look for yourself. You'll hear it in a second."

She turned back in the direction of Ruala in time to see an entire slab of the mountain slowly sliding downward, gathering momentum and speed.

Mac announced in disgust, "I had no time to assess the rock face before I set that explosive. I hit a fault line and started a freaking avalanche."

The rumble reached them the same instant that the ground began to shake. The last thing Susan saw as she turned to run for her life was the four white blobs turning to sprint back up the hill toward them in a desperate effort to avoid the rock fall.

She took two steps before her leg locked up and toppled her flat on her face. And then she was on her hands and knees, scrabbling as best she could until she topped the ridge.

Mac's voice reached her, low and urgent. "You're clear, Suzie. Get up and go. As fast as you can."

She came to her feet on the steep incline. Her leg moved like a clumsy block of wood attached to her body. She stumbled forward, half sliding and half falling down the mountainside. She felt her fingernails tearing as she broke her momentum against rough boulders. All her limbs protested as she braced herself, desperate to stop her madcap descent from becoming an out and out fall down the slope.

She slammed into a boulder, knocking the breath out of herself. She somersaulted once, but flung out her limbs and managed to halt the tumbling. Still the descent went on. The drop became sharper. She gasped for air and picked up even more speed. Stiff-armed, her legs thrust out in front of her, she slid the rest of the way down the mountain on her behind.

She landed on her back with a thud. C'mon, self. *Breathe.* Painfully, she dragged herself a few feet to the deep shadows of a looming rock formation. She looked back up the hill. Nobody had followed her. Had Mac gotten away from Ruala and his men? Had they caught him in their unexpected sprint back toward him? Was he up there right now, in trouble because of her? Did she dare try to reach him on her throat microphone?

Better not try it in case the noise in his earpiece was audible to other people. She wouldn't want to give him away if he were hiding in a tight spot. Worry for him tightened her chest until it was hard to breathe.

She lifted the field glasses, which had miraculously managed to stay around her neck during her descent, and watched the slope—practically a cliff—behind her. No movement. She leaned back against the rock and caught her breath. She did not need to do anything like that again anytime soon.

Seconds stretched into minutes, and then into longer than she cared to think about. Where in the world was Mac? He said he'd meet her here. What if something had happened to him? She had absolutely no idea where she was right now. She couldn't find her way back to their camp if she had to. Mac had to be safe. He had to come find her. He *had* to.

Maybe she should risk using the microphone to call him. She debated the idea until she couldn't stand it anymore. She pressed her throat button and whispered, "Mac, where are you?"

Nothing.

She tried again. Still nothing.

"Dutch, Mac. Anybody?"

There wasn't any sound at all in her earpiece. Not even the faint static she remembered. And she couldn't hear her own breathing like she had before. Oh no. Her radio was broken. She must have hit it on something coming down the mountain. Great. She pulled her good knee up to her chest and hugged it while she watched the hillside glumly for Mac.

Suddenly a hand slammed across her mouth and yanked her back into the deep shadows. She screamed against the big, hard palm, but no sound escaped.

"It's me, Suzie."

She sagged back against Mac while her terror abated. His hand eased away from her mouth, and she hissed, "You just scared ten years off my life, Mac Conlon! Don't you ever pull a stunt like that aga—"

His hand went back over her mouth.

He pulled her against him, tucking her body close against his. His heat was as soothing as a warm bath. His mouth moved against her ear as he murmured very low, "We've got a little problem. Our four goons have split up to look for another way out of the canyon. The avalanche blocked the entrance they used. They're wandering all over the place."

Susan frowned. Then why didn't she and Mac make their way to the other end of the valley and get out of here?

Mac continued, his voice so quiet she had to strain to hear it, even though his lips were tickling her earlobe. "Thing is, the other exit has no cover at all. It's right out in the open. We wouldn't stand a chance of getting out of here unseen. Plus, it leads straight to our camp, where the other two hostiles are parked."

A heavy feeling settled in Susan's stomach. What were they going to do now?

Mac anticipated her unspoken question. "I need you to hunker down in a safe spot while I go help these idiots find their way out of here. Once I've herded them out of the canyon, then we'll leave. Can you stay put for a while?"

She nodded beneath his hand.

"You need to be absolutely silent. One of the thugs is about a hundred feet from us behind some rocks. Understood?"

She nodded again, and his hand eased away from her.

He murmured, "I lost the infrared blocking blanket on the way down the hill. You'll need to hide."

Mac looked around. He pointed at a crevice in the boulder at her back and then pointed at her. The opening was barely big enough to hold her if she curled up in a ball on her side. Moving quietly, he reached into his backpack and pulled out a fist-size black bundle. He picked at it until a matte black piece of silk unfolded, flowing over his hands like a ripple of water. It was a good two meters square. He gestured for her to pull it over herself.

She took the silk and wrapped the cloth around herself, plunked down on the ground, and wedged herself backward into the crack.

She felt Mac's hands adjust the other end of the cloth about her. He made a small opening for her to see out of, then picked up a handful of dirt and sprinkled it over her. He flashed her a quick thumbs-up, and he was gone.

Silence settled around her, heavier than the stone pressing down against her back and shoulders. She wasn't particularly claustrophobic, but being wedged into the base of this boulder was unnerving. She just prayed no rattlesnake made this little hollow his home. He'd find a nice warm bed waiting for him when he came home tonight if this was his hangout.

The snap of a twig brought her to full alert. She gazed out at the little piece of the valley she could see, waiting for a stranger to materialize. Nobody appeared, and she eventually relaxed. But then the wind blew, and the ominous moan of it alarmed her anew.

There were four men out there, a killer plus three more who were heaven only knew how violent or how well trained. And Mac was out there all by himself trying to lure them away from her. He was good, of that she had no doubt, but it was four against one.

And here she was, hiding in a crevice that would barely conceal a rabbit. She had no radio and no idea where she was. One of the bad guys was going to find her and kill her.

In all her life, she'd never felt so alone or vulnerable as she did now. Her life depended on a flimsy piece of silk, and the skill and dedication of a single man. But as the waiting stretched out, along with her nerves, her thoughts drifted.

She didn't remember much about the last time she'd been this scared; the night of the shooting. One second she'd been listening with utter absorption to Eduardo Ferrare making a deal with a band of terrorists to finance their overthrow of the government of a tiny, South American country called Gavarone. Then that horrible, sudden flash of Ramon Ruala's face in the van's window. And the next second, the entire interior of the van exploded.

She only vaguely remembered the shot that hit her knee, and she had no idea how she got to the floor. She did remember curling up with her hands over her head and praying for all she was worth as bullets and pieces of destroyed electronics equipment flew everywhere. She'd been going into shock by the time the second bullet grazed her neck and just missed killing her.

When she woke up in the hospital, Captain Folly told her Mac was in Gavarone shaking every bush and turning over every stone, looking for Eduardo Ferrare and his gunman, Ramon Ruala. Tex and the rest of Charlie Squad had hovered over her constantly, until she finally had to throw them all out of her room so she could have a little privacy to grieve and rage over losing Mac. By the time Mac got back to the United States, an ugly red scar puckered her neck and she knew she'd never run or dance again. She'd been the one who refused to see him when he came to the hospital. She hadn't been ready to face him, yet. Heck, she wasn't sure she was ready now.

Every time over the last ten years Tex mentioned that Mac had asked about her, which happened often, she'd been overcome by an urge to run and hide. She'd never wanted him to see her scarred and crippled. But Ruala took that choice out of her hands by showing up again.

Looking back, it had been patently ridiculous of her to jump to the conclusion that Charlie Squad would ever walk away from a criminal like Ferrare. But she hadn't exactly been thinking straight after Mac made love to her and then dumped her like a hot potato.

Honestly, she couldn't say if she'd ever really had her act together since. Something in her heart died that night, and she'd never gotten over it. Pathetic. No wonder Mac walked away from that hospital and never looked back. From his point of view, he must see her doing the same thing she had the last time—pushing her way into a dangerous op that she wasn't remotely prepared to handle. Why was she driven to put herself into these insane situations?

Mac had called her a groupie and a wannabe. He'd probably been right. A shrink told her right after the shooting that she'd pushed her way into working with Charlie Squad to be with her brother, to gain approval from him. While it was true she'd been an incredibly annoying big sister who hovered over her baby brother everywhere he went, fussing like a nervous mother hen, she could hardly be accused of being obsessed with Tex. Had she replaced her mother henning for Tex with doing the same to Mac? Was that why she'd taken that van out by herself that night? To cover for Mac's inexplicable failure to do his duty?

As painful as it was to admit, loving Mac hadn't been enough to hold him. It wouldn't be enough now, either. Problem was, now she was crippled and couldn't be the equal he so obviously needed a woman to be to love her. She was deluding herself if she thought she could hold on to Mac for keeps.

The sound of gravel rolling underfoot snapped her attention back to the present. Her nerves couldn't take much more of this. This tiny space was smothering her. She reached for the edge of the cloth.

A pair of designer lizard skin boots stepped into view, not ten feet away from her nose. She froze. *Cowboy boots.* Mac was wearing combat boots with green nylon tops.

She inhaled lightly, careful not to make even a whisper of sound. An urge to squeeze her eyes tightly shut and pray came over her. But the compulsion to watch those cowboy boots take a step, and then another, was even more overwhelming.

A slight movement caught her eye. At the same ground level she was at. Ohmigosh. It was Mac. Lying on his belly under a bush, not more than three feet from the boots. What in the world was he doing? In horror, she watched his hand ease out from under the scrub toward the man's ankle. Holding a knife. It struck like lightning, jabbing the side of the cowboy boot through the thin leather so fast Susan barely saw the motion.

A shouted profanity. The boot leaped straight up in the air. ''Carlos! Carlos! Come quick. A rattlesnake bit me!'' Good God. That was Ruala's voice. Not six feet from her. Terror ripped through her, tearing the air right out of her lungs. She couldn't gasp for breath or the killer would hear her. She could only lie there in frozen agony, praying he'd leave so she could breathe again.

His frantic yelling was accompanied by his hopping out of her line of sight. She dragged in a sobbing breath. Any second, he'd turn around and see her.

She jumped as Ruala called out abruptly, his voice irritable, "You idiot! I'm injured! Come over here!"

Apparently Carlos was not forthcoming, because Ruala limped off into the night, losing a stream of invectives against his companions, who were going to let him die out here in this godforsaken wasteland.

Susan all but fainted in relief, her head spinning and pinpricks of light dancing before her eyes. Lord, that had been a close call. For her and for Mac. She looked for him in his hiding place under the bush, but he was gone. She hadn't seen or heard a thing, and she'd been looking right at him as he lay opposite her. How in the world had he managed to disappear in the blink of an eye?

It couldn't be a good sign that Mac was blatantly risking his neck like that. Dismayed by the chances he was taking on her behalf to herd these guys out of the valley she did the only sane thing she could think of. Clamp down on her panic and hunker down to wait out this nightmare.

Chapter 9

Mac watched the last thug stumble out of the valley. He sat down heavily, leaning against a boulder. Exhaustion pulled at him. What a night. Not only had it been dicey to subtly prod four separate, roaming men into simultaneously heading the right direction, but two of them had practically tripped over Susan. He never, ever, wanted her in danger like that again.

He closed his eyes and leaned his head back against the rock, letting fatigue wash over him. What in the world was he going to do with her? One minute she drove him crazy with her fierce independence and the next, drove him crazy with desire.

Face it pal, you're hosed.

He had learned one important thing about Susan's pursuers from this night's work. Ruala's minions were also serious criminals who'd kill her in a heartbeat. He had to nail them *all* to ensure her safety.

Some objective operative he was turning out to be, living

in a constant state of half panic and full arousal. He grimaced. He'd promised Colonel Folly he could pull off this mission.

First things first. He'd better go get Suzie. She was no doubt scared to death out there by herself. He stood up slowly, stretching out the kinks of a hard night's work. He made his way silently toward her hiding place. He'd long since figured out her radio was broken, or he'd have called to warn her of his approach. But as it was, he had to sneak up on her and get a hand over her mouth so she wouldn't scream if he scared her. Ruala and his men were out of the valley, but not necessarily out of earshot.

Sure enough, she started every bit as badly as he expected when he slapped his hand over her mouth. Poor kid. He picked her up, parachute silk and all, cradling her in his arms. Sleek heat and soft curves curled against him, and despite his exhaustion, his body responded powerfully to her.

He murmured into her silky hair, "I've got you, baby. It's all over. The bad guys got tired of playing cat and mouse."

Her arms looped around his neck, half choking him. He held her close as she sobbed out her fear. He muffled her sounds against his shoulder, soaking up her tears with his black shirt. Each racking breath she took called to something deep within him—an urge to protect her, to surround her, to absorb her entirely into himself. So much for the tough facade she'd worn ever since he arrived at the ranch. His relief was enormous to know that this vulnerable side of Susan still existed within the capable, independent woman she'd become. A guy liked to be needed a little bit, after all.

Finally she lifted her head. Her eyelashes were dark, wet spikes, and tear tracks shone on her cheeks in the first, faint easing of the night into dawn. She gazed up fearfully into his eyes, her heart an open book. ''Mac, promise me you'll never leave me alone again.''

He stared down at her. Many possible layers of meaning to her words leaped into his head. What, exactly, was she asking of him? Was that a simple plea not to be stashed under a rock again by herself? Or was it something else? A deeper request not to walk out of her life again? To stand beside her forever?

''Promise me,'' she whispered urgently.

''I promise, Suzie.''

The second the words left his mouth, the same questions popped back into his head. Exactly how much had he just promised her, consciously or unconsciously? It felt like a hell of a lot more than not leaving her under a rock again.

She hugged him tight, murmuring against his neck, ''I've never been so terrified in my life. I was so worried about you taking such crazy risks. I saw you jab Ruala's ankle to make him think a snake bit him…''

She was too scared. It was no good working with panicked civilians. Time to lighten the mood. He grinned down at her. ''That was cool, wasn't it? I've always wanted to poke someone like that.''

She frowned. ''You've been that close to bad guys, before?''

He chuckled. ''More times than I can count.''

She shuddered in his arms. He squeezed her close. ''I'm still here, aren't I?'' He had to admit it. He liked the way her arms tightened protectively around his neck. ''What say we head back to camp, Suz? Dutch says the hostiles have left to go lick their wounds.''

''Will Ruala come after us again?'' Susan asked.

''I don't think he knows what hit him. They'll spend most of the day trying to figure out what happened. By the time they muster up the nerve to come play again, we'll be long gone.''

"Won't they follow us?"

He hesitated. Standard procedure dictated that the civilian under protection be kept calm, relaxed and able to follow instructions. The rule was Never Panic the Protectee. And telling Susan that Ruala most certainly would follow them and try to kill her again would definitely panic her. Damn. He really didn't want to lie to her. But he was required to follow the rules. He couldn't count how many times he'd heard Colonel Folly say over the years, "Procedures are what they are because they work."

Mac sighed. And lied reluctantly. "Nah. Ruala and his men won't mess with us again anytime soon. Don't you worry about it."

God, he hated lying to Susan. A lie ten years ago, in the name of following procedure, had cost him her love. Standard ops or not, he didn't like doing it. *You owe me one, Colonel Folly. I followed your damn procedure again.*

He felt her draw breath to question his statement that Ruala would leave her alone. No surprise there. She was smart as a whip. He spoke quickly. "It's almost sunrise. What say we go catch some shut-eye? We'll need to ride again tonight."

That snapped her out of her dangerous train of thought. She lurched upright in his arms. "Gosh, I didn't even think about the horses! Are they okay? Did those jerks leave them alone?"

"Dutch hid them well. Ruala and his thugs didn't get anywhere near your babies."

She sagged in his arms. "Thank goodness."

He set her down gently. "Let's go."

To Susan's surprise, the walk back to camp took only a few minutes, even at the snail's pace her knee would tolerate. The joint was stiff and unbendable after the night's acrobatics. Thankfully, Mac didn't make a big deal of it; he just kept pace beside her.

She was surprised to see Dutch efficiently taking apart the tent and packing it when they got there. "Why are we breaking camp?" she asked the tall Viking.

Dutch glanced over at Mac, who sent him some sort of hand signal. A slight nod from the blond giant, and then he answered her. "We're moving. Ruala and company tromped right through here last night and know where to find us."

Mac asked his partner, "Have you got a new spot in mind?"

Dutch pointed over his shoulder. "There's a side canyon up that way. It's where I've got the horses stashed. I thought we might park close to them today. Plus, we'll hold the high ground if it comes to a shoot-out."

Susan blinked. A shoot-out? As in right out of a bad western movie? This wasn't happening to her. Any moment now, she was going to wake up from this insanity and resume her real life. *Her real life.* The thought was sobering. This would all go away—*Mac* would go away—as soon as Ruala was caught. She'd testify against the assassin, and then she'd go back to the same old solitary grind of everyday life. She jumped when Mac's fingers touched her arm.

"Need a hand?" he asked quietly.

She realized she'd stopped at the foot of a high scree slope. "Thanks." His hard palm was dusty and callused against hers, but it steadied her gently as she picked her way up the unstable slope. When they reached the top, she ventured a smile at him. His answering smile crinkled the layer of dust around his eyes. Dark circles showed through the dirt, testament to how little sleep he'd gotten the past couple of days.

"Mac, when this is all done and we get back to the ranch, I'm putting you to bed and making you stay there for a week."

He grinned broadly. ''Will you be joining me?''

Heat rushed through her at the idea. She replied gamely, ''If I do, you'll need another week to recover.''

''Done,'' he answered promptly.

Her pulse skittered wildly. But she managed to retort lightly, ''Men. You've got to be so tired you can hardly walk, but you're still thinking about sex.''

''Honey,'' he murmured, ''if I stop thinking about sex when I'm around a woman as hot as you, it's time to bury me.''

Dutch called out low, ''Are you two coming or not?''

Mac grinned ruefully and turned away from Susan. Mildly in shock, she followed him. A woman as hot as her? She couldn't help but smile. It had been a long time since a man had desired her. Since Mac had desired her.

A tap on his foot woke Mac up. He lifted his head and saw Dutch squatting at the opening of the tent. The blond man gestured for him to come outside. Mac slid his arm carefully out from under Susan's head. Even though his side was sweaty where she'd been plastered against him, he already missed the feeling of her. He stepped out into bright sunshine. It must be approaching noon.

''What's up, Dutch?''

''Ruala and his gang just packed up and drove away.''

Mac stared. ''You're kidding. Why?''

Dutch shrugged. ''Your guess is as good as mine.''

Mac swore under his breath. They didn't have the manpower both to protect Susan and track Ruala to figure out what he was up to now. ''We need Doc and Howdy back here ASAP. Have you called headquarters? We need an estimated time of arrival on those two.''

Dutch nodded grimly and held up his cell phone. ''I was just getting ready to make the call. Thought I'd let you know what was up first.''

Mad nodded his thanks. "I'll make the call. Why don't you hit the rack? You look beat."

"You look worse, you old fart." Dutch grinned as he crouched down in front of tent. "Mind if I cuddle up with your girl?"

Mac snorted. "You wanna die young?"

Dutch's chuckle was joined by a distinctly feminine sound of surprise. Mac looked down guiltily as Susan stared up at him incredulously from the opening of the tent. Whoops. "Uh, hi, Suzie. I was just about to call headquarters." Flustered, he made a big production out of taking the cell phone Dutch held out to him.

He frowned down at the phone. Digital technology. State-of-the-art satellite reception. *And transmission.*

He said low, "I think I know how Ramon Ruala found Susan out here so damn fast."

Dutch poked his head out of the tent. And glanced in the direction of Mac's gaze. He grunted in surprise. "You think Ruala got this phone number?"

Mac nodded grimly. "It would explain a lot."

Susan peered up at him. "What's wrong?"

"Nothing," he commented lightly. "I'm about to call Colonel Folly."

She nodded, but the worried expression didn't leave her eyes. Damn. And then a male voice spoke in his ear. Colonel Folly.

"Identify yourself."

"Mac Conlon here, sir. We need an ETA on Doc and Howdy. Ruala's made contact with us but he just bugged out. Could be headed back to the ranch. We could use some backup. Go ahead." The phrase *go ahead* signaled the colonel that he wasn't in a position to say much and that the colonel should ask some yes-no questions for Mac to answer.

Folly asked on cue, "Did Ruala make an attempt on Susan's life?"

"Yes," Mac answered.

Alarm laced the colonel's voice. "Are you in danger, now?"

"Not right away," Mac answered vaguely.

"But soon," Folly replied grimly.

"Oh, yeah."

"Does Susan want out of the op?"

"No way."

"Any chance you could talk her into leaving?"

"Not a chance."

Folly swore under his breath. Then said, "I assume a full-blown FBI SWAT team would send Ruala running for the hills, never to be seen again?"

"Undoubtedly," Mac replied.

Silence at the other end of the phone while the colonel chewed on that. "Okay. Ruala's seen the bait. And he's seen the minimal protection around her. If he's spooked and takes off now, there's nothing we can do about it. But if he hangs around, looking to make another try at her, then we know he thinks he's got more firepower than you and Dutch. I'll send Doc and Howdy into the ranch in full-stealth mode. They can clear it and let you know it's safe to come in. If we can sneak them in without Ruala seeing them, we'll have doubled the force against him without him knowing."

His boss's logic was sound. Although, knowing Ruala, the bastard would probably come in with a small army the next time. The assassin was a bulldog when it came to getting the job done. It was part of what had made him one of the deadliest killers in the world. He'd keep gunning for a guy until he got his kill.

The colonel was speaking again. "Will the four of you have sufficient juice to take on Ruala and his men?"

"I think so," Mac answered.

Folly replied, "We were hoping to get the indictment handed down by a grand jury tomorrow. Let me call the judge and see if I can get the whole thing expedited. Either way, I'll put Doc and Howdy on a plane for Texas as soon as I get off the phone. They'll be in place no later than midnight tonight."

Mac breathed a sigh of relief. The odds for the good guys had just gotten measurably better. He thanked his boss and terminated the call.

Susan gave him a funny look. "Is now a good time for that talk I asked for last night?" she asked.

His pulse jumped in consternation. He had no clue what to do about her, and he certainly wasn't ready to talk about it. Keep the Protectee Calm. He nodded in resignation and led her away from their camp.

He moved out of earshot of Dutch and picked a spot where he could scan the area with the binoculars he'd brought along. He gave Susan a hand in sitting down and was surprised that she let him help until he looked down and saw the swelling under her pant leg. "Jeez Louise, Susan! Why didn't you tell me your knee was in trouble?"

She glanced down at the melon-size lump where the joint should have been. "It does this whenever I seriously over-use it. It's no big deal."

"No big deal? That's got to hurt like hell!"

She shrugged.

His generalized worry for her safety metamorphosed abruptly into anger. "You ought to take better care of your leg," he growled. "When's the last time a doctor saw it? Hell, with all the new medical advances these days, I bet there's some way you could get a joint that's fully functional for heavy athletics."

"I'm fine the way I am," she retorted.

''How can you say that?'' He waved a hand at her knee. ''Look at that. It's a wreck!''

''Why do you suddenly give a damn about my knee beyond its impact on the mission, Mac Conlon?''

He stared at her, frozen by her pointed question. Why *was* he so worked up all of a sudden? The answer came to him, and his anger drained away as quickly as it had come. He answered quietly, ''Because we're not just talking about your knee, here.''

She looked as if he'd just slapped her. Her voice shook when she spoke, but he couldn't tell if it was in outrage or hurt. ''Why should I take better care of my knee? So I can look pretty and walk nice for all the hundreds of guys who are busting down my door trying to get to a scarred cripple like me?''

Outrage. That was definitely outrage in her voice. Which meant she was trying to hide the hurt. ''A scarred cripple?'' he asked gently, his heart breaking a little. ''Is that what you see when you look in the mirror?''

''I don't live my life feeling sorry for myself, if that's what you're asking. I'm okay with who I am and I have a decent life. But the fact is, I don't happen to perform well in the dating and marriage market.''

He snorted. ''Good grief, woman. You're drop-dead gorgeous. You've got a sensational figure and the most remarkable eyes I've ever seen. They look right inside a person's soul. You're smart. You're funny. You're kind and honest. What the hell makes you updateable or unmarriageable?''

She shook her head, a look of exasperation on her face.

''Suzie—'' he dropped to a knee in front of her ''—listen to me. I'm not BSing you, here. I'm not suggesting you have lousy self-esteem. I'm saying you have a lousy opinion of how smart men are. When they—we—

look at you, we see a woman who completely qualifies as girlfriend or wife material.''

"Yeah, and that's why I've been beating off swarms of them with sticks over the past ten years.'' She glared at him. "You're so blinded by your compulsion to fix everything that you can't see what's right in front of your eyes.''

He frowned. "What compulsion?''

"It's called a superhero complex. You believe you can fix everything that's wrong with the world. While I admit that sort of self-confidence probably comes in handy in the course of doing your work, there's a limit to your powers. You can't fix my life. I'm responsible for me. Not you.''

He protested, "I'm not trying to fix your life. I'm only stating the facts.''

She went on the offensive. "Like the fact that you're darn near drowning in guilt that you broke up with me right before I got shot? Look me in the eye and tell me you don't think you drove me to get in that van and land in the middle of the Ferrare sting.''

He stared at her, flummoxed. "But I did drive you to do it.''

"Mac Conlon, you did no such thing. You told me in no uncertain terms to go away from you *and* from the op. It was purely my decision to go solo and do the surveillance on Ferrare that night.''

"But you weren't thinking clearly. You didn't know about the sting. If I'd told you—''

"I might very well have decided you were lying about there being a sting operation and done exactly what I did, anyway,'' she declared.

He frowned. She was arguing for the sake of argument here. Her logic wasn't sound. "You had no reason to think I'd lie to you about there being a sting operation.''

She stared at him coldly. "Wanna bet?''

He met her glare with one of his own. "Yeah. Why in the hell would you think that?"

"Because you'd already lied to me that night when you said you were over me."

He rocked back on his heels. She might as well have punched him in the solar plexus. He stood up, struggling to breathe, too agitated to sit still. She knew all along? She *knew?* He slogged back and forth across the gravel-strewn slope.

And finally he sat down heavily beside her. "How did you know?" he asked in dismay.

"I might have been young, Mac, but I wasn't stupid. I knew what we had going between us. I wasn't a groupie chick any more than you were having a casual fling with me. But for some reason, you decided to walk away from me. So, you lied through your teeth and came up with that lame story to get rid of me."

He stared at her in open shock. Sonofa—

She interrupted his train of thought. "Why wouldn't you have thrown in some equally lame claim that you and Charlie Squad were going to take out Ferrare, just to make your lie about dumping me sound more believable, or at least more macho? Telling me about the sting wouldn't necessarily have changed anything I did."

Astonishment rendered him equal parts numb and stupid. It couldn't be. For ten years he'd wrestled with what happened that night, with the guilt of pushing her into a situation that maimed her and nearly killed her. And here she was, claiming he'd done no such thing! It was too much for his mind to take in.

"Why'd you do it, Mac?"

He looked up at her. "Do what?" His brain felt like mush and was processing information about as well as mush at the moment.

"Why did you lie to me? Why did you break up with me like that?"

"I was ordered to. Folly had a feeling the sting was going to go down ugly and he needed to get you far away from it for your own safety. He told me to drive you off, to push you away from the op, and to use whatever means were necessary to do it." God, it was a relief to have finally said that to her.

Susan stared at him, absorbing the information. Funny, but she didn't act nearly as surprised as he'd thought she'd be. In fact, she nodded as if she'd expected those very words. And said, "I thought that might have been the case. I hoped it was, at any rate. I'd hate to think you believed all those awful things you said about me."

He exploded. "If you knew, then why in the hell did you barge into the middle of the sting and get yourself shot?"

She smiled sadly. "You were partially correct. I wasn't thinking clearly that night. It didn't occur to me as I watched you walk out of my apartment that you guys would move so aggressively to set up the sting that fast. That part I didn't see coming. But afterward, in the hospital, I had a lot of time to think about everything. That's when I figured out that Folly must have ordered you to dump me."

Mac sighed. "In the colonel's defense, he didn't order me to dump you. He only told me to push you far, far away from the op, and to do it before the sting went down."

Susan stared at him for a long time in silence. And then she asked abruptly, "Why didn't you ever come back to me?"

"After what I did to you? If you'll recall, before I left your apartment you did say you never wanted to see me again. Plus, I felt responsible for thrusting you into the middle of the shoot-out. I figured you'd hate my guts for that. And then when I tried to see you at the hospital, you told me to go away."

"And that was enough to drive off the superhero for good?" she asked derisively. "Maybe it's just as well you never came back if you're that easy to discourage."

Her words stung like needles. He spluttered, "But Tex… He said you were furious…said you refused to talk about me—"

Susan interrupted. "I was furious. Furious you were avoiding me. Furious you didn't come back for me sooner after the op was over. That you preferred to run around a jungle chasing Ferrare and Ruala than spend time with me."

Her words hit him like body blows. Gut punches that knocked the wind right out of him. Made him sick to his stomach. "But I did that for you. I thought you'd want them caught."

"I did—I do—but I needed you with me more."

"Well, hell," he managed to gasp. "I really blew that one but good."

She glared at him.

Sonofagun. She'd wanted him. Loved him even after he shattered her world and her knee. After he'd lied to her and walked out on her. But she hadn't forgiven him for feeling too damn guilty to come back and face her immediately. For not fighting harder.

Where were they supposed to go from here? Was there a chance he could salvage the relationship with her? But how? He'd been a complete shmuck without even realizing it. Dammit, he thought he'd done the right thing by staying away from her. He thought he'd done a noble thing to suck up his grief and loss and pain and leave her alone.

Susan shook her head. "I can practically see your mental wheels turning. You're sitting there, trying your damnedest to figure out some way to make it up to me, aren't you? Well here's a news flash for you, big guy. *Don't bother.* I don't need an apology, and I got over you a long time ago. You and I are ancient history.''

Now who was the one lying? Maybe he was just in denial, but he'd bet his life savings she'd been waiting to deliver that line for a good part of the last decade. He'd also bet it was just a line. Delivered out of wounded pride and anger. He'd seen the way she looked at him when she thought he wasn't looking. He'd felt the way she unraveled in his arms. They had an ancient history to be sure, but they had something powerful now, too.

Question was, would she admit it? Would she let what was simmering between them grow into something more? He'd hurt her. Bad. It was a lot to overcome.

He looked her square in the eye and said patiently, ''Yeah, I deserve that line. But honey, I don't buy it for a second. Go ahead and take your mad out on me. When you feel better and are ready to move ahead with our relationship, you let me know. Because I'm not going anywhere this time.''

She scowled at him. Apparently not the reaction out of him she'd been hoping for. She said raggedly, ''If you want to do penance for your sins, do it somewhere else. I don't need to go down this road with you again.''

Her words were dagger blows straight to the jugular. Damn, she was sharp. He *was* here looking for forgiveness. He *had* thought at some subconscious level that if he could save her this time, they'd be even somehow. As if bailing her out of this jam could make up for his playing a part in wrecking her life before. Right.

''I'm sorry, Susan,'' he mumbled. ''So sorry…''

''Don't.'' She cut him off with a sharp gesture of her hand. ''No apology, nothing you could say, will ever make up for the past ten years.''

He staggered from the blow of her words. ''You're absolutely right,'' he ground out. He whirled away, slipping and sliding toward the bottom of the hill. He paused maybe thirty feet away from her. And forced words past the silent scream of agony tearing at him. "Ruala and his men have left. The coast is clear for us to head back to the ranch. After Dutch catches a nap and the horses get some more rest, we can go."

Susan nodded fractionally, her face averted from him.

Mac gritted out, "I'll be back before dark."

Unable to hold it together for another second, he whirled and headed away from her. Into the mountains. God, it was tempting to just keep on walking. To lose himself in the maze of gullies and canyons. To disappear forever.

But the toy soldier was too damn well trained to do that. Bitterness soured his stomach. Mechanically, he found a high perch with good cover and panoramic visibility. He lay down and peered through his binoculars, not seeing a blessed thing before him. Instead, wounded, angry eyes stared back at him, wide and green.

Sonofabitch. He'd really screwed things up good this time. He really ought to just pack up and go home. Leave the mission to Dutch and the others. It wasn't as if he was in any shape to do a bit of good out here.

But dammit, he couldn't walk away from her again. He *wouldn't.* Even if she cracked his chest open and physically tore his heart out, if that's what it took to make it up to her, by God he'd let her do it.

How in the hell was he supposed to keep her safe when she was busy destroying him from the inside out? He was going to blow this mission. A Tango One down the tubes because he was self-destructing over Susan Monroe.

It was a quiet ride home. Really quiet. Even after sleeping most of the day, Susan felt like she'd gone ten rounds in a boxing ring and didn't feel much like talking. What the heck did Mac want from her? Absolution?

It wasn't hers to give.

He didn't owe her anything. He'd only followed orders—thank God that's what his verbal attack on her that night had been, and not an actual case of him losing interest in her. If Mac had been honest with her instead of pretending to dump her, if he'd told her a dangerous sting operation was about to go down and they needed her to go away, would she have gone meekly like he asked? She'd been pretty brash in her youth. Pretty confident. Pretty sure she was immortal back then.

She'd also been violently protective of her little brother. She'd all but raised Tex herself when their mother abandoned them on an isolated ranch in West Texas with their depressed, overworked father. She couldn't honestly say that she wouldn't have sneaked up on the sting and tried to be there to save the only two men in the world she loved.

Why did Mac have to go and be so blasted understanding and patient on her now? It was almost as if he wanted her to fall in love with him again. Or more accurately, to rekindle the love for him that she'd never lost. But what earthly purpose would that serve? A man like him could have any woman he wanted. Surely he could do better than her. Her thoughts whirled, tangling into ever messier knots until she developed a throbbing headache.

Mac and Dutch were tense and stilted throughout the ride back to the house. She knew why Mac was wired, but Dutch? Were they worried about what they'd find when they got back? Mac said Ruala wouldn't mess with them again for a while. Had he lied about that, too? Was he lying about everything? Damn him for confusing her like this!

The horses held up well for the return trip. It was mostly downhill, and once they got the scent of home in their noses they were hard to hold back. Her glowing watch declared the time to be about 1:00 a.m. when, in front of her, Mac held up a closed fist. Apparently, that meant to stop, since

Malika all but ran into the rear end of his horse when it skidded to an abrupt halt.

He and Dutch slid off their horses. Her knee was having no part of dismounting right now, so she stayed in the saddle, alarmed at the sudden stop. They were no more than a half mile from the ranch. It was just over the next big rise.

She leaned down toward Mac. "What's up?" she murmured.

"I'm going to check out the ranch before we barge in as proud as you please," he murmured back.

She rolled her eyes. These Special Forces guys seemed to enjoy making everything as difficult as possible. "Why don't you just call Frank on your cell phone and ask him if anything's going on? He's staying at the house until we get back," she asked with imminent logic.

"Can't use my cell phone just now. It's turned off. Doc and Howdy should have returned this evening. We need to make contact with them. I'd hate for them to shoot us as we ride in. Dutch is going to radio and get position fixes on them, and then I'll have a look around for traps or other surprises from our end."

"Can I come with you?" she asked, nervous at the prospect of sitting out here alone for any extended period of time.

Mac shook his head regretfully in the negative. "On this recon, I'll be moving fast and quiet. But Dutch will stay with you."

The rest of his answer hung unspoken in the cold night air. He'd be moving fast and quiet, *and she wasn't up to that sort of physical challenge.*

After her terrifying experience the night before, she wasn't quite as militant at the thought of hanging back while Mac went ahead and did a bit of his fancy commando stuff. But she still didn't like the idea of not being able to keep up. She covered up her frustration by sighing and saying, "Let me guess. I'm supposed to stay here with Dutch and keep the horses quiet while you play cowboy and go scout for Indians."

The distant manner he'd taken with her ever since their argument this morning softened a bit. He even cracked a tiny smile for her. But his instructions were businesslike. Impersonal. "You catch on fast. Stay mounted, and if the slightest thing looks or sounds weird to you, bolt for the hills. Do you remember that Charlie Squad phone number you called the night Ruala broke into your house?"

"How could I forget it?" she asked dryly.

"Call that number when you can and someone will come find you. I'm sorry to have to leave you here like this, but it'll be just a little while. I promise I'll come right back as soon as we know it's clear to move you into place."

"Okay," she answered gamely. She was already scared. Afraid to be alone. But that sounded so bloody weak. "I'll be okay by myself for a little while. I didn't mean last night that you could never leave my side again."

He peered closely at her in the dark for a moment. "Just remember what I said. If anything spooks you, get out of here. Dutch will cover your retreat. I don't want anything bad to happen to you, got it?"

She cleared her throat and reached for his horse's reins. "Right. Well, you have fun and don't stay out too late or you'll miss your supper."

Mac grinned. "Aww, come on. It's not a school night, Mom."

For just a second she smiled back. "I'm a lot of things, Mac Conlon, but I'm definitely *not* your mother."

"Thank goodness for that," he murmured.

Did his hand actually caress her thigh as he moved past her? When she was done gaping in shock, she glared at his retreating silhouette. First he made some clumsy attempt at an apology to her, then he ignored her the whole way back to the ranch, and now he had the gall to cop a feel? He had some nerve.

If only her nerves were half as bold as his. The minutes dragged on, and an hour passed. The horses grew as antsy as she was. They smelled supper and were not amused at being kept away from it like this. Gradually a breeze began to pick up. It had a heavy, wet smell that presaged rain. The horses sensed the storm coming, too, and Malika shifted restlessly beneath her.

"Easy girl." She patted her mare's neck. "I know exactly how you feel. But we ladies have to humor the men, you know."

"Oh, yeah?"

The quiet voice made her jump practically out of her skin. Malika shied hard, too. Susan managed to stay on her horse and hang on to the other horses' reins. Barely.

"You're lucky I didn't scream, Mac Conlon," she replied.

"Nobody would have heard you but the rest of Charlie Squad, and they'd have figured we were having wild sex out here."

"You wish," she retorted.

"You say the word, and I'm there."

There was an undertone of seriousness to his flip response that silenced Susan. Her world tipped off balance once more. Would she ever feel stable and in control of her life again? She was still reeling mentally when Mac mounted his horse and took the reins of the packhorse from her.

When they reached the barns, she slid out of the saddle and into Mac's arms. She'd have fallen flat on her backside if he hadn't been there to catch her. Yet again, he'd anticipated her need and was there for her. She really wished he'd quit doing that. It made being mad at him darned difficult. Fortunately, he set her away from him immediately and stepped back to a safe distance. As it was, her pulse betrayed her by pounding at the brief contact.

Gratefully she handed Malika over to Frank, who passed her a cane. As humiliating as it was to use it in front of Mac, there was no other way she'd make it up to the house tonight. But as he walked beside her to the house, he seemed completely oblivious to the cane or her limp.

A long soak in a hot tub sounded wonderful, but bed sounded even better. Her knee would have to wait until tomorrow to be pampered back to a semblance of functional. Mac followed her inside. She stopped in front of her bedroom door, surprised that he was still right behind her. "What are you doing?" she asked.

"Going to bed."

"Where?" she asked, suspicion blossoming.

He gazed at her solemnly. "Where do you think?"

Alarm roared through her. "No. Absolutely not. Even if I was interested, and I'm not, I'm dead tired."

"So am I. And you're not sleeping alone until we catch these jokers. You're at maximum exposure here at the ranch, which translates to maximum danger."

"You're still not sleeping with me!"

He shrugged. "Well, it's me or one of the other guys. I just thought you might be more comfortable with me since we're not strangers. Who would you like me to get to sleep with you instead? I'd recommend Howdy. He's the lightest sleeper of the bunch, and he's the best sniper I've ever seen."

Her alarm threatened to become panic. "Are you serious?" squeezed out of her tight throat.

He looked straight at her. "Yes, Susan, I am. Someone's sleeping in your room until this is over. I know that's a pain in the butt for you, but we're moving into the final phase of this op. Now's when the risk goes sky high for the bait. And that's you.''

The finality in his voice left little room for argument. And, when she stopped to think about it, she probably would feel more comfortable knowing somebody was nearby to protect her. But did it have to be Mac? Except the thought of anybody else sleeping in her room was even more weird.

She sighed. "I'll get you some blankets and a pillow."

When she stepped into her room with an armload of bedding a minute later, Mac was sprawled out on the floor beside her bed, wearing only a pair of gym shorts, fast asleep. He looked exhausted. Gently she covered him and put the pillow beside his head in case he wanted it later. Limping around him carefully, she took off her clothes, pulled on an elastic knee brace and an oversize T-shirt and crawled under her own covers.

As exhausted as she was, she lay in bed for a long time, listening to Mac's quiet breathing. It was unsettling having him so close. How many years had she dreamed of him in the dark like this, imagining him near enough to touch, to kiss, to...

She had to find a way to get over these errant thoughts of him! She'd be lying to herself if she didn't admit she lusted over him. But the other feelings that kept flooding her... Dang it, *she didn't love Mac Conlon!*

Her mental outburst subsided, and she resumed listening to him breathe. Imagined the rise and fall of his muscular chest. Her whole body felt hot and flushed. Shoot. She was never going to get to sleep at this rate.

The wind rattled her window, and she snuggled deep under the covers to listen to the storm come. A spatter of raindrops hit her window. There was nothing quite as majestic as a thunderstorm rolling across the high plains of West Texas. The storm cut loose all at once with a flash of light and an immediate crash of thunder, right outside her window.

Susan jumped, or would have jumped if two hundred pounds of brawn hadn't landed on top of her just then. A hard hand landed on her mouth and pushed her head back into the pillows.

A harsh, male whisper grated in the echoing silence. "Don't move."

Chapter 10

Panic slammed into Susan, and she fought like a wildcat. She grabbed the first weapon that came to hand, a feather pillow, and bludgeoned her attacker with it.

"Damn, Suzie," Mac complained. "Don't kill me! I'm one of the good guys! I was dead asleep and that crack of thunder sounded like a gunshot."

He rolled off her, but she continued to pummel him with the pillow, her fear melting into fury at the fright he'd given her. And something began to break loose inside her, heaving in her chest like a huge logjam about to bust free. "You scared the living daylights out of me!"

He threw up his hands, covering his head as she flailed at him with the heavy pillow. His big frame was an easy target for her assault. Why didn't he fight back? Why was he just lying there? She *wanted* him to fight. *Needed* him to. So she could vent her fury without guilt. Ten years' worth of it. "Come on. Grab a pillow and take a swing at me," she panted.

He peered out from under his elbow. "I don't want to hurt you."

The logjam gave a tremendous groan and ripped loose, sending splinters of pain and grief and anger shooting every which way. He talked such a big line about her being attractive and marriageable, but then he turned around and treated her like a cripple. God, how she hated that!

"Damn you, Mac," she ground out, "fight back!"

"No."

She hit him harder. The pillow landed with heavy whumps against his chest and arms. "Stop...treating me...like a damned...invalid," she grunted between swings.

That snapped him out of his infuriating passivity. He stared at her in the blue strobe light flashes of lightning. "What the hell are you talking about?" he demanded.

"You always act like I'll break at the slightest jostle. I'm not made of glass, you know. I won't shatter, and I'm sick of you pussyfooting around me! Now pick up a damn pillow and show me what you've got, or I'm going to march downstairs and tell all your buddies you're a coward."

That did it. With a move so fast she didn't see it in the single flash of lightning it took, he flipped her on her back and pinned her to the mattress. He loomed menacingly over her. And snarled, "I...don't...hit...women."

"Well, hallelujah. He finally admits that I'm a woman. We have a breakthrough!"

His hands fell away from her shoulders and he sat back on his heels, straddling her hips. "Susan, don't push me. I'm trying hard to be a gentleman here, but you're making it real damn difficult."

She was *really* getting tired of his whole "good guy responsible for everyone in the world" routine. He couldn't have made her madder if she'd been a bull and he'd just waved a big, fat red flag at her. She punched his chest, almost too irate to notice his sharp intake of breath as she surged beneath him. Her knee shouted its protest, but she ignored it. "Oh stop it, already! I'm sick of this honorable unto death martyr act out of you."

"Martyr? Me?" He gathered an indignant head of steam fast. "You're the one running around trying to be so damned independent every minute of the day—"

"You are such a jerk!"

"I am not!"

"Are, too."

"Am not!"

"Shut up and kiss me." She reached up, pulled his head down, and plastered her mouth against his. Whoa. All that heat and passion and masculine energy completely stole her breath away. She pulled back a few inches to gasp for air.

He stared down at her for one endless moment, his eyes burning like brimstone. And then his arms swooped around her, drawing her to him in a crushing embrace. His mouth claimed hers with carnal fury, moving across hers like a river of fire, his tongue plunging inside the dark, wet places of her mouth possessively.

Another blinding flash and a tremendous crack of thunder exploded right outside the window. He jumped, breaking the kiss. A second flash of lightning illuminated the rippling set of his jaw. His control was tenuous at best right now. If her intent had been to wake the sleeping tiger, she'd succeeded. Spectacularly.

The thrill of him finally cutting loose, of finally letting go of the passion inside herself, was almost too much for her. The room spun around dizzily, and she clung tightly to him. He was as solid as a rock. His raw physical power sent her already-scattered thoughts spinning further astray in a blistering vortex of need.

Another bright flash. A stillness came over her as she waited for the thunder to follow. Mac froze as well, listen-

ing, sprawled protectively over her. He pressed her deep
into the mattress, fitting his body to hers, making her viv-
idly aware of how slender and soft she was in comparison
to him.

His breath was warm against her temple. His wood
smoke and leather scent filled her nostrils. Her chin tucked
perfectly into the crook of his neck, and his skin was bare
centimeters away from her mouth, from her taste and touch.

How many times had she imagined him with her in her
bed just like this? A hundred? A thousand? It was enough
that the reality blended seamlessly into all those fantasies.
Her mind spun off into possibilities that left her breathless.

Another flash of light, more distant. She counted silently,
one-one-thousand, two-one-thousand, three-one-thousand...
The thunder started low, rumbling in the distance, rolling
over the wide-open range like a slow-moving train. It broke
over her like her dreams of Mac, vibrating low in her belly,
deep and potent.

The anger she'd held tight inside her heart for the past
ten years drained away as she gave in to the inevitability
of this moment. Mac must have sensed it, because he relaxed, as well. The tension left his hard frame and he
shifted slightly, fitting their bodies more perfectly together.
She didn't even think about it. She just looped her arms
around his neck and speared her fingers into his hair the
way she'd imagined for a decade.

She whispered, "Do you feel it? The storm's coming."

He gazed down at her, his eyes pools of black fire burning her to cinders. "Yeah. I feel it." His voice was rough.

Her lips curved into a smile. "There's nothing quite like
riding out a West Texas thunderstorm. They're as big and
wild as they come. Sometimes they just sweep away everything in their path."

His eyes flamed even hotter. In the intermittent flashes
of lightning, she saw his gaze drop to her mouth. Her

throat. His stomach muscles contracted against her belly, and his hips ground slightly against hers. Exhilaration rolled through her. He wanted her as much as she wanted him. Lightning flared, one blinding burst on top of the next, as the thunder rolled, painting her room in surreal strobe flashes of blue white. Fascinated, she watched her hands move in jerky snapshots from his hair, down to his broad shoulders, along his arms and then disappear as she wrapped her arms around him.

Mac rose up on his elbows, staring down at her. "Are you sure about this, Suzie? There'll be no going back this time. We aren't kids anymore. This will be the real deal."

He was right. The stakes were a lot higher this time than they'd ever been. She knew what heartache felt like now, how loneliness ate at a soul. She'd spent years looking for someone who could replace the empty spot for him in her heart, and she'd failed. Nobody had ever made her feel the way he did. If she—if they—blew it this time, there could very well be no more chances at love for her.

The magnitude of the moment struck her. And then Mac shifted, all heat and muscle and impatient man. She had to go for it. The alternative—living like she had for ten years—was unthinkable. Her arms tightened around him. "I want it all, Mac. I want the real deal." Her voice caught. "I want you."

The dark shadows enshrouding his face gave way to a slow smile. "So, show me how we're supposed to ride out this wild West Texas storm."

Susan closed her eyes and opened them again. He was still there. This wasn't a fantasy. The thrill and hunger shooting through her weren't purely her imagination. "Are you sure?" she whispered in turn.

A chuckle shook his chest. "Oh, yeah. I'm sure."

"No pussyfooting with me?" she asked.

"No pussyfooting," he answered firmly.

And then his head descended toward hers. Their lips touched. Blinding light—heat, lust and ecstasy all in one—exploded inside her head. He lifted her T-shirt off her in a single, swift movement. And then he touched her skin directly, kissing her and caressing her, relishing her body. His hands were everywhere, stroking her, cupping her flesh, exploring. His mouth followed, warming her with his breath and his kisses.

Pressure began to build inside her, an impatience for more, a need for release. And yet he drove her farther, pushed her higher. It was as if she'd become the growing storm, raging and roiling within its cloudy prison, demanding escape. Mac was wind and heat, molding and building the storm, whipping it up into a barely contained frenzy. He was motion and sensation, smoothness and power, throbbing need and controlled violence. He was everything she'd imagined and more.

''Please,'' she gasped. She pulled him close, wrapping herself around him, arching up into him in a silent agony of wanting as the swift rip of foil tearing made her smile in the dark. Still protecting her. He didn't keep her waiting any longer. He lowered his glorious body to hers, gifting her with all of himself in a single hot, slick slide of flesh on flesh.

The storm broke outside, and the rain came in a rush, pounding down upon the roof, matching the surging rhythm of their movement as their bodies became one. Wild gusts tore at the trees outside, flinging the branches against the house.

She twisted and turned with equal abandon, flinging herself against the rock that was Mac. He gave and took in equal parts, his pleasure hers, and hers his. Lightning flashed and thunder roared, the wind howled and rain slashed at the windows.

The two of them rolled through the blackness like the

storm, surging ever forward, sweeping away everything in their path. Only the fury and the grandeur of their love remained. They cried out together, their voices mingling with the night, their hearts pounding with the rain.

Slowly the storm abated. The rain became a gentle patter on the roof, and then it became nothing more than a quiet dripping now and again. Mac lay still and silent, tangled with her across her bed. His body relaxed against hers, but he was as lethal as the tiger he resembled. A lazy kiss touched the side of her neck. "Am I hurting your knee?" he murmured.

"Not at all. Don't move," she murmured back.

His mouth curved into a smile against her skin. "I'm glad you said that. I don't think I could if I wanted to."

She smiled over his shoulder into the velvety darkness of her room. Heaven. She was definitely in heaven. She kneaded the ridge of muscle along his spine with her fingertips. He groaned with pleasure. She lifted her other hand and massaged more of his back.

"Let me die, right now," he sighed.

"Die?" she asked, surprised.

"When I go, this is exactly how I want to feel."

"How do you feel, Mac?" As soon as the words were out of her mouth, she regretted them.

He paused before he answered. When he finally spoke, his words came slowly. "Like I've come home."

She let out the breath she realized she'd been holding.

"How about you?" he asked.

He sounded a tad cautious.

"I feel better than I have in years." It hit her that it was absolutely true, too.

"No regrets?"

She smiled. "No regrets."

He rolled to the side and pulled her close against him.

"Well, I've got to hand it to you. Those West Texas storms are something else."

"They kind of grow on you, don't they?"

She heard a grin in his voice when he answered. "Yeah. I'd almost forgotten what they're like."

She snuggled against his warmth as he pulled a blanket up over them both. His breathing settled into the slow, even rhythm of sleep. Good. She'd already cost him a lot of rest, and she was glad to see him catch up a bit.

She lay there in the dark for a long time, listening to the slow thud of his heart under her ear. Utter contentment settled upon her, and a peace she'd never known before seeped through her. Mac had been correct. This was the real deal, all right.

Mac was so comfortable when he woke up the next morning that he had to spend a moment figuring out just where he was. Ahh, yes. The storm. A magnificent night with Susan. And peace. He hadn't slept so well in years, and it had nothing to do with being tired or sleeping in a good bed.

A sound intruded on his lazy contentment. He frowned. Instinct told him that a similar sound had awakened him in the first place. It came again, a little louder, more insistent. Someone was knocking on Susan's door. He slid his arm out from under her carefully and stood up. She looked like an angel with her hand curled under her chin and a faint smile on her lips. He hunted for his discarded shorts and yanked them on, hopping to the door as he did so. He cracked the door open. Dutch was standing there, looking exasperated.

"What's up?" Mac murmured.

"Finally, Sleeping Beauty," Dutch groused. "There's a phone call for you downstairs."

Mac frowned. "I'll be right down."

As he pulled on his T-shirt, it struck him that in all the years they'd been apart, all the times he'd lain in a jungle distracting himself from his misery, he'd never imagined that making love with Susan could be like that. He thought he had a pretty good imagination when it came to her. But he'd completely failed to factor in her growing up and becoming a woman.

He slipped out of Susan's room quietly and bounded down the stairs three at a time. The other guys were sitting at the kitchen table, drinking coffee. Dutch pointed at the phone on the desk in the far corner of the living room.

Mac picked it up. "Conlon here."

"Mac, it's Tom Folly. We got positive IDs on the photos Dutch sent us last night of the guys who followed you into the canyons with Ruala. They're thugs on the payroll of Eduardo Ferrare."

"Killers?" Mac asked tersely.

"Definitely. Nearly as nasty as Ruala himself."

Mac let loose a heartfelt curse at the confirmation of what he already suspected.

"I hear you," his boss commiserated. The colonel paused for a fraction of a second. Not many people would have noticed it, but Mac had worked for Tom Folly for eight years. He knew that pause. Bad news was forthcoming.

"We have a source inside Ferrare's organization, and Ruala has asked for additional firepower from his boss. Should be headed your way in a couple of days. These guys seriously want Susan dead. I think we need to pull her out. Go ahead and put her in the witness protection program somewhere on the other side of the world."

Mac's gut clenched. Witness protection meant she'd leave behind everyone she knew, forever. *Everyone.* Including him. How could he lose her after he'd just found her again? Not to mention witnesses against Ferrare had a way of ending up dead. "I'd hate to see Susan have to abandon her life…" The second the words left his mouth, Mac knew they were a mistake.

Colonel Folly jumped all over it. "Dammit, I need you operating at one hundred percent. This case is huge. If you can't maintain objectivity, tell me now."

Mac sighed heavily. "I honestly don't know if I can do that, sir. But I do know this. Susan can be damned stubborn. She's probably going to refuse to go into protective custody or witness protection. But, if it's the only way to keep her safe, then I'm the best chance we've got to talk her into it."

There was a long silence at the other end of the line. Then, "All right. But don't screw it up. Get her to agree. Understood?"

"Yes, sir. I copy you loud and clear." Sonofabitch. Standard procedure and the colonel's orders were going to force him to drive her away from him. *Again.* She'd never forgive him if he pushed her away a second time in one lifetime.

The colonel was businesslike. "All right, then. I'll get off the phone and let you get to it. And Mac—" a slight pause "—be smart. If you give a damn about her, stay focused on the mission."

Mac set down the receiver. Yeah. Focused. Keep Susan alive. Nuke their future together. No problem. He felt like he was going to throw up.

Chapter 11

Susan floated down the stairs, as giddy as a teenager. It was a beautiful morning, the sun was shining, and somehow, someway, she and Mac had managed to find their way back to each other after all these years. It was a miracle. For the first time since the shooting, she'd woken up feeling pretty. Lovable. She was still whole beneath her scars. The revelation was liberating. And she owed it to Mac.

Dutch, Doc and Howdy sat dourly at the kitchen table. "You guys look like you've been sucking on lemons," she joked as she breezed into the kitchen.

They all made a momentary effort to look more congenial. And they all failed. She shrugged. She was too happy to be dragged down by a bunch of grouchy commandos. "Where's Mac?" she asked, her head inside the refrigerator as she rummaged for breakfast.

"He went out for a walk," Dutch answered.

Susan popped her head up over the refrigerator door. "Great. Thanks."

"I wouldn't follow him, if I were you," Doc commented.

She turned around to look at him quizzically. "Why not?"

Dutch answered quickly, "He's setting up trip wires and traps around the perimeter. It could be dangerous."

Her enthusiasm waned a bit. "Oh. Well, that makes sense."

She began peeling an orange. It sprayed a fine, citrus mist into the air. "So. Are you guys excited about becoming ranch hands?"

Dutch looked up. "I beg your pardon?"

"Well, Mac sent all my help away, and it's been three days since any stalls got cleaned around here. Plus, there's a shipment of hay due today. It has to be unloaded and stacked in the barn."

She grinned at the dismay that flickered across the three men's faces. "Cheer up. You're gonna love it. It's lots of good, hard exercise in the fresh country air. Think how well you'll all sleep tonight."

Dutch rolled his eyes. "Just what we need. Fresh country air."

The other men snorted and pushed away their cups of coffee.

"Let's get to it, then, gentlemen," she said briskly.

She had to admit it. She enjoyed ordering around a big, tough squad of macho, Special Forces soldiers. And good grief, were they ever fit! They got the chores done in half the time her regular workers would have taken.

There was no sign of Mac all morning. A tendril of doubt wove its way into her joy. Was he regretting last night? Surely it wasn't so. He'd been completely at ease afterward. He said he'd come home. She was just being paranoid. And goodness knew after the week she'd just had, that was no big surprise.

At lunchtime, Dutch, Doc and Howdy headed for the house and showers. While they recovered from fun with stacking two thousand bales of prickly alfalfa hay, she made them lunch. The guys came downstairs, smelling suspiciously of calamine lotion, and ate a leisurely meal. But there was still no sign of Mac. Her exuberance dimmed. Surely Mac wasn't avoiding her. He'd seemed so at peace, so certain they were doing the right thing.

She asked Dutch, "If I stay on the gravel footpaths between the barns, will I be clear of Mac's traps and trip wires?"

The blond man nodded. "He's ringing around the buildings with his toys. And he won't arm them until tonight after everyone's inside for the night."

She told the men, "When you're ready to get back to work, go find Frank. I'm sure he's got plenty for you to do."

The men groaned but dutifully got to their feet.

Susan grinned. "Thank Mac for this. He's the guy who sent all my workers away."

The glint in the three men's eyes boded ill for Mac the next time they saw him. She chortled to herself and went upstairs to change into clean clothes. She stood in her bathroom a few minutes later, brushing her hair, putting on a touch of makeup and actually dabbing on perfume. She stopped and stared at her reflection in the mirror.

She was only going outside to find Mac. It really was ridiculous to do all this primping just for that. But it was Mac. She was willing to pull out every stop to make it work for them this time around. And then what? If—big if—Mac did fall for her again, what did she want from him? A long-term commitment? Fantasy sex for as long as he was here? A casual, ongoing fling? It was nearly impossible to think past the residual glow left over from last night.

One step at a time. It was how she'd learned to walk

again against the odds. How she'd made peace with her broken heart and gone on with life.

She found Mac sitting next to the pond. Big, old cottonwood trees hung over the water's edge, casting flickering shade over the glassy water. He looked up briefly when she approached him but then went back to staring at the pond.

"Hi, stranger," she said softly.

"Hi," was his short response.

He didn't sound mad, just distant. "Mind if I sit down?"

He didn't even glance up. "Nope."

She sat beside him for several minutes, enjoying the quiet of the place. Finally she commented, "We missed you at lunch. I brought you a snack." She held out the turkey club sandwich she'd made for him.

"Thanks." He took it, unwrapped it and bit into it.

"You know, the guys are plenty mad at you. They got stuck mucking stalls and stacking hay while you skipped out on them."

Mac shrugged. "I was busy."

"Are the traps and trip wires set?" she asked.

"Yeah. They're all laid. I won't arm them until later, when Ruala makes his move. You can move around your ranch for now without blowing up."

She smiled. "Good to know."

He nodded and looked back out over the crystalline surface of the pond. Man, he was really making her work hard to keep dead silence from falling between them. "Help me out here, Mac. I'm trying to have a conversation with you."

He shot her an unfathomable look. After a moment he leaned back against a tree. "Okay, I'll play ball. Tell me why you wanted to act as bait for Ruala in this op."

She blinked. That wasn't what she'd expected. "You need the help if you're going to catch him. I volunteered to give it. What more is there to say?"

"Why did you volunteer to help?" he asked.

She stared at him. "You have to ask?"

He stared back. "I'm asking."

Her gaze narrowed. She was *not* going to give him the satisfaction of admitting she might have done it partially to be with him again. Instead she asked tartly, "It didn't occur to you that the same patriotic zeal to nail Ruala that burns in your chest might burn in mine?"

"What occurred to me was that working with the Squad nearly got you killed the last time. Why in the hell would you come back for more?"

"Why are *you* still chasing Ruala? He's already burned you once. Why come back for more?" she retorted.

His eyes flared in anger and he gestured at her leg. "Because I want to nail the bastard who did that to you."

She stared back at him significantly.

His brows came together in a dark frown. He growled, "It's not your job to go after Ruala, Susan."

"Why the heck not?" she demanded.

He opened his mouth, but apparently thought better of what was about to come out of it.

"Exactly," she snapped. "I have the right to avenge my own wrongs, Mac. I was thrilled to death when you offered me another shot at Ruala."

Mac opened his mouth a second time, but she cut him off.

"Don't you dare tell me that women aren't supposed to take matters like this into their own hands, Mac Conlon."

He subsided, but the mutinous glint in his eyes said he disagreed with her.

"How in the world did you get to be such an overprotective chauvinist, anyway?" she asked, frustrated.

To her surprise he actually considered the question seriously. Her surprise transformed to shock when he answered slowly, "My father left my mother for his secretary when I was twelve. It destroyed my mom. Somebody had to step up to the plate and take care of her, and the job fell to me. It's what I do. I look out for the women I care about.''

Whoa. Not what she'd expected when she flung out the accusation. If they were laying out their cards like this, she might as well go for broke. She cleared her throat. ''If you don't mind my asking, why is it you care about me again?''

Mac looked at her sharply. ''You have to ask?''

She threw his own words back at him. ''I'm asking.''

He shrugged. ''We fit. You hold my interest. You make me laugh—hell, I don't know. You turn me on.''

Not going to admit he had feelings for her today, was he? She pressed, ''But why? Why would a guy like you, who can have any woman he wants, choose someone like me?''

His head snapped up. ''Can it with the crippled, ugly-me act. I'm getting real damn tired of it.''

His words slapped at her, and she gasped at the sting.

He glared at her. ''You're even better looking now than you were ten years ago, and you're a far sight sexier. Hell, I thought we were good together before, but last night blew my mind. When are you going to get it through your stubborn skull that you're a stunningly attractive woman?''

She touched the scar on her neck. ''Most people think this thing is rather stunning. Repulsive, in fact.''

Mac snorted. ''Have you seen the scar on my chest? It's twice the size of that puny thing.''

Susan stared at him, dumbfounded. He was serious! He honestly didn't think her scar was all that ugly, or interesting for that matter. Most people couldn't take their eyes off it. Entire conversations were known to take place with her scar. Not to mention people's squirming discomfort and solicitous fussing over her limp.

''What is it about having a fancy scar or a limp that made

you believe you can't ever get married or have a family?'' he asked, cutting straight to the heart of the matter.

She winced. Boy, his aim was dead-on today. She answered lightly, ''It takes two people to pursue getting married or having a family. I've never found any man who could take his eyes off my scar or get over my limp long enough to be interested in *me*.''

''Then the men you've dated are blind idiots,'' he growled.

His outburst sent warmth shooting through her. ''What about you, Mac? Any thoughts of marriage and family?''

One corner of his mouth twitched into a humorless smile. ''Hard to do the marriage thing when you're out of country two hundred plus days a year. Not many women will put up with that.''

If a guy like Mac Conlon wanted to marry her, she'd certainly wait for him, even if they only had a few months a year together. Just knowing that someone like him loved her would be infinitely better than the lonely existence she led now.

Mac changed subjects abruptly, which was just as well. That line of thought had been leading her in a truly dangerous direction. ''Colonel Folly called this morning. The guys chasing us around the back forty with Ruala were definitely Ferrare's men. So, we've got positive proof the two of them are still in cahoots. Makes our legal case against Ruala that much stronger.''

Like there had ever been any doubt that Ruala and the shadowy, international crime lord, Eduardo Ferrare, were still working together. She asked reluctantly, ''So, what comes next in this little cat-and-mouse game?''

Mac hesitated. And she knew him too well to miss it. ''Don't even think about feeding me another lame line about being safe. Give it to me straight.'' She added earnestly, ''Please.''

He sighed. "Look, I'm not supposed to talk to you about this stuff. I'm supposed to be keeping you calm and relaxed." He frowned. Paused. And then, "I'm sick and tired of playing games with you in the name of procedures."

She blinked in surprise as he continued.

"After our encounter out in the canyons, Ruala and his men know you're being professionally guarded. They know they can't just waltz in here and knock you off. My best guess is they'll hit us with a well-planned and executed military-style strike next time. It's our assessment that the addition of the extra thugs has raised the threat to you to an unacceptable level."

She swallowed hard. Maybe demanding to know everything hadn't been such a great idea. Maybe this was one of those times when ignorance was bliss.

Mac sighed. "I don't want to scare you, but the truth is, this is a no-kidding, serious situation we're heading into."

Her innards felt wobbly and her hands shook. "What do you need me to do next?" she choked out.

Mac jumped on that one. "I need you to leave. I need you to go into protective custody a long ways away from here so Charlie Squad can nail this bastard once and for all without putting you in danger."

Frustration swirled through her. That was the last thing she wanted to do! She'd just found Mac. No way was she walking away from him and letting a mission tear them apart again!

"Don't give me that look," he warned. "You're not a trained Special Forces soldier. And believe me, it's gonna take all our training to get through the back end of this mission. Leave this to me and the Squad."

Susan scowled. He might be right, but that didn't mean she had to like it.

Mac balled up his sandwich wrappings and shifted his weight like he was going to stand up. "Come on. I've got stuff to do to get ready for our visitors. The colonel said to expect them within a couple days.''

A couple of days? Folly thought the assault would come that soon? Oh, God. She wasn't ready for it! Hah. Like she'd ever be ready for a bunch of criminals to try to kill her.

"I'm not leaving," she said warningly.

He glanced over at her. She'd swear that was a momentary glint of pride in his eyes. "I warned the colonel that you'd probably feel that way."

Mac popped to his feet easily. A twinge of jealousy touched her. What she wouldn't give to be as athletic and graceful as Mac again. She sighed and took the hand he offered her.

He lifted her lightly and she came upright only inches away from him. His eyes had gone a dark, midnight shade of blue. It was a color she could happily lose herself in forever. No matter what had gone on between them, past or present, there'd never been another man like him in her life. Never would be.

"Mac," she whispered. "I lo—"

His mouth swooped down on hers, stopping the words before they crossed her lips. His arms came around her, dragging her up against him in a crushingly tight embrace. She looped her arms around his neck, pulling his head closer, deepening the kiss.

Their mouths slanted across each other, wet and hot, tongues tangling in a wild dance. Mac's embrace lifted her completely off her feet. She felt the desperation coursing through him. It vibrated in every fiber of his being. Was he that worried about her safety? She fought off the answering panic that flitted through her. She held him close, cradling his body with hers, silently reassuring them both that everything would be fine. She was his and he was hers.

Eventually he relaxed, accepting what she offered. His

grip on her loosened enough for her to slide down his body until her feet touched the ground. "God, I can't get enough of you," he groaned. "But unfortunately, duty calls. I'm still under orders to talk you into leaving the ranch ASAP. What's it going to take? I'll do anything to keep you safe and get you out of here. You name it."

She looked deep into his eyes. And said quietly, "Wild horses couldn't drag me away from you. I'm sorry, but I'm not going anywhere."

Chagrin filled his dark gaze. "Dammit, Susan, if you stay because of me and get killed, how am I going to live with that?"

She smiled gently. "Then I guess I better not get killed."

He swore under his breath. But at least he had the good grace not to argue with her any further. He mumbled, "Colonel Folly's going to have my head on a platter for screwing up this mission."

She asked reasonably, "How can he blame you? I'm the one refusing to leave."

He answered heavily, "I'm the one who gave you a reason to stay."

She frowned and tugged him to a stop. He pivoted to face her in surprise. "Once and for all, Mac Conlon," she declared, "get over it! I'm a big girl and I make my own decisions. You did not force me into this situation. I'm here acting as bait for Ruala because it's the right thing to do and because I'm the right person to do it."

He still looked unconvinced. Nonetheless, he tucked her hand in the crook of his arm and held it there until they came into sight of the house. Then he let go and stepped away to an impersonal distance. Even that tiny loss of his nearness caused an ache in her heart.

He couldn't leave her—or make her leave him—again. She'd never survive another messy ending with him. So *why* had she hopped on this runaway train…again?

* * *

Mac tried to catch a nap after supper before his turn at the night watch, but he couldn't sleep. He tossed and turned in Susan's bed, the scent of her heady in his nostrils, his thoughts a jumbled mess.

He kept circling back to the same question. *What was he going to do if anything bad happened to Susan?* He knew better than to fixate on something like that. It could paralyze him if and when the time came to save her life for real.

Colonel Folly had told him to stay focused. *Focused* definitely didn't include sleeping with the woman he was supposed to be protecting. Nor did it include putting his career or the lives of his teammates at risk. If he blew a Tango One mission, particularly because he'd gotten involved with a woman in the middle of an op, he'd be bounced out of Charlie Squad so fast it'd make his head spin.

The only option was to give up Susan. Right now. Cold turkey. At least until the mission was over. Problem was, if he abruptly cut things off with her she'd be devastated.

He could explain it to her. She was a smart cookie. She'd understand that he had to concentrate completely on his work for now. But once this mission was wrapped up and she was safe again, he'd take some time off. They'd go away somewhere, just the two of them, spend some time together. Find out if what they had between them was strong enough to last a lifetime.

It was dark and quiet when Susan slipped into bed beside him sometime later. He must have dozed off because he woke up just enough to be aware of her presence. Her body slid over his in the same silken dream he'd imagined a thousand times, seducing him and loving him. Her mouth was warm and sweet and lured him slowly toward consciousness. Finally, when every nerve was tingling, every muscle clenched, his blood pounding hard and fast, he rolled over with a growl, trapping her beneath him.

She looked up at him innocently in the scant moonlight seeping past the drapes. "I'm sorry. Did I wake you?"

He gave her a dark look. "I thought I warned you before not to tease me."

"Who's teasing? I'm prepared to follow through," she purred.

"About that—" He cleared his throat. "We need to talk—"

"Later," she murmured. She wound her arms around his neck and arched up into him in the way that drove him crazy.

Discipline, dammit! He had to stop this. But then her thigh rubbed against him and his body revved to full alert, demanding her hungrily. His heart warred with his logic. His desire for her ran as deep, as fundamental, as his need to breathe.

"Don't tease me either, Mac," she pleaded. "I want you. Tonight I don't want any holding back. No boundaries, no limits. I want all of you. As wild and free as that storm."

He groaned as his sanity slipped another notch. He had to have her. Just the way she'd said. *Now,* his heart prodded him. Aww, hell. He was so going to lose the battle with himself. He could feel his resolve slipping, inch by hard-fought inch.

"Come on, Mac. Fly with me," she whispered.

She had no idea what she was getting into. He was edgy and tense right now. The violence that had been so thoroughly trained into him was bubbling close to the surface tonight.

He grabbed her wrists in a one-handed grip, stilling the delicious roamings of her fingers against his chest. "Suzie, you don't know what you're asking. I can't let go all the way."

"Why not?"

"I don't want to hurt you."

"Ohh, puhlease. We've been over that ground already."

"I'm serious. I've changed a lot in the past ten years. You don't know me as well as you think you do. Don't push it."

"Ohh, you've gone all dark and dangerous on me, have you?" she teased.

He scowled at the laughter in her voice.

"Susan, you need to stay away from me for your own well-being."

Her voice caressed him like velvet. "Mac, I hate to tell you this, but for my own well-being, I can't possibly stay away from you. I need you like I need air to breathe."

He closed his eyes, experiencing actual physical pain at the temptation she offered. What sane man could walk away from a woman like her when she said something like that?

"You're killing me, Susan," he groaned.

"Then let me give life back to you like you gave it to me," she murmured right before she arched up into him again. Her arms wrapped around his neck, and although he refused to sink down into her, she rose to meet him.

It was too much. He couldn't resist her forever. She was the only woman he'd ever loved, and no matter what he told himself was right, he still wanted her beyond all reason. He gave in to the kiss. Gave in to Susan. Always Susan. Only Susan.

Liberated by the surrender, he cradled her close, savoring every inch of her satiny sleek body pressed against him, enjoying every soft breath she took. He rolled onto his side so he wouldn't crush her and tucked her close against his body. He murmured into her hair, "What am I going to do with you?"

"Make love to me until we're both too exhausted to walk."

In spite of everything, she still made him laugh. "Until we can't walk, eh? A tall order, but I think I'm up to it," he joked back.

She groaned and jabbed his ribs. "Behave yourself, Mac Conlon. I'm a lady, and I won't have such crass innuendoes in my bed."

He laughed and pulled her down on top of him. "A lady, indeed. Come here and teach me some manners, ma'am."

Their gazes met and he watched the humor fade from Susan's eyes. Her pupils slowly dilated, and the expression in their black depths grew limpid. They looked at each other for a long time. There was no need for words. Unspoken promises hung between them as real as if they'd been uttered aloud. Duty be damned. Some things were more important than duty, bigger than notions of right and wrong.

His hand slid under the heaviness of her hair and slowly he pulled her down to him. It was an exquisite journey of slow torture and joyous anticipation. Their lips met and the world fell away, leaving them perched on a summit of their own making, beyond the realm of other mortals. They soared on currents of heat and passion, ever higher.

Their joining took his breath away. It was so perfect it was frightening. Their movements synchronized in a stunning symphony that crescendoed until he thought he would blow into a million pieces. They hurtled over the edge and out into space together, drifting back down slowly in a fog of pleasure for he knew not how long.

They slept.

Mac woke up sometime later and retrieved the blankets. Taking care not to wake her, he arranged them into some semblance of order over Susan's sleeping form.

He lay beside her for a long time, staring at the ceiling

bleakly. After loving her like that, how could he even consider calling their relationship off, even for a few days until the mission was over and Ruala neutralized? He sighed.

He slid out of bed and donned his clothes. Quiet as a cat, he slipped out of the room and eased the door shut behind him. Gliding down the stairs, skipping the step that squeaked, he headed for the kitchen. The other guys were still up, clustered around terrain maps of Susan's ranch spread out on the kitchen table.

"Hey," he mumbled. He felt guilty as hell that he'd been making passionate love to Susan while his teammates sat down here and worked. Hoping against hope they didn't notice the heat in his cheeks, he turned his attention to the battle plan they were carefully shaping.

It was almost 1:00 a.m. before Mac pushed back from the table, shaking his head. For the dozenth time he protested, "There's got to be another way."

Howdy spoke patiently. "If Susan won't leave, then we have to stick with the original plan and lay a trap for Ruala here. We've been over a dozen different options. And every one of them keeps coming back to using Susan. She's the only person who will work as bait."

"Can't someone dress up to look like Susan?" Mac asked.

Dutch piped up. "Ruala and his men will see right through something like that. They're not amateurs. They will all have studied pictures of her and will know what she looks like."

Howdy again. "Face it Mac. The bait's got to be Susan."

The other men were unanimous that if Susan wouldn't go into protective custody, they had to nail Ruala now. And that meant using Susan to lure Ruala to show himself. No matter how much he argued, he failed to budge any of them on that one.

He scowled in frustration. "Look. Susan functions amazingly well, but I don't think you guys realize just how serious her knee injury is. She's ambulatory, but not a hell of a lot more. Just because she lives a day-to-day life without much trouble doesn't mean she can handle the kind of acrobatics that might be necessary to pull her out of an ambush safely.''

Dutch sighed. ''We don't need the bait to run. We just need it to sit there looking tasty and lure in the sharks.''

Mac's voice rose. ''And I'm telling you she's going to get hurt. She's not going to be able to get out of the way once the shooting starts.''

Dutch argued back. ''You're underestimating her, man. I know you're all hot and bothered to keep every little hair on her head safe and sound, but a certain amount of risk is necessary here!''

Mac stood up, leaning his hands on the table. ''Dammit, Dutch! It's not her job to die out there. It's mine!''

Howdy intervened. ''Nobody's going to die, Mac. We'll put Susan out for bait, and as soon as Ruala and his men move in, we'll pull her out. It'll be fine.''

They didn't get it. She couldn't defend herself. And *nothing* could happen to Susan!

Mac's thin control finally snapped. ''For God's sake,'' he shouted. ''She's crippled!''

An abrupt, deep silence fell over the room. The kind that falls when people are horribly uncomfortable and don't know what to say.

Mac looked up.

Susan stood in the doorway to the kitchen. Staring. At him.

She'd heard.

Her face was ashen and her eyes way too big as she gazed at him in dismay. Without a word, she turned around and disappeared down the hallway.

Sweet Mary, Mother of God. What had he done?

Chapter 12

Susan stood frozen in the doorway to the kitchen, staring at Mac. Shock numbed her body. She couldn't believe he'd just said that. After everything she'd shared with him, after the way they'd made love… He *didn't* see her that way. He *couldn't* think of her as a cripple. He *wouldn't* have lied to her about it. About everything.

He stared back at her, guilt written in every line of his body.

He did. And he had. He'd lied to her about it all. His own words from yesterday came back to her with painful clarity. He said he'd do *anything* to get her to leave. Apparently including sleeping with her and playing her emotions like a concert violinist. The bastard!

Anguish sliced her heart into tiny shreds. She turned and fled, hop-skipping down the hall. She headed for the stairs but then she heard a chair push back abruptly in the kitchen. Instead, she fumbled at the lock on the front door. She paused just long enough to slip her feet into a pair of sandals on the mat by the door, and then she was outside, fleeing clumsily into the night, its blackness enveloping her. Fleeing from the man who had just broken her heart. Again. Oh, Lord. Not again.

Tears streamed down her face. She could barely see where she was going. She didn't care where she went, as long as it was far, far away from him. She heard footsteps behind her. Shouting. Mac wanted her to stop. Fat chance. She might not be an Olympic sprinter, but she knew every inch of the ranch. She stuck to the gravel paths to avoid Mac's various traps, and the smooth footing helped her make better time. She slipped past the barns, past the pond, out toward the thick tangle of scrub pines and live oaks that passed for a forest in this part of the country.

The footsteps were closer now, Mac's voice clearer. She put on an extra awkward burst of speed and ducked under the first branches. Shadows closed around her and she slowed down to catch her breath and ease off her protesting knee. She followed winding paths she'd trod since her childhood, heading for her and Tex's secret playhouse deep in the heart of the woods. Dodging limbs and stepping over logs as much by feel as by sight, she pressed forward in a blind fury of grief.

Mac wasn't bothering to yell anymore, and she no longer heard his pursuit, but she felt his presence behind her as surely as if he was breathing down the back of her neck.

She made it into the playhouse her father had built for her and Tex not long after their mother left. She ducked inside the child-size door and into the musty darkness. Leaves littered the floor, and she kicked them aside with her good foot. Her knee creaked warningly and gave an ominous hitch. She sat down on one of the low benches built into the walls.

She never heard him coming. One second she was alone, and the next, a black shape loomed in the door. Terrified, she looked up. His eyes were pools of black rage, promising her unthinkable bodily harm. Violence fairly radiated from him. She'd never, ever, seen Mac Conlon this angry.

When he spoke, his voice was a sibilant hiss. "If you ever pull another damn fool stunt like this again, I'll kill you myself. Understood?"

Her eyes widened as she nodded. He looked like he meant it, too. She began to shiver as the shock of reaction began to set in. He moved fully into the tiny room, filling it with his furious presence. He glanced around and sat down on the only other bench in the space. She watched fearfully as he propped his elbows on his hiked-up knees. But then he let his head hang down, slumping between his hunched shoulders. The fight rushed out of her in a whoosh. Apparently, she'd scared the living heck out of him with her flight from the house.

But then her own pain came raging back full force. "How could you do that to me?" she whispered painfully.

"Do what to you, Susan?" he replied wearily. "Fight to save your life? Argue with my own teammates because they want to expose you to more risk than I'm willing to? Throw my career away because I can't make the tough decision to put you in harm's way when I have to?"

"How could you have used me like that? Did you have to play on my emotions to get me to do what you wanted?" she half sobbed. "Don't you know I'd give my life for you if you asked me to?"

He ran a hand through his dark hair, a gesture of frustration and pain. "But that's the point. I would never ask that of you. I'm here to keep you safe. My life is the expendable one."

"Why?" she cried out. "Because you think you owe me one after I got shot the last time? You think this time it's your turn to dance with death?"

He looked up at her bleakly, and his eyes were pools of

black. She battered him with her words. "Does that give you the right to manipulate me like this? Is this what you've become?"

He swore under his breath. "I have not manipulated you. I've done my damnedest not to act on my feelings for you, but I lost the fight. You're right. It is my fault that I wasn't strong enough to resist you. But I swear, I never used you."

Each word he uttered bit like a knife in her heart. She cried out, "Why should I believe you? You lied to me the last time you were ordered to drive me away from a mission."

"This time I told you what my orders were. I told you I was supposed to make you leave. I was straight with you, which is most definitely against my orders."

She shrugged. "I'm older and smarter. You needed a new tactic. It almost worked, too. I came real close to agreeing to leave. I was actually coming downstairs to tell you I'd thought it over and I'd do as you asked." She laughed at the irony of it. "And then I walked in on you expressing your real feelings about me to your buddies."

Mac surged to his feet, but sat back down abruptly when he nearly banged his head on the low ceiling. "How the hell do you know what my real feelings are? You've spent the last ten years believing I was a coward. Did it ever occur to you that I stayed away because I loved you? Because I thought that was what you wanted? That I ripped my heart out and let it bleed for ten years so you could have some peace?"

She stared at him in shock. Surely it wasn't so… But his voice was ragged, and agony fairly poured off him. "Why should I believe you now?" she asked past the constriction in her throat.

He swore violently. "I lied to you once, ten years ago, in the name of following orders and keeping you safe. Why are you so determined to believe I'm not telling you the truth now? Are you afraid to believe me? Are you the one who's been the coward all this time?''

She reeled from the accusation. It cut bone deep, the way the truth always did. Was he right? Had she hidden behind anger at him to avoid facing her own fears? Her own inadequacy? Her own insecurity over whether or not she was a lovable human being?

She stared out the tiny window for a long time, but no other answer came to her beyond a silent certainty deep down in her gut that he was right. Finally she released a shuddering breath. She'd blown it. She'd hidden behind her scar and her limp rather than face her feelings for Mac. She'd latched on to the fact that he'd lied to her as a defense against allowing herself to love him without reservation. She'd blamed him for their breakup, when it had been her fault all along. He'd waited for ten years for a sign from her that she still wanted him, and she'd never given it. In her selfishness and fear, she'd hurt him far worse than he'd ever hurt her.

She half whispered, ''You're right. I was afraid to let you love me. Afraid I'm not worthy of your love.''

''But…''

''Don't say it. I know you're going to try to take the blame again. But it was my fault all along. Oh, Mac, I'm so sorry. How can I possibly make it up to you?''

He reached forward across the small space. She'd love nothing more than to curl up in his lap while he wrapped his strong arms around her, but she dared not. She slid down the bench, away from his hands. They fell back down to his sides.

''At the risk of completely pissing you off,'' Mac asked quietly, ''could you please explain something to me? Why is my wanting to protect you and keep you safe such a bad thing?''

She sighed. ''It's not a bad thing. But you deserve a

woman who will love you with no strings attached. Without bringing all my hang-ups to the relationship."

"My need to take care of you runs a lot deeper than mere responsibility. Deeper than my guilt over having a part, however small, in getting you hurt the last time around. But I have no idea how to convince you of that." He stared out the same window she had a minute before. But then his gaze swung back to her, pinning her in place. "So how do we move forward from here?"

Her throat ached. "I don't know," she whispered.

He closed his eyes briefly. "Great. I screwed it up this time, too."

"Stop it, Mac. I don't want your guilt. We've both lost too much already. It's time to put the past behind us and move forward."

"How? Am I supposed to just walk away from you?"

Hearing the words said aloud brought anguish bubbling right up to the surface of her heart. She felt ready to collapse on the floor. She'd seen the truth too late. Realized her mistake too late. She'd inflicted too much pain on him and he was throwing in the towel. Somehow she managed to choke out, "It's for the best, don't you think?"

He leaned across the narrow space and grabbed her by the shoulders, forcing her to meet his urgent gaze. "Susan, I'm not going to let you throw everything we've ever had between us away, dammit!"

He yanked her close and his mouth closed upon hers, hot and angry and desperate. She couldn't bear to tear herself away from him. Most of her adult life had been tied up with this man one way or another. Cutting him out of her world would be like chopping off her right arm.

His mouth lifted away from hers. "Does this feel like pity?" he demanded harshly.

He kissed her again, more gently this time, absorbing her into himself with his whole body. His hands roamed up and down her back and his arms pressed her close against his glorious heat. His tongue invaded the most intimate places of her mouth, giving as well as taking, evoking erotic sensations all over her body.

"Does this feel like guilt?" he growled.

With a quick bunching of muscles, he carried her down to the pile of old blankets on the floor in the corner. He discarded her clothes with quick precision, and she burned everywhere he touched her. She couldn't help responding to him any more than a flower could help turning toward the light. He'd always been her sun, the center of her universe.

"Does this feel like obligation?" he whispered.

And then he was inside her, all heat and friction and driving passion. Her universe expanded until it combusted in a supernova of blinding pleasure, catapulting her out of herself and up into the diamond-studded blackness of space. How could she turn her back on this? On him? She strained ever closer to him, willing him to understand what she felt for him. Willing him to understand that she needed to trust him. Needed to find the strength in her own heart to allow them to be together.

He froze for a second, staring down at her like he'd consume her, and then they both plunged into the abyss together, pleasure shuddering through them as one.

She floated, disembodied in his arms for an eternity, wandering slowly through the dark, starry vastness of the universe, back toward the tiny, distant speck that was reality.

"How can you doubt my feelings for you after that?" he murmured.

And the lovely starlight shattered around her like the illusion it was.

Chapter 13

Susan closed her eyes against the hot tears threatening to spill over. "It's not about my doubting your feelings. It's about me coming to grips with mine. After what I've put you through for all these years…"

He drew breath to argue with her, but she laid her fingertips across his mouth, stopping the words. "Do we have to go there again? I can really do without the whole fight, fall into bed, then fight again routine."

He rolled over on his back and drew her across his body, off the cold, scratchy blankets. "I agree," he replied. "Next time let's skip the fighting and go straight to the making love part."

She had to smile. But she replied wistfully, "Mac, great sex doesn't solve anything."

He raised his head and stared down his chest at her darkly. "What you and I have between us goes a hell of a lot deeper than great sex."

She shook her head, denying the truth of his words. "There's got to be more. Friendship. Mutual respect—"

"We've got those," he interrupted.

"—equality," she finished. "If you think you've got to protect me constantly, and I think I don't deserve you, then the relationship can't ever work. You can't save me from every possible accident life might throw at me, and I'll always be trying to live up to some impossible standard to earn your love and respect. We'll both fail because perfection isn't attainable."

"Dammit, Susan, why can't you stop beating that dead horse?"

"Because I'm right. You're just too wrapped up in your overdeveloped sense of duty to see it."

"Oh, like you're not wrapped up in your whole, I'm-too-flawed-to-be-loved-by-anyone thing?"

Her heart wrenched. They'd blown it. They'd been unable to overcome the mistakes of their past. "Mac, I care about you—about us—too much to let us destroy each other."

He snatched up his jeans and threw them on, zipping them angrily. He stared down at her bleakly. "I swore I'd do whatever it took, anything, to clean the slate between us and give us a new start. Even if that meant letting you tear my guts out and stomp them into the ground."

She blinked, startled. He'd wanted a second chance for them all along?

"But I gotta say, babe. If you were looking to get your pound of flesh back out of me, you're doing a hell of a good job of it. Honest to God, I hope this makes you happy, because you're killing me."

She got dressed in numb silence while Mac finished doing the same. How could two people love each other so much and still not manage to find a way to be together? *I won't cry. I will not cry.*

She followed him out of the playhouse and back through the woods. He took it slow and held out a hand to her occasionally to help her over a log or past a rough spot in the trail. Bone-deep weariness coursed through her, making her limbs as heavy as stone. Blessed numbness began to creep over the torturous pain of loss twisting and writhing in her gut. They emerged from the woods and headed toward the house in silence. How she managed to stay upright, to keep putting one foot in front of the other, she had no idea. She just wanted to collapse in a heap and cry for days.

When the body blow came from her left, knocking her completely off her feet, shock rendered her mind completely blank. She pitched forward onto the soft ground, gasping for air, but nothing came. *What had just happened?* She tried to breathe, but it felt as if an anvil was sitting on her chest, crushing her lungs. Belatedly, panic slammed into her. It ripped through her like a tornado, tearing up her thoughts and emotions and jumbling them in a chaotic mess. The dead weight rolled off her, and her ribs expanded hungrily, finally letting her pull in a sobbing breath. The smell of dirt and wet grass filled her nose.

Mac, still lying half-across her, murmured in her ear in the barest whisper, "We've got company."

Soul deep fear detonated inside her. Not now! Not yet! It wasn't time. Ruala wasn't supposed to be here for a couple more days!

"Stay here. Don't move. I'll be back," Mac murmured tersely.

Oh, God. Ohgod, ohgod, ohgod...

She realized he was staring at her expectantly, so she nodded her terrified understanding. He slithered away on his belly. She lost sight of him as he melted into the shadows a few yards beyond her. And then she was alone. There was a bush a couple yards to her right. Should she crawl under it or stay where she was? She remembered Mac saying once that it was possible to hide right out in plain sight as long as a person didn't move a muscle. She plastered herself to the wet, cold grass and made like a rock.

She lay there for several long minutes. And then, without warning, Mac was back. Just like that. She felt his presence an instant before his whisper came out of the dark only feet away.

"It's me."

She sagged with relief as he made his way to her on his belly, stopping only when he was plastered against her side from head to toe, an arm across her protectively. His mouth moved against her ear. "Ruala and his men are here."

She'd known it the second Mac tackled her, but hearing the words sent an icy, ominous chill through her.

"He's between us and the house, and I don't think we can get around him so we can't head back there."

"Can we go back into the woods?" she breathed.

"One of his guys is circling out that way right now. Our best bet is to head for the barns. It looks like they've already searched that area and are fanning out away from it. We can slip in behind them and take cover."

She nodded against his shoulder. Oh, Lord. Mac didn't have any of his gear with him. No weapons, no night-vision goggles, no radio to let the rest of Charlie Squad know what was going on. Her mind threatened to vapor lock completely at the danger they were in.

As if he'd read her mind, he whispered, "We've got our brains and my training going for us. We're going to have to out-think the bastards until I can get the squad's attention."

She nodded again.

"When I tell you the coast is clear, we're going to jump up and run like hell for the broodmare barn."

"Uh, problem. I can't run."

"How about if I hold your elbow and take the weight from your left side?"

She nodded gamely, gulping. It was anybody's guess as to whether her knee would cooperate or not. But it wasn't as if they had any choice. She had to try. If she couldn't cut it physically, she or Mac could get seriously hurt. Or worse. Warning bells clanged wildly in her head at the prospect of so much depending on her completely untrustworthy knee. He nodded tersely. She pushed herself to her feet. Her knee hitched ominously before it unfolded. Oh, God. It was already being cantankerous.

"Let's go," he murmured. He grabbed her left arm and hoisted about three-quarters of the weight off her left leg. She hop-skipped forward beside him, her left foot barely touching down. Had she not been fleeing for her life, the sensation of moving like this again after all these years would have been exhilarating.

Thin clouds obscured most of the moonlight, but she still felt practically lit up by spotlights on the wide expanse of grass separating them from the barns. She felt Ruala's gaze boring into her back, right between her shoulder blades. Despite a sharp stitch in her side, she hop-skipped even faster. She did her best to keep up with Mac in the race to the first barn, but she wasn't used to such strenuous exercise. A bad cramp stabbed her under the ribs. But Mac dragged her forward while she concentrated on keeping her feet under her and letting him do most of the work. Finally they reached the blackness of the barn's alleyway.

She stopped the second they hit the dark shadows. Mac's arm fell away from her elbow. She stood there panting for several seconds. Abruptly a powerful arm snaked out and snagged her around the waist, yanking her to the ground. She'd have screamed if she had a single molecule of air left in her burning lungs.

Mac. One of these days, she was going to deck him when he scared her like that!

''Don't move,'' he breathed in her ear. ''We're not alone in here.''

Great. Just great. Her eyes began to adjust to the thick darkness of the barn. A long row of stall doors became discernible. She strained desperately to catch any sign of movement in the shadows. The smells of hay and horse sweat tickled her nose. How did he know there was some-one here? She glanced over and realized Mac was in that Zen listening state of his. Finally, he gestured at her to go into the nearest stall.

Assuming that he wanted her to do it stealthily, since that seemed to be how these guys did everything, she rolled gradually onto her side. Then onto her back. Another slow roll to her other side. She lifted herself enough to grasp the latch on the stall door. Thank goodness Frank kept them well oiled. She opened the door, inch by agonizing inch, praying the horse inside wouldn't notice the opening and come barreling out. Finally it was wide enough for her to slip inside. She closed the door slowly behind her.

The mare, quiet little Moofah, came over to investigate. Susan reached up and patted her neck. Moofah recognized her and returned to chewing hay on the other side of the stall. Susan sat down in the sawdust and leaned back against the wall, quietly going crazy. What was going *on* out there? The silence was absolutely maddening. She rubbed her throbbing knee and talked herself out of peeking out of the stall at least twenty times. Curiosity was all well and good, but there were real men out there with real guns. With orders to kill her.

Susan started. She thought she heard a noise. Kind of a gurgling sound. But then it went away. Her pulse subsided.

Then Moofah's head jerked up, her back rigid. The mare blew hard through distended nostrils. Something had spooked her but good. The mare trembled violently across the stall. There was lots of stamping and snorting throughout the barn. All the horses were spooked by something. Her heart pounded even harder.

"Suzie, come out slowly and stay low like you did going in." It was Mac. Murmuring from the other side of the stall door.

Relieved finally to be moving again, and even more relieved that he was all right, she did as he instructed.

"Come down to the far end of the alley. Walk, but stay low."

Her knee threatened to collapse with every awkward, bent-over step, but thankfully it held until she reached the far end of the barn.

"Over here." His voice sounded as if he was right beside her, but darned if she could see him. She moved toward it and jumped out of her skin when a shadow cast by a rack of saddles detached itself from the wall and held an arm out. She flung herself into Mac's embrace. He felt so warm and strong and solid. She just wanted to grab on and never let go. He wrapped both arms around her and squeezed her so tightly she could hardly breathe. He dropped a kiss in her hair, and then he gently set her away from him and settled a rifle he'd apparently just acquired at the ready.

"It's almost time to go," he muttered. "We're heading straight for the next barn this time." He nodded at the second, larger horse barn. "No crouching or anything. Just run as fast as you can and I'll keep pace at your left elbow. Okay?"

She nodded.

"Remember to breathe."

Breathe. Right. They waited just inside the barn for Mac to decide the coast was clear. And waited. She had no idea what he was looking for, but she trusted his instincts implicitly. She could swear she saw him actually fidget for a second as the wait for whatever he was looking for dragged out.

''What happened in here?'' she murmured while he peered outside. ''Did you find anyone?''

He gave her a hard look. Then he nodded shortly and gestured in a slashing motion across his throat. She blinked. He'd slit a man's throat? Surely that cutting motion was a euphemism for something less lethal than killing somebody. Except the horses had reacted violently. *Just like they would if they'd smelled blood.* Holy cow.

The absolute lack of emotion in Mac's expression as he pantomimed the fate of the intruder was chilling. This was not the same man who had made love to her less than an hour ago.

This man was dangerous.

He interrupted her train of thought by nodding at her and then at the door. Time to go. She took a deep breath. She took off hop-skipping again with Mac supporting her left side. She tried to remember to breathe, but that awful itchy sensation between her shoulder blades was too much for her. She tensed up, and all hopes of breathing deeply were gone.

She was about three-quarters of the way to the next barn when she ran out of oxygen. Her feet became heavy and clumsy. She wasn't going to make it. She was going to die out here, and Mac would die trying to save her. His hand lifted even more powerfully under her elbow and propelled her forward. He all but carried her the last thirty yards. He kept going until they were well into the bowels of the darkened barn before he released her arm and let her take her own weight on her knee.

At least he was breathing hard, too. It was a small consolation.

''Stay here until I sweep the trainer's apartment upstairs. I'll come get you when it's clear to come up.''

She nodded and sagged against the wall at her back. Her

legs felt like rubber and her chest felt like huge steel bands were squeezing it until she couldn't inhale at all.

She still wasn't recovered when Mac said quietly from off to her right, "Come on up."

She climbed the stairs laboriously. "Where are you?" she murmured into the inky blackness.

"Over here," was Mac's quiet reply. "By the bed."

She made her way cautiously to him. She bumped into him and his arms came around her.

"Hi, gorgeous. Wanna dance?" he whispered.

The incongruous remark made her smile against his chest.

"I've made you a nest," he said, gesturing at the bed.

She made to sit down on it, and he stopped her with a hand on her arm. "Under the bed, sweetheart."

"Of course. How silly of me," she remarked wryly.

His quiet chuckle was a breath of fresh air in the middle of this nightmare. Thankfully, it was an old-style metal cot with a good eighteen inches of clearance under it. Mac had, indeed, laid several thick blankets underneath the bed and even provided a pillow and another blanket to cover herself with.

"Lie on your side, sweetheart. That way if you fall asleep, you won't make noise breathing."

"You mean I won't snore," she commented.

"Well, yes. I was trying to be delicate."

"You were wonderfully delicate, Mac."

"Thanks. But don't get out from under that bed under any circumstances unless one of the four of us tells you to. Okay?"

"Okay."

"This is really important. You need to stay out of our line of fire."

"Got it. I'm not budging from here until you guys say so."

"Okay. And don't be afraid…"

He sounded so worried for her. Her heart melted a little. "I'll definitely be afraid, Mac. But I trust you." *To keep her safe.* She'd just finished ranting about him letting her stand on her own two feet, and now, when the chips were down, she caved. Sheesh.

"Just out of curiosity, why are we up here?" she asked.

"The plan Charlie Squad agreed upon earlier tonight was to stash you here when the attack came, but make it look like you were still up at the house. We want Ruala to focus his attention there. When the squad realizes what's going down, they'll know I've put you in here to keep you out of harm's way."

She nodded. "And just how do you propose to let them know what's going on? It's not like you can just shout it up to the house."

"I thought I'd set off one of my traps. A couple of them will make plenty of noise to get the guys' attention. Thing is, I'm going to have to get away from this barn a bit to detonate my traps. I don't want to draw Ruala's men right to you."

She stared hard at him in the dark. No, he was just going to draw Ruala's men right to *him.* "Mac, don't do anything stupid and heroic on my account."

Mac kissed her hard on the lips and murmured, "Stay put. I have to go make some noise. I'll be back in a few minutes."

A few minutes. Right. The next ten minutes took a veritable eternity to tick off her wristwatch. She was going to go completely, screaming crazy long before he ever got back.

Mac crouched in the shadow of a fat, bushy juniper. Any minute now. He'd shown himself to one of Ruala's men for an instant, just a flicker of movement, to draw the guy's attention. Enough to get him to come this way to investigate, but not so big a movement as to truly alarm the guy.

Ruala's man stooped and peered between the slats of wood at the far end of the paddock fence. *C'mon, already. Climb the damn fence and come investigate me.* There. The guy put a foot on the first fence rail. Then shouldered his rifle and reached out with both hands to grasp the top rail of the tall fence.

Mac nodded in satisfaction as the night's deep silence was ripped asunder by a horrible screaming noise. The guy sounded like a rabbit in its death throes with the same eerie pitch of agony in his voice. The noise trailed off into a choking gurgle and then silence. He moved away fast because Ruala and his men would surely come investigate that scream.

He glanced over his shoulder at the main house. All the lights were going out. Fast. The squad had heard Ruala's man hit the electric fence he'd juiced up earlier that day. Well, maybe that wasn't the word for it. He'd run enough electricity through the wire to kill a man in a few seconds. The last light blinked out in the house. Charlie Squad would be tossing on its gear and coming out to play any second. Thank God. Now maybe they had a fighting chance of keeping Susan alive tonight.

He spent the next half hour creeping around on his belly outside the barn, trying to spot one of the guys on Charlie Squad to let the team know where he and Susan were. Unfortunately, his teammates were too good. He couldn't find any of them.

He'd better head back to Susan. She had to be freaking out by now. After that guy's screaming death and then the long, loaded silence that followed, he could imagine how wired she must be. She'd been damned brave up till now, but she'd trembled like a leaf when he told her Ruala and his men were at the ranch. Even she had her limits.

He low-crawled on his belly toward the main horse barn and Susan. It was slow, painstaking going. Move. Pause. Move, move. Pause. He avoided any rhythm in his motion, any large movements that would attract Ruala's attention. The bastard or one of his men could pick him off like a duck in a shooting gallery if they spotted him right now.

It took almost twenty minutes to move the full length of the fence whose shadow he followed. A grassy, open space about a hundred feet across separated him from the yawning blackness of the barn's alleyway. He scanned the whole area slowly. Ruala was out there. He could sense the killer nearby. Could smell him.

He pressed into a slow motion push-up, easing himself toward vertical, inch by agonizingly slow inch. There was no help for it. He was going to have to make a run for it across that expanse of grass. He took a couple of long, deep breaths and leaned forward to launch himself at top speed.

And froze. A flash of black moved in front of him. A lone figure. Slipping around the corner of the main barn and into the alleyway. Swift and silent. Too fast for him to see a face or make an ID of friend or foe. He swore under his breath. Was that a Charlie Squad member gone to check on Susan or one of Ruala's men?

He leaped toward the barn. And all hell cut loose around him.

Chapter 14

The firefight exploded without warning. A single burst of gunfire became a raging torrent of lead flying faster than the ear could comprehend. Automatic weapons spit out their staccato rhythms. A pair of grenades exploded in white starbursts, throwing clods of dirt high up into the sky to rain down around him and on him.

Flares popped overhead, their sulphurous pink sizzle casting the landscape in bright focus. Standard tactic for blowing night-vision and making night-vision goggles useless. He ducked as something whizzed past, dangerously close to his head. Rocket-propelled grenade, maybe. A booming concussion behind him knocked him off his feet, blasting him forward and slamming him flat onto his face again. *Damn, that hurt.* He rolled and regained his feet in one movement and resumed running toward the barn and Susan. He dropped the rifle into a firing position at his right hip and randomly returned fire in the direction of Ruala and his men.

A hail of bullets rained around him, and he changed course, zigzagging back and forth. But then a second barrage of gunfire erupted and the lead whizzing around him diminished. Suppression fire from Charlie Squad. His guys had gotten position fixes on Ruala and his men from the muzzle flashes of their guns and now were pinning down the assassin and his men. Hallelujah.

An ominous sense of déjà vu assaulted him. It was just like ten years ago. A firefight flying all around and Susan at the middle of it all, in deadly danger. The barn loomed before him. He ducked as something hot brushed his cheek and wood exploded off the corner of the barn at face level. Damn, that had been close.

Only a few more yards to go. And then a flash grenade detonated practically beneath his feet. The blue-white strobe of light blinded him, and the blast knocked him flat on his back. Damn, that had been close. If it had been an explosive grenade, he'd be minus his legs or dead right now. He staggered to his feet and stumbled forward, pressing on doggedly for the barn and Susan.

He might just make it after all. The black maw of the alleyway entrance loomed. He dived for it. And landed awkwardly, slamming his shoulder into the hard dirt floor. He rolled up against a stall wall and lay there breathing hard. He was as blind as a baby bird. He squinted, begging his eyes to adjust while he strained to hear anything at all that might indicate the whereabouts of the shadow he'd seen entering the barn.

The alleyway came into focus painfully slowly. Deserted. No sign of the guy he'd seen slip in here. Not good. He crept stall to stall, checking inside each for the intruder. Nothing.

The guy had to be upstairs. Dismay slammed into him, and a string of curses ripped through his head. The trainer's apartment was a single, spacious room. Susan didn't stand a chance of hiding from Ruala's man up there!

For the first time in his career, he very nearly panicked. Only years and years of intense training prevented him from tearing up the stairs, shouting her name. Hanging on to his cool by a thread, he glided up the steps, one at a time. The agony of taking it slowly all but killed him. But he managed not to rush headlong into surefire disaster. Barely.

He reached the top of the stairs and stopped, listening. Over the sounds of the firefight outside, he couldn't hear a blessed thing. He eased down onto his belly and inched his head far enough around the corner to peer into the room.

He'd have roared his rage aloud if it wouldn't have gotten him and Susan both killed. She was seated on the bed, and one man held a gun to the side of her head. Another man was peering right at the stairs—right at *him*—through a pair of night-vision goggles.

The man in the goggles spoke in heavily accented English. "Come join us, G.I. Joe."

His gut fell like a brick. *They'd made him.* All chance at stealth was gone. With that gun at Susan's temple, there was nothing he could do but surrender and hope for a miracle to get her out of there alive before they killed her. He'd always known this moment might come, where he'd be out-maneuvered and outgunned and there'd be no way out. He just hadn't expected Susan to be there, too. A strange calm overcame him as he stood up and stepped into the room with his hands on the top of his head.

Susan moaned aloud when she saw him.

He shot her a crooked smile. "Sorry, sweetheart. My fault."

"I'm the one who charged outside in the first place. Don't apologize to me," she replied.

''Shut up. Both of you,'' the man in the night-vision goggles spit out. ''Drop your weapon, G.I. Joe.''

He dropped the rifle and held his hands away from his sides.

The silent one frisked him. Rudely and painfully. Bastard.

''Now take off your belt. And your shirt,'' goggle guy ordered. ''Get down on the floor with your hands behind your back, American.''

Mac knew the drill. He'd done this to other people a hundred times. The silent one slapped a pair of metal handcuffs on him. Mac tested the rigid restraints cutting into his wrists. Standard police issue. With time and a little pain, he could get out of them. But he probably wouldn't get the opportunity. They'd shoot him first. He eyed the guy in the night-vision goggles, who was alert and wary. The guy's attention never wavered, and neither did the muzzle of his pistol, which remained pointed at Susan's head. Which left him no options at all.

The pair withdrew to a corner to whisper to each other. Mac strained to hear them. He heard enough of the two men's conversation to figure out that these jokers weren't the brains of the operation. But they were smart enough to realize they weren't going to walk out of this firefight alive unless they had hostages. He and Susan were the thugs' ticket out of here.

Sure enough, he was dragged to his feet moments later and shoved down the stairs. Susan slammed into him from behind, and he barely managed to maintain his balance. He half turned to help right her with his shoulder.

''Sorry,'' she mumbled.

''Shut up,'' goggle guy hissed. He smacked her across the back of the head.

''Quit slapping around the lady,'' Mac growled. ''Or

aren't you man enough to pick on somebody your own size?''

"Don't do it, Mac," Susan murmured.

He should have guessed she'd recognize that he was trying to channel the men's anger away from her and onto himself.

The blow to the back of his head with a pistol butt exploded agonizingly inside his skull. It sent razor-sharp shards of pain shooting through his eyeballs. Had the blow been a little to the left, it would have knocked him out cold. Had it been a little lower, it could have killed him. A gun barrel poked him hard in the ribs, and he stumbled forward once more.

Goggle guy snapped at the one who'd clocked him. "Not yet, you fool. We need them to shield us until we're out of here."

If only Susan knew the first thing about military tactics. She'd know once they were outside and in sight of Charlie Squad to drop to the ground and give the team clear shots at their captors. Howdy and the guys could have them free in no time.

But she didn't know to do that, and he dared not try it by himself. If he pulled a shooter's drop, Susan would get shot long before Charlie Squad could get a clear line of fire at her captor.

Mac was startled when Ruala's men prodded them to the rear of the barn instead of the front. He caught sight of an open-topped Jeep parked outside. Must have been driven back here during the first few seconds of the firefight. He and Susan were shoved into the vehicle. He did his best to cushion her body against his when the Jeep lurched forward. As he expected, the two of them were forced to stand up like rag dolls for the drive across the ranch compound. He flinched every time the vehicle hit a rut. That gun to the side of his head made him damned nervous. It didn't take a lot of pressure to fire a weapon. A hard jostle of a finger on a trigger…

Fortunately, the gunfight ceased as they made their way toward the driveway. Charlie Squad wasn't going to shoot while he and Susan were being used as human shields, and Ruala probably wanted to kill her himself. The bastard. Mac was surprised when Ruala didn't take a shot. His own men must be blocking his line of fire to Susan.

Sometimes being as highly trained as he was turned out to be a strange blessing. He knew almost to the moment when the blow was coming just behind his left ear. He even turned slightly at the last second to better position the blow and minimize the risk of brain damage.

His last conscious thought was that he hoped Susan was as lucky if they knocked her out.

The first thing she became aware of was pain. A sharp ache behind her right ear. Blood throbbed through the tender spot with each beat of her heart. The second thing she became aware of was light behind her eyelids. Then, a hard metal chair beneath her bottom. It felt like a standard folding chair. Her hands were handcuffed behind her back with metal bracelets and felt as if they were attached to the chair. Her mouth tasted like stale blood.

Where was she?

She slitted open one eye. Cardboard boxes? She opened her eyes all the way. Tall piles of brown boxes were stacked along the walls. It looked like a storeroom of some kind. It smelled like a basement.

Then it came back to her. She and Mac were prisoners of Ruala's men. They'd found her underneath the bed in the trainer's quarters and there'd been nothing to do once they pointed a gun at her but crawl out and surrender.

A careful look around the dimly lit storeroom showed it to be square and spacious. Deserted. But then, a slight movement behind her and to her right startled her. She turned her head carefully in that direction. Her stomach heaved and she barely managed not to gag at the sight that met her eyes. Mac sagged in a chair, his head lolling on his chest. A blue bruise discolored a lump on his left temple, and a trickle of blood had dried down the side of his face.

"Mac," she whispered.

Nothing.

"Mac!" she whispered more urgently.

He stirred infinitesimally.

"Mac, wake up," she urged in a low voice.

His eyelids fluttered and then his eyes opened fractionally.

"We're alone," she murmured.

His eyes snapped open, alert and wary. "Are you all right?" he asked curtly.

She recognized that brusque tone of voice. He was in work mode. Definitely a good thing in the current situation. She answered him in as businesslike a fashion as she could muster. "Yes. I've got a bump on my head, but I'm fine."

He nodded once. "Any sign of our captors?"

"Not since I've been conscious, which has only been a minute or two."

"They probably didn't have the manpower to post guards both in here and outside. That's good news."

"What do we do now?" she asked.

"We get out of here one way or another."

"How?"

"The first order of business is to get our handcuffs off. Can you wiggle your wrists much in yours?"

She tried to move her hands, and her cuffs rattled musically against the frame of the chair. "No, they're really tight."

She saw Mac's shoulders strain, and a similar metallic

clinking sounded. "Okay. I've got some room to work in mine. I'll see what I can do. Look around for any small metal object on the floor or sitting around somewhere. A paperclip or a wire, maybe."

The light came from a single fixture overhead, and it was hard to see much. She strained to see into dark corners and crannies between boxes. "I don't see anything like that, Mac."

"Keep looking. I'll keep working on these cuffs."

For several minutes there was silence while she scanned the room and he rattled and strained against his handcuffs.

Susan's head continued to clear and her thoughts became more logical. And more worried. "Why haven't they killed us yet?" she asked.

"Ruala probably wants to do it himself," Mac grunted.

Oh, God. "What are we going to do?"

"I'm going to do my damnedest to keep the other thugs' attention on me for as long as possible, then I'm going to hold out as long as I can against whatever they do to me."

"Like what?"

"Like get even for all the misery we've put them through the last few days."

She felt sick to her stomach. "I'm so sorry I ran out on you and the guys like that. It never occurred to me that Ruala might come back so soon. God, I was stupid."

He shrugged. "Don't beat yourself up over it. Hell, it didn't occur to me, either. I shouldn't have made love to you in the playhouse and kept you outside so long. My fault."

"Don't apologize for that," she replied. "I'm going to hang on to the memory of it to keep me strong. We have to survive this! We've got so much to live for—"

Mac cut across her babbling sharply. "Susan."

There was something in his tone that made her stop abruptly.

"We're both likely to die before this night is over. Whether or not you should have left the house or we should've made love isn't all that important right now."

"But I— We— No!" she stuttered.

"Listen to me." His gaze bored into her like steel-blue fire. "There's a chance that Ruala won't kill you right away. He may want to rough you up or have sex with you. Maybe film you to prove to Ferrare he caught and killed the right woman. Whatever he does, I need you to hold out as long as you can. Time is your best friend right now. The more of it we can buy Charlie Squad to find and rescue us, the better. Understood?"

"No! No, I don't understand!" she cried.

He spoke succinctly, with terrible urgency. "Don't give the bastard any reason to kill you. Draw out whatever he does for as long as you possibly can. Delay him. Distract him. Play dumb. Whatever. Just buy yourself more time. Your life depends on it, Susan."

She stared back at him. She heard his words, but their import simply refused to sink in to her brain. Blankly she said, "But what about you, Mac?"

He frowned. "I'm a dead man. Just promise me you'll do whatever it takes to stay alive. Even if that means ratting me out. If you tell them I'm Charlie Squad, that should buy you a good long reprieve. They'll work me over until they kill me. And I'll hold out for you as long as I can."

Maybe it was denial of the situation they were in. Maybe it was her need to feel something other than choking terror. Or maybe it was just that she'd reached the end of her rope.

But she leaned forward in her chair, glaring daggers at him. "Mac Conlon, now you listen to me. I am *not* going to rat you out. Ever! How *dare* you believe that I would even consider such a thing!"

He opened his mouth to speak, but she kept right on going.

"Don't you go all martyred and honorable on me! And don't you *dare* tell them who you are just to buy me more time. Have you got that? You fight to stay alive, damn you!"

"It's not about me living. It's about you getting out of here alive—"

She cut him off. They might not have much more time together. She fought back the tears that rushed to her eyes at the thought. She was going to have her say before he went and got himself killed.

"I love you, you muscle-bound jerk. I even thought we might finally have a permanent future together. But if you can't bend your stiff spine enough to avoid suicide in the name of protecting me, then maybe you don't deserve me! Getting yourself killed will prove you're stupid, not that you love me. Dammit, if you do love me, fight! Live!"

He looked completely broadsided. "Susan, I…"

A noise stopped him in midsentence. She looked up at the source of the noise.

Dear God.

The door at the top of the stairs creaked open.

Ruala was coming.

Chapter 15

She loved him.

In spite of it all. And he'd let her down. Hell, let *them* down. He almost did deserve to die tonight. Here he'd been, running around, acting like a complete jackass, and she still loved him! A moment of elation soared through him. But, he reminded himself sternly, they were in very deep doo-doo at the moment. If he didn't buckle down and concentrate, her declaration might not matter one damn bit.

Mac watched Ruala and two of his men come down the stairs. Not the ones who captured them. These guys looked tough. Casual about pain. Pros. This was going to go down *so* bad. He closed his eyes, steeling himself for the agony to come. He could do this. He *would* do this. For Susan. No matter what she said, his primary goal was still to get her out of here alive.

If Ruala recognized him as a Charlie Squad type, this would get real ugly real fast. If not, he still had a shot at buying Susan some time. He took a deep breath to clear his head. Focus. He had to empty his mind of everything but the situation at hand. He dug deep inside himself for discipline. Calm.

"So, the little birds are awake." The guy who spoke was big and burly. Bouncer material. Wore a ridiculous little pair of wire-rimmed sunglasses that got lost in his ham-size face. Apparently it was important to look cool while beating the tar out of someone. Mac mentally labeled the thug "Crew Cut." Probably the interrogator, since he was the one who spoke first. Interesting. Ruala wasn't going to do the grunt work himself. Not yet, at any rate. Cagey bastard. Mac wiped all expression off his face and glanced over at the talkative one. No telling at a glance what would set off Crew Cut. Better not provoke him, yet.

Big, strong-looking thug number two, "Muscles," met and tried to hold Mac's gaze. Mac let his slide away. Not time to tangle with that guy just yet, either.

Ruala stepped back into the shadows beside the stairs, but Mac still was able to get a decent look at him. Man, the guy looked like hell in person. Had really let his health go to pot. Probably couldn't beat up a prisoner on his own if that sallow, soft look about him was any indication. Clearly, Ruala's plan was to hang back, call the shots, and let his guys get their kicks before he offed him and Susan.

Crew Cut came over and put his hand under Mac's chin. Mac didn't resist when the guy lifted his head to look in his face.

"Who are you?" the guy asked.

Mac nodded lightly toward Susan. "The boyfriend."

"The stupid boyfriend. The stupid, toy-soldier boyfriend."

Mac allowed himself a mental snort. A toy soldier? If that's what they thought of him, they were in for a surprise.

"Who do you work for?" Crew Cut barked.

"Allied Import/Export Company," Mac answered. It

was an old joke in Charlie Squad. Import Charlie Squad, export criminals in body bags.

"And where did you get all your fancy toys, soldier boy?"

"From my boss. He dabbles in, uh, exotic exports."

Still Ruala hung back, not reacting at all. Crew Cut had to think about that answer for a second. "You mean to tell me you're an independent?"

Mac shrugged. He let the guy's mental wheels spin a bit.

Crew Cut continued. "Then who were the other guys with you?"

"My buddies."

"Your soldier buddies," Crew Cut stated.

"A couple of them," Mac answered vaguely. He didn't stand a chance of convincing these guys that the force they'd been up against wasn't military.

Ruala spoke from the shadows. "He's lying."

Crew Cut turned to his boss as if looking for instructions.

"Get to the point, Carlos," the ringleader said.

Mac took a long, deep breath and exhaled slowly. The preliminaries were over.

Crew Cut—Carlos—turned to him. "You've been a pain in the ass, toy soldier."

Mac shrugged. "Sorry to inconvenience you."

The guy's voice rose. "Don't get smart with me."

The guy was working himself up into a rage where he'd enjoy beating the tar out of him. He knew techniques to diffuse the guy's building frenzy, but tonight he had to let it roll.

Carlos slapped the cardboard box beside him. The loud smack made Susan jump. *Steady, Suzie. Stay out of this. Let me handle it.* Mac willed her to hear his thoughts. He knew what he had to do. He had to drive the guy over the edge into violence. It was going to get him messed up bad, but it would shift the focus away from hurting Susan and buy them crucial minutes for Charlie Squad to get here. The guys would have followed Ruala and his hostages as they left the ranch. They'd have hung back at a safe distance so Ruala didn't kill his human shields until he stopped somewhere. He had no doubt Charlie Squad was nearby, assessing how to attack while they moved in for the kill. Because Ruala had hostages, they'd have to come in using stealth. And that took time. It all boiled down to whether or not he could buy his teammates enough time to save Susan.

"If I'm supposed to be impressed by you, I'm not," Mac commented blandly.

Carlos tore off his sunglasses and threw them down on a box in exasperation. Nasty little pig eyes. No wonder the guy wore shades. If he could turn this into a one-on-one honor duel with Carlos, the other thug and Ruala might stay out of it long enough for Carlos to avenge the insult to his manhood.

Mac said pleasantly, "You're not man enough to take me."

Ruala scowled.

Muscle-bound thug number two stepped forward, blatantly flexing his biceps. Mac ignored him.

Carlos went red in the face. "You American prick!" he screamed. "I'll show you!"

There. Now the guy was where Mac wanted him. Mad as hell and not thinking calmly. Time to push the button. He laughed.

That did it. Pulling a John Wayne act always did, in these situations. The fist came from his left. It clipped him sharply in the jaw and snapped his head back. Damn, that first hit always stung.

Another meaty fist to his eye this time. And then a solid blow to the gut. He grunted and hoped Carlos would uncuff him out of the chair and stand him up soon. He'd be able to absorb the blows better on his feet. Thankfully, it only took one more blow for Carlos to decide he'd get better results if the punching bag was vertical.

Mac assessed damage while his cuffs were rehooked to a metal water pipe running up the wall. Not bad so far. Maybe a cracked tooth. But from the look of those biceps, it was going to get worse. Much worse. At least he'd gotten free of that chair. Although it wasn't likely he was going to get a shot at escape now.

Carlos got right in his face and snarled, "You're going to die real slow, gringo."

"Kiss. My. Ass," Mac replied succinctly.

The beating continued. Time stopped for Mac, and he counted its passage only by the landing of another punishing blow to his body. He did his best to detach himself from the pain. So far, none of the damage was life threatening. There'd been one moment when he was worried, though. A vicious hit to the torso broke at least one rib, and he was unable to draw in his next breath. For a second he'd thought maybe his lung had collapsed. He might not be so lucky next time.

Random thoughts passed through his mind in slow motion. *Tough. Think tough. Pain is temporary. Ride it out. Be worthy of Charlie Squad. Be worthy of Susan. Buy time for her. She loves me.*

He didn't know how long it went on. He might even have passed out briefly. But suddenly Mac was aware of Ruala stepping forward out of the shadows and moving near. He came into Mac's limited range of vision, cocked his head sideways and looked up into Mac's battered face.

The assassin spoke curtly, in accented English. "You're either one stupid SOB or a hell of a smart one. Which is it?"

"Wha'?" Mac mumbled. He didn't have to put on much of an act to sound dopey with pain.

Ruala stepped back in disgust. "Let's go get the video camera. The boss wants pictures when we kill the woman. We'll make the boyfriend scream before we kill him, too."

The three men turned and filed up the stairs and out of the room. The door creaked shut behind them.

"Oh, my God, Mac. Are you all right?" Susan cried out softly. Her handcuffs rattled.

"Not 'xac'ly" he managed to force past his bloody, swollen mouth. Even thinking hurt. He fought to clear his brain. There was something important…something he'd seen that had registered subliminally….

It came back to him.

"Su, can mov' your chair?"

"Yes, I think so." She looked as perplexed as she sounded. At least it wiped the horrified expression off her face. He'd made sure not to look at her for most of the beating. He didn't know if he could have borne seeing her pity.

"Carlos took off…glasses. They still on…box?" He gestured with his head and then winced as pain screamed from a dozen locations in his body.

"Yes. I see them."

"Slide your chair…can you reach 'em?"

He waited impatiently while she inched her way across the room. They didn't have much time.

"Hurry, swee'hear'," he urged softly.

"I'm going as fast as I can."

The sob in her voice broke his heart. "I know, Suz'."

She managed to get herself turned around with her back to the box. She pushed off the floor with her feet and arched her back up awkwardly, trying to raise her hands high enough to grasp the glasses. Mac watched in an agony of suspense. On the third try she got them. She collapsed back onto the seat with a sob of relief.

"Bring…to me."

It was awkward, and she jostled him hard enough to wring a groan from him, but the hand-off eventually got made.

"Go back...where you were."

While she inched back to her original position, he snapped one of the earpieces off the glasses. It wasn't the world's best lock pick, and he fumbled with it for several minutes, feeling for the right angle, but he got it. The handcuff fell away from his left wrist.

He hugged himself carefully, stretching out the cramps in his shoulders as he moved to Susan's chair and knelt behind her. And unleashed a foul curse.

"What?" she cried out.

"Your cuffs hav' differen' lock...can't open without real picks. Can't get you loose."

"That's okay. You go get help," she murmured urgently.

He moved around in front of her, kneeling so he could see her face. "I'm not—" he enunciated carefully "—leaving you here alone."

"Are you nuts? Get out of here!"

"No. I promised I'd never leave you alone again, and I'm not breaking that promise."

"Don't be ridiculous. Save yourself!"

He stood up shakily and staggered across the room.

"Mac, you'd have died if you'd been in that van with me all those years ago, and you're going to die if you stay with me now. Climb out of that morass of guilt you're drowning in and *go get help!*"

Ignoring her wrenching pleas, he put the broken pieces of the glasses back on the box where Susan had gotten them. He moved painfully back toward the pipe on the wall where he'd been cuffed before.

"Mac, what are you doing?" Susan all but sobbed. "Go! I can't stand watching them do this to you anymore. Please!" she begged him.

His brain felt clearer by the second. Clear enough to know what he was doing was completely insane and absolutely right. "I know this is hard for you, Susan. But we're buying a lot of time here. Hang in there a little longer. And remember what I said. After I'm done for and they turn their attention to you, hold out as long as you can."

A squeak from above announced the return of Ruala and his men. Mac jumped into position and grabbed onto the pipe behind him with both hands. He leaned against the cold steel. Hopefully his body would hide the fact that his handcuffs were unhooked. Now the key was to stay conscious for as long as humanly possible and hang on to that pipe.

The punishment resumed, along with suggestions this time from Ruala on how to inflict maximum pain. He was vaguely grateful Carlos wasn't trained in true torture, but brute force was managing to deliver enough pain that it was becoming almost more than he could stand.

Finally there came a point when his body just turned off. No matter how hard he willed himself not to, he felt himself slipping into unconsciousness. With every ounce of his remaining strength he controlled his fall to the floor, managing to collapse with his back still plastered against the pipe and his hands gripped around it.

He'd done his best. Hopefully it was enough.

The darkness was cool and soothing. Reluctantly he let it overwhelm him.

Susan lurched against her bonds when Mac collapsed, sobbing her relief that his agony was over.

Carlos kicked Mac's prone body.

"Stop it!" she screamed. "You've already killed him!"

Through her tears, she saw all three men's heads swivel in her direction. She gulped. Now it was up to her to buy time for Mac. Time for him to regain consciousness and maybe muster up a little strength. Time for Charlie Squad to find them before these animals killed them both.

A calm clarity came over her. Mac had been willing to die for her. To stand there, uncuffed, and take a brutal beating rather than break a promise to her. He'd sworn she wouldn't ever be alone again. The least she could do was honor his choice and return the favor to him. If he had to die here, tonight, he was going to do so with her at his side. And with that knowledge came peace.

"So, the little woman speaks," Ruala snarled. "Perhaps she would like to join the fun."

She remembered Mac's advice. "Maybe I would at that."

Ruala gave her a startled look before he glared and stepped forward. She held his gaze gamely.

"Do you want to suffer the same fate as your boyfriend?"

She glanced over at Mac's crumpled form and shrugged. "Guys like him are a dime a dozen," she said scornfully. *Please, please, please, let them buy her act.*

"You were all concerned about him a couple minutes ago," Carlos piped up suspiciously.

She snapped, "A couple minutes ago he was alive and could have helped me. Now he's not." She thought she saw Mac's rib cage rise, and she prayed with all her strength that she'd seen the slight movement. "I'd like to offer you a deal."

Ruala took another step closer. "What kind of deal?" he demanded. "Tell me or I'll kill you."

She gave him a long, steady look and said slowly, "A deal concerning my testimony to the grand jury. Why kill me when I can clear your name and save you a world of hassles with building a new identity from scratch and going through more reconstructive surgery?"

Ruala blinked. In his artificially smooth face, the gesture

looked downright reptilian. "Indeed? You bring up an interesting possibility. Did the boyfriend think that one up?"

She glanced down at Mac's battered form and snorted. "You honestly think he had enough brain cells underneath all those muscles to come up with something that intelligent?"

Ruala blinked a couple more times. Lord, that was creepy. She restrained a shudder as he said slowly, "I think my employer and I may have underestimated you. Wait here. I'll be back."

Duh. Like she was going anywhere handcuffed to a chair. He and his flunkies left the room once more.

She waited in an agony of suspense until the door closed behind them at the top of the stairs. Then frantically she slid her chair in jerky lurches over near Mac's body.

"Mac," she whispered frantically. "Mac, can you hear me? Oh God. Please be alive."

He exhaled. A bare thread of rattling breath escaped him, but at least he was breathing. She had no idea if he was remotely conscious or not, though. She tried to get through to him anyway. "I'm going to try to convince Ruala you're dead and to leave your body here. So don't wake up on me when he comes back. Okay? Did you hear me?"

"Yeah." It was so faint she could barely hear it.

"Oh, Mac, why didn't you leave when you could have? I can't believe you let them do this to you. What were you thinking?"

His voice was weak, but clear. "I love you, Susan. I was thinking about buying you time and keeping you alive."

He *loved* her? After all the horrible things she'd said to him? And still he'd sacrificed himself like this for her? Her composure threatened to shatter completely.

Not yet. She couldn't let down yet. She had to do her best to protect him, to give him a fighting chance to survive. She drew in a wobbly breath. "Well, good grief, Mac Conlon, you've got a strange way of showing you love me," she quipped gently.

His painful, bloody smile tore her heart in two and made it whole again, all at the same time. "I'd kiss you if I could get to you to do it," she said softly.

"I'd let you if...wouldn't make me...pass out," he mumbled, his strength starting to fade.

"Any bright ideas to share with me before that jerk comes back?" she asked.

"I heard you... Did good. Stick...with offer. Bargain for as long as possible. Leave me...for dead..." His voice trailed off.

"Don't talk if it hurts," she murmured to him. "I'll buy us however much time it takes for Charlie Squad to find us."

He took several careful breaths and visibly gathered his strength to speak one more time. "I doubt you'll get...chance, but in my right boot...under liner...homing device in heel. If they move you, take it..."

A homing device? No wonder he'd been so sure Charlie Squad would find them. A brief spark of hope lit in her heart. Maybe, just maybe, they would get out of this alive.

And then, in the very next second, the lights went out. The room plunged into total blackness.

Chapter 16

Mac heard Susan's gasp of alarm in the dark. "'Bout damn time," he murmured in a flood of relief.

"What are you talking about?" Susan whispered tautly out of the darkness.

"Charlie Squad…here."

"How do you know?" she asked.

"Who else…take lights out?" *God, it hurt to talk.* "We like…work in dark."

If Ruala had wanted the lights out, he'd have taken them out when he got here. It had to be Charlie Squad. And he was feeling stronger by the second. Apparently, knowing a rescue was on the way did that to a guy.

"Thank God," Susan murmured.

She sounded close to tears. Damn. He needed her to hold up just a little while longer. He gathered his strength to talk some more. "Susan, we're not out…yet. Don't let down." He took as deep a breath as his busted rib would allow. "I need you…be strong…li'l while longer. Okay?"

He wished he could see her face to read her emotional state more precisely. Her voice sounded reasonably steady, though, when she answered, "I'll try."

"Good girl."

There was something about knowing he might actually live that made the pain more tolerable. He eased his arms from underneath his body and pushed carefully to a sitting position. He felt nauseous. By sitting very still until the dizziness passed, he managed not to hurl the contents of his stomach across the room. Barely. After a few more minutes, his stomach settled enough for him to move. Gingerly he tested his limbs. Sharp pain shot through his left forearm, but otherwise he was functional.

"So what do we do now?" Susan asked quietly.

Even his broken mouth was feeling better. "Sit tight and wait for the cavalry to charge in to the rescue," he replied.

"Shouldn't we try to get out of here?" she suggested nervously.

"And go where? We don't know where we are, what the layout of this place is, where the good guys and bad guys are and we've got no weapons."

"Good point," she answered dryly.

"What we can do is take cover. Ruala will probably sweep through here to kill us."

"Ohmigosh."

He rolled over onto his hands and knees and dragged himself up the very pipe that had held him captive earlier. He was glad Susan couldn't see his clumsy movements in the dark.

"Sit tight, Suzie. I'll move a few boxes and make us a hiding spot." He tried to envision the room as it had looked with the lights on. He picked a spot out of the line of fire from the top of the stairs and felt his way slowly in that direction. His outstretched hands encountered cardboard.

He groaned when he tried to lift the box and was appalled that he actually lacked the strength to do it. He settled for pushing that box and the one it was stacked upon aside. As quickly as he could in his wrecked state, he rearranged boxes until he'd made them a child-size fort behind the boxes.

"Talk to me, Suzie. So I can find you again."

"I'm over here, Mac."

He stumbled into her and moaned at the jolt.

"Mac, are you all right?"

"I've been better."

"There was a moment earlier when I thought you were dead."

He snorted and then bit back a groan of pain. "There were a couple moments when I thought I was done, too." He moved around behind her chair. "I'll push and you scoot. Let's get you and your throne over behind those boxes."

"Some throne," she grunted a minute later as they struggled to move her across the room quickly and quietly.

"We're almost there, I think," he replied. Normally his orientation was flawless in total darkness, but he wasn't doing anything in top form at the moment. His breath was short and he was getting dizzy again. Just a little bit farther.

"Ouch!" Susan yelped.

"Whoops. I guess we found the boxes."

"Yeah, with my shins." Good. He heard a smile in her voice. Her morale was better already.

He managed to stay upright long enough to help slide her chair into the makeshift fort. Gritting his teeth, he pulled a stack of boxes across the entrance to their hiding spot. Then, gratefully, he slid to the floor. "This could take a while. If Charlie Squad's engaging Ruala and his men out there, the team may have to finish off all of them before they come in looking for us."

"You rest a bit, then. I'll keep watch," Susan announced.

"Do you know what to keep watch for?" he asked skeptically.

"Nope," she replied cheerfully, "but I'll figure it out."

"Getting cocky, are we?" he joked weakly.

"Should I keep you awake? Do you have a concussion?"

He managed a chuckle for her benefit. It was probably just as well she couldn't see him right now. He could feel swelling setting in all over his face. "I don't think I have a choice. I think I'm going to pass out again."

"Go ahead and pass out. I'll guard you."

She sounded as fierce as a she lion with her cub. He smiled and then winced in pain as his split lips protested. "Yes, ma'am," he sighed before he slipped into unconsciousness.

Susan sat in the dark for a long time, listening to the labored quality of Mac's breathing. He moaned now and then. She realized just how badly he was hurt when he couldn't stay lucid in the middle of a crisis. He needed medical care, and soon.

Frantic to help him and terrified of what might come out of the dark and the silence, she sat there, reliving the horror of watching Mac get beaten within an inch of his life. She'd *never* forget it, nor forget the raging guilt screaming through every cell of her being. This was all her fault. If she'd stayed put in the house, everything would have been fine. Her foolishness had led to this.

A faint rumble came to her. She wasn't sure if she felt it or she heard it. She froze, listening. There it was again.

"Mac," she whispered, reaching out with her foot to nudge him.

"Hmm?" he answered groggily.

"I heard something. A low rumble of some kind."

She felt him snap to full consciousness beside her, listening as hard as she. Another sound. Louder this time.

"Machine-gun fire," he commented. "Sixty caliber."

"Ours or theirs?" Susan asked.

"Theirs."

"How can you tell?"

"The rounds aren't firing evenly. That gun's mechanism is fouled. It won't fire too much longer before it jams."

"So how do you know it's theirs?"

"We keep our weapons in perfect operating condition."

She smiled in the darkness.

A creak sounded. She froze, choking on abrupt terror. Oh, Lord. The door at the top of the stairs.

Her insides turned to water. It was either a rescue or a death squad. Mac's hand came to rest on her thigh. He squeezed her leg reassuringly while she held her breath.

A male voice spoke very quietly in the darkness. "Mac, check off."

Mac spoke quietly from beside her. "Check."

Silence.

What in the heck was going on? Obviously, that had been one of the good guys or Mac wouldn't have said anything. So where did the guy go? A hand slapped over her mouth and she about jumped out of her skin. Man! She hated it when these guys did that!

A man's voice whispered in her ear. "Don't make a sound. Understood?"

She nodded under his hand. She was surprised when the hand didn't move away from her mouth.

"Hi, sis."

Tex! She'd have squealed for sure if his hand weren't over her mouth. She shook his hand off and demanded in a whisper, "Where did you come from? How long have you been back in Texas? Thank God you're here! I've been so scared—"

Mac's low murmur cut her off. "Not now, Susan."

She stopped babbling abruptly. He was right. They weren't out of here, yet.

Mac continued in a whisper, "Good to see you, Tex. What's up?"

Her brother answered, "It's a mess out there. Quite a fireworks show. The hostiles are armed to the gills. And this building's laid out like a plate of spaghetti."

"The building's not secure?" Mac murmured in surprise.

"Not even close."

Susan's heart dropped to her feet. Great. Now her brother's neck was on the line, too. "So what are you doing down here, then?" she interjected.

"I heard a rumor that my sister and my best buddy were prisoners in here somewhere. That was reason enough to invite myself in."

"I'm going to kick your butt when we get out of here for taking such a foolish risk," Mac growled under his breath.

"I'll let you," Tex murmured back, "*after* we get out of here. What's your status? You look like death warmed over through these IR goggles."

"I feel worse. Susan's cuffed to a chair. Have you got your picks on you?"

"You bet," Tex answered. "I'll have her loose in a sec."

Susan waited impatiently while Tex worked on her handcuffs. It took under a minute for the metal bracelets to fall away from her wrists. "I didn't know you could pick locks," she commented.

Tex chuckled quietly. "I can do all sorts of things you don't know about."

"So I gather from talking to Mac."

"I know you two are glad to see each other, but we need to get out of here," Mac reminded them.

"Right," Tex answered. "One escape coming up. I've got two sets of night-vision goggles for you guys. They'll work once we get out of this dungeon. There's a little ambient light in the halls upstairs."

What felt like a set of heavy binoculars was thrust into Susan's hands. She felt for the head strap and pulled the goggles on over her head. She didn't see anything until she looked up at the exit. But then she made out a faint line of green coming from under the door.

"I've also got throat mikes for you guys."

"Great." Mac's relief was audible.

Susan took the jumble of wires Tex handed her and managed to sort it out and don the microphone all by herself. She was getting pretty good at this special-ops stuff.

"I see you've been playing with Mac's toys," Tex remarked.

She sputtered and couldn't come up with a response to that one. She *truly* hoped blushes didn't show up through his infrared goggles.

Mac covered up his abrupt cough by asking Tex, "Have you got any heat to spare?"

"Of course," Tex answered casually.

Susan heard several metallic clicks. "What's that noise?"

Mac answered. "I'm checking to make sure there are bullets chambered in the pistols your brother just handed me."

"Oh." She gulped. "Are we going to have to shoot our way out of here?"

"Let's hope not," Mac replied. "But you know us. We plan for the worst and…"

"…hope for the best," she finished for him.

"Exactly. Tex, if you don't mind taking point, I'm not at a hundred percent."

"You got it. Susan, stay right on my heels, and Mac will follow you. Okay?"

"Okay."

She heard the frown in Tex's voice. "It could get sporty out there. Do exactly what I say as soon as I tell you to do it. Got that, sis?"

"Yeah, yeah. I've crawled around with Mac, avoiding these guys before. I know the drill."

They eased up the stairs and Susan held her breath while Tex pushed the squeaky door open slowly. Silence. Nobody shot at them. They moved out into the hallway on their hands and knees, and it jumped into dim, green focus. Doors and signs came into view. She put all her weight on her arms and her good leg, and Tex remembered to set a slow enough pace for her to keep up.

Tex whispered into his throat mike, "We can't go back the way I came. Too much company for the three of us."

Especially since she was a noisy amateur with a bum knee, and Mac was badly hurt. She made the mistake of glancing back over her shoulder in his direction. She felt physically ill at the sight of him. He was covered in black, which had to be dried blood. What she could see of his face around his goggles was monstrously swollen and misshapen. If she ever got the chance, she was going to kill the guy who'd done that to Mac. Painfully.

Mac tapped her foot and pointed forward. She jumped, remembering abruptly that she was supposed to be sticking close behind Tex. She sped up as best she could on her tripod arrangement of limbs and moved back into position behind her brother.

They crawled down the hallway until the first intersection, where Tex motioned her to stop and stand up. It felt really good to unbend her aching knee.

"Wait here while I check it out," Tex murmured. He crouched low and disappeared around the corner.

Susan glanced over her shoulder and was surprised to see Mac facing the other direction, pistols at the ready in front of him. Had he heard something?

She strained to hear anything. The rat-a-tat of distant gunfire was the only noise she picked up.

A finger tapped her on the shoulder and she whirled around, terrified. Tex. He motioned her to tap Mac on the shoulder and then to follow him. She did as he instructed. They repeated the same drill a half-dozen times, Susan and Mac stopping and waiting while Tex went ahead to scout. But when Tex returned the seventh time, he ducked around the corner fast and uttered a single word.

''Run!''

She followed Mac clumsily back in the direction they'd come from with Tex supporting her left elbow. The sound of shouting behind them in Spanish spurred her forward.

''Hit the deck!'' Tex ordered.

Susan mimicked Mac's rolling dive as bullets slammed into the wall above her head with a sickening thud. Bits of plaster flew at her, stinging her face. Her knee was screaming bloody murder. Tough. It wasn't like they could stop and rest it right now.

''Follow me,'' Mac called over his shoulder while Tex returned fire. She hop-skipped after him, and then Mac took a running dive in front of her and landed beside an office door. Somehow he managed to open the thing from his prone position on the floor while he shot a pistol down the hallway. She dived through the opening that appeared behind him. Mac followed right on her heels, and Tex dived in behind him, closing the door fast. Then her brother sped over to a heavy filing cabinet, which he immediately pushed over in front of the outer door.

She looked around. It was a plainly appointed office, with tall filing cabinets ringing the walls.

Tex crawled to the window and peeked over the sill using a small periscope thingy. "Good news," he transmitted over his throat mike. "We're on the ground floor on the back side of the building. Most of the shooting is around front. We ought to be able to get out of here."

"Great," Mac grunted. "'Bout damn time some luck went our way."

Susan's head swiveled sharply in his direction. He sounded bad. He slumped weakly, sitting against a filing cabinet, one hand holding his side and the other arm cradled awkwardly across his chest. The side of his head was bleeding again, and even through her night-vision goggles, he looked pale. She made out big beads of sweat on his forehead.

"Good grief, Mac! Are you trying to kill yourself?" she demanded as she hastened to his side. "Why didn't you tell Tex you needed to rest?"

Tex materialized at her side. He took one look at Mac and let loose a stream of curses. "Mac, you know better than to press so hard in your condition. Why didn't you say something?"

"I thought getting out of here alive was a higher priority than my current…discomfort."

"Yeah, and what if you went into shock on us or passed out from loss of blood? Then where would we be? I'm calling in a full assault team and we're yanking you out of here."

Mac's response was immediate and sharp. "No, you're not. Susan would be put in too much danger."

"So what do you suggest, tough guy?" Tex asked irritably.

Mac was silent for a long time.

"What's on your mind, my friend?" Tex asked. "When you're quiet this long, you're usually cooking up something diabolical in that twisted mind of yours."

Mac frowned. "I was thinking that Ruala is going to

keep coming at us until he takes out Susan. He'll never back off and leave her alone. If he doesn't kill her tonight, he'll try tomorrow or the next day or the next until he succeeds."

Tex scowled. "That bastard's not walking out of here alive."

Mac replied slowly, "True. But we've got another problem. Ruala said tonight that Ferrare wanted film of Susan being killed. And if Ferrare has decided she needs to die, he's not going to back off until she's dead, either. He'll keep sending thugs after her until she's history."

Susan frowned. If he was right, then she was never going to be free of this mess!

Tex nodded slowly at Mac. "Yeah, you're right about Ferrare. He must have figured out she's my sister. He can get even with me for stealing the RITA rifle from him if he kills her." He frowned. "What else were you thinking about?"

"Killing Susan."

"What?" she squeaked.

Mac sent her a pained smile. "Faking it. Making Ferrare *think* you're dead."

Tex nodded slowly. "It would back him off."

Mac frowned. "She'd have to stay dead until we kill Ruala and his pals outside. And we'd need to stage a funeral—maybe send Ferrare word that we're coming after him to get even with him for killing your sister."

Tex nodded slowly. And turned to look at her.

"I'll do it if you guys think it's best," she said bravely.

Mac reached out a bruised hand to squeeze her fingers. There wasn't anywhere near enough strength in his grasp. "Think this through before you decide, Suzie. If we don't manage to kill Ruala tonight, you'll have to completely disappear, sweetheart. You'll have to cut off your family, your friends, everyone you've ever known. You'll have to quit your job. Give up your entire life.''

It wasn't like her life or her job was anything to write home about. And if it would stop Mac from flinging himself into danger… She stared at him for a moment and then asked, ''If I pretend to die, could you stop putting your neck on the line for me?''

He frowned. ''I suppose so.''

''Then I'll do it,'' she answered emphatically.

''You sure?'' he whispered weakly.

''Mac, you were willing to give your *life* for me tonight. I'm certainly willing to give up a job and a few friends for you. Besides, Tex will know I'm alive. And you will.''

His battered fingers touched her cheek lightly.

Tex cleared his throat. ''Look. Whatever we decide, we need to get on with it. The guys who chased us in here will no doubt be back with reinforcements soon.''

Mac's voice was fading badly. ''Give me a second to rest. And then we'll figure out how to kill Susan.''

Tex dug in a pouch at his belt and held out a small packet in his palm. ''Can I interest you in a spot of morphine?''

Mac smiled lopsidedly. ''I thought you'd never ask.'' He tore open the packet and popped the pills in his mouth, dry.

Tex went over to the window and peered outside cautiously.

''How's it look?'' Mac asked.

''Real quiet. Too quiet if you ask me.''

Mac nodded. ''That's what I was thinking.''

Susan frowned. ''What are you guys talking about?''

''Mac and I are guessing that most of Ruala's men are out front putting on a big show, while he and maybe a couple of his best men cover the back of the building,'' Tex explained.

''You mean there's an ambush waiting for us out there?'' she asked, dismayed.

Mac answered, "In a nutshell, yeah."

She gasped. "What are we going to do about it?"

Mac actually grinned. "We're going to sit tight and let Tex watch out the window. In case you didn't know it, your brother has the best eyesight of anyone I've ever met. Give him a few minutes and he'll know the position of every shooter out there."

Susan looked over at her brother who was standing beside the window, staring outside with total concentration. "Really?"

"Yup," was Tex's absent reply. "I've already spotted two men. But the way they're positioned, there should be one more guy out there."

About two minutes later Tex stepped away from the window and shook out his shoulders. "Got 'em all," he announced casually. "Whenever you're ready, Mac, we can blow this joint."

Susan jumped. "You're not literally going to blow it up, are you?"

Mac and Tex looked at her sharply.

Tex commented slowly, "You know. That's not a bad idea…"

"The timing would be tight," Mac answered.

"Hell of a diversion, though. Great way to kill her."

Mac grinned at Tex. "Great way to flush out Ruala and his men, too. How much go-bang have you got on you?"

"A couple pounds of C-4."

Mac nodded. "That's a little shy of what I'd need to drop the building, but I could start a nice fire with it. That way, if any of Ruala's men get away, word will get back to Ruala that she was waxed here."

Susan couldn't stand it anymore. "What *are* you two talking about?"

Mac smiled. "You'd be a natural at special ops, Suzie.

We're going to do what you suggested and blow up the building.''

"The building we're sitting in?" she asked, incredulous.

"The very same."

"With us still in it?"

"Well, with you still in it. Tex and I will bail out just as it blows up. The blast will mess up the night vision of the snipers out there and cover our movements. They won't know if you're still inside or not."

"Pardon me, but won't the blast mess me up, too?"

Tex grinned. "Ahh, sister mine. Allow me to introduce you to one of the best explosives men in the United States Armed Forces. He's a veritable artist with C-4. He'll set the charges to blow away from our position. You'll be in a dead zone right in the middle of the blast."

Susan glanced at Mac. "Dead being the operative word. Sounds awfully dangerous to me."

He flashed a wolf-like grin at her. "Trust me, baby. The place will go up in flames around you, and you'll be able to stroll out of here as pretty as you please."

"Mac, you're terribly hurt. I don't want you roaming around the hallways trying to set charges with Ruala's men out there, too."

"That's my job. I know how to do it."

"Mac, you can hardly move. You show Tex and me where to set the charges and we'll do the work."

"She does have a point, Mac."

Mac glared at Tex. "I don't like it."

"Well, buddy, I've got the C-4 and you're outnumbered by Monroes, two to one."

Mac's swollen eyes still managed to narrow menacingly. "If anything happens to Susan, I'll break your neck."

Her brother laughed at Mac. "If anything happens to Susan, we'll see who breaks whose neck first. You ready to go?"

Mac drew in a slow, careful breath. "Yeah. Let's do it."

The next ten minutes were a nightmare. Susan rapidly thought better of her earlier bravado. Every little noise made her jump, and Mac was in no shape to be moving at all, let alone crawling around messing with explosives and detonators. Tex shot at something behind them once, but when Susan turned around to see what it was, he grabbed her shoulders and pushed her in the other direction.

"Don't look back," he bit out.

He must have killed someone. Although she was getting pretty immune to that idea at this point. Nevertheless, she spared herself the sight and followed Mac into the next stairwell. They high-tailed it back to the office they'd come from as soon as the wiring job was done.

Mac rested while Tex manhandled a half-dozen heavy filing cabinets onto their sides and created a bunker for her beneath their metal frames. Mac explained that the paper-filled cabinets would protect her from the dynamic over-pressure of the blast—the air recoiling back into the space where the explosion had just blown outward. It was mostly a precaution. When the C-4 blew, it would create a ring of fire well away from this office and give her plenty of time to get out.

Susan watched as Tex followed Mac's directions in laying a line of thin, rope-like explosive he called det cord around the window. Tex pulled a grenade off his belt and passed another one to Mac. "My last two flash-bangs," he announced.

Mac nodded.

"What's a flash-bang?" she asked.

Mac replied, "A grenade with very little explosives in it. It makes a bright flash and then a loud noise, but does practically no damage. Wrecks night vision like a charm."

"All set," Tex announced.

Mac helped Susan into her makeshift foxhole. His hand

trembled on her back. Clearly, he was at the very end of his formidable strength. She paused to look up at him.

"Are you sure about this, baby?" he asked.

She nodded firmly at him. "I'm sure, Mac."

He leaned down and kissed her briefly, gently. His lips were swollen against hers, and she tasted blood. As much as she wanted to fling her arms around him and never let go, she refrained. He was in too much pain already.

"Stay flat against the floor, Susan," Mac directed. "Heat and pressure from the explosion are going to be bouncing around over your head and will scramble your brain if they hit you."

"Lovely," she remarked dryly.

Mac flashed her a smile, but it was weak. Far too weak. "Just sit tight after the blast, and I'll come back for you as soon as the coast is clear."

She nodded her understanding.

His voice was starting to falter. "The filing cabinets are…dense enough to absorb…most of the shock. Just stay down, cover your ears, and…you'll be fine."

He had to get out of here. Now. She was *not* going to stand around twiddling her thumbs while his life slipped away.

"This better work, Mac," she declared. "Because if it doesn't, I'm taking your gun, shooting all those snipers and calling you an ambulance. That's all there is to it."

Mac nodded at Tex. "You heard the lady. Let's do it."

The two men took off their night-vision goggles and put their hands over their ears. Tex nodded at Mac. Susan watched his finger depress the button on the small remote control in his hand. There was a bright flash as the det cord blew a door-size hole in the wall. Tex jumped through it, tossing his flash-bang out in front of him as he went.

Mac paused just long enough in the gap to glance over his shoulder at her. He mouthed the words, "I love you."

And then he was gone.

There was another bright flash outside, and then she ducked down way back underneath the filing cabinets. She slapped her hands over her ears and screwed her eyes tightly shut.

First there was a jolt as the floor jumped beneath her. Then came a blindingly bright light through her eyelids, followed instantly by a deafening blast so loud it made her whole body ache. A ferocious wall of heat struck her, slamming her flat against the floor.

Chunks of plaster and concrete rained down on the cabinets above her, and the opening in front of her filled with dust and debris. She felt buried alive.

Mac knew she was here. He said he'd come back for her. He and Tex wouldn't let her burn alive. They'd be back. She repeated the words over and over in her head, a frenzied litany that kept her from losing her mind with fear. Barely.

The minutes ticked by and smoke began to creep through tiny openings in her shelter. "Oh, God." She was going to die in here, and Mac would never know how very much she loved him.

And then she heard a noise. Someone was tearing at the pile of debris in front of the opening. She scrambled forward and shoved on it with all her might. Her knee protested violently, but she ignored it. Wrecking the joint completely was preferable to burning up.

Slowly, with a reluctant cracking of wood, the pile in front of her gave way.

"Susan, are you okay?" came Mac's ragged voice.

She sobbed aloud in her relief. "I'm here," she cried.

A piece of drywall lifted away, and Mac's hand was there, reaching in for her. She grabbed it and held on for dear life as he dragged her clear of the mess. He wrapped his arms around her and held on like he was never going to let go. The gunfire and destruction around her were eerily reminiscent of that night ten years ago. She looped her arms around Mac's neck and buried her face against his chest. He'd come back for her. Saved her. Again.

"Let's go!" Mac shouted over the growing noise of the fire.

Susan jumped through the hole in the exterior wall and fell to the ground in an unceremonious heap. Mac landed beside her with a grunt of pain.

Tex spoke fast over her headset. "I got two of the snipers for sure, Mac. Had to try twice for the third. I hit him but I don't know if he's down or not."

"Roger," Mac replied tersely. "His last position?"

"Your two o'clock, one hundred yards. In that stand of trees."

"Got it. Stay down flat, Susan, while we look for this guy."

She didn't have to be told twice. She plastered herself against the ground. Within a few seconds, heat from the burning building blistered her back. She ventured a glance back behind her. "Uh, Mac, I think we'd better get out of here. The fire's about to come out the window."

Mac swore beside her. "There were more flammable materials in the construction than there should have been. We've got to move, Tex. We need about a hundred feet more to clear the secondary blast."

"Secondary blast?" Susan squeaked.

Mac nodded. "Yeah. The rest of the flammables in the building, like gasoline or cleaning solvents, are gonna blow soon the way this building's going up. That's why I came back for you before we took out the last sniper."

Great. Susan mimicked Mac as he inched forward on his belly, propelling himself with his elbows and toes. It was slow and painful going at best. But each yard put them farther away from the inferno blazing behind them. How

Mac managed to keep moving with his injuries eluded Susan.

The ground exploded in a puff of dust in front of Susan's face. She flinched, startled. "What was that?" she whispered.

"Don't move!" was Mac's sharp reply.

He propped himself up on his elbows beside her, and something hard rested across the back of her thighs. Cold metal jumped away from her flesh as Mac pulled the trigger once. The barrel of Mac's pistol touched her legs again, warm this time.

"Nice shot," Tex commented.

"Hello? What just happened?" she demanded.

Tex answered succinctly. "The last sniper took a shot at you and missed. Mac shot back. He didn't miss."

"Oh. Uh, thanks Mac."

"Anytime," he replied casually.

"Why don't we get out of here, boys and girls," Tex suggested, climbing to his feet with his rifle at the ready before him.

Mac and Susan stood up, as well, and headed for the same trees the sniper had been hiding in moments before. Even with her knee in open revolt, Susan had no trouble keeping up with Mac's shambling gait. She actually put her hand under his elbow to support him the last few yards.

The building behind them made an ominous whooshing noise and then sent a huge plume of smoke and flame shooting up into the night sky, lighting it as bright as day.

They reached the shadows of the trees, made all the darker for the light behind them. Mac stopped just inside the tree line and slid down a tree trunk to the ground. She hovered over him, hating the helpless feeling of not being able to do anything for him.

Tex materialized out of the darkness. He squatted beside them, talking quietly into a handheld radio. He put it away and said to Mac, "Doc's on his way. He'll be here in a minute."

Susan blinked. "Doc, as in Joe Rodriguez?"

Tex frowned at her. "How do you know Joe?"

"Doc, Dutch, Howdy and Mac have been at the ranch for the last week."

"Doing what?" Tex sounded surprised.

"Well, they weren't on vacation," Susan replied tartly.

"What the hell's been going on since I left?" Tex demanded.

"It's a long story. Once we get Mac taken care of, I'll tell you all about it."

"You bet you will," Tex growled. He looked back and forth between them. "Then, everything's all right between you two?"

Mac looked as uncomfortable as she felt at that one. She was relieved when he broke the silence that abruptly descended by saying, "Hey, Tex. Why don't you go do a quick body check while we wait for Doc?"

"Good idea. Don't go anywhere, old man."

Mac chuckled and then grabbed his side.

Susan winced for him. He must have some broken ribs the way he kept holding his side like that. "What's a body check?" she asked to distract him.

"You have a look at the bodies to verify they're dead."

"Oh." She was sorry she'd asked.

She jumped when Tex appeared beside her a couple minutes later. When had he learned to move so quietly? He'd bombed around the house like a minor tornado as a kid.

"Look who I found," Tex crowed.

Doc appeared beside her brother. She grabbed the medic's arm and all but shoved him at Mac. She waited anxiously while Doc examined him.

Finally the dark-haired man leaned back on his heels. "I

don't know how you did it, Mac, but you've got no life-threatening injuries that I can see. Your left forearm's broken in a really nasty location. Gonna need pins if I had to guess. You need an MRI to make sure you didn't rupture anything under those busted ribs, too. But you'll live.''

Susan sagged in relief.

Doc continued. ''You're going to need stitches over your right eye when we can get that swelling down a little. I'm going to tape your ribs right now, and that's going to hurt like hell's own fury, but you'll be able to breathe better after I do it. Beyond that, you need about two weeks of bed rest and a trip to the dentist to cap that cracked tooth you've got.''

Susan gasped. ''That jerk cracked your tooth?''

Mac grinned crookedly. ''Hey, at least the dude wasn't a professional interrogator. Otherwise, he'd have been pulling my teeth out.''

Doc nodded. ''Along with a dozen other interesting forms of torture you were lucky to avoid.''

Susan shuddered at the thought. She stayed out of the way while Doc taped Mac's ribs. How many times in their lives were she and Mac going to get this lucky? First she'd survived the surveillance van getting shot up, and now he'd survived being beaten half to death. Except this time Mac's injuries were her fault.

It was all her fault.

Chapter 17

Mac fidgeted in the white hospital bed, frustrated by his enforced stillness. Two weeks of bed rest had all but killed him. His arm still hurt under the cast where the pins had been inserted, but he'd been through worse. He looked out the window at the darkness outside. Somewhere out there was Susan. What was she doing tonight? Was she thinking of him? Counting herself lucky to have gotten rid of the bastard who messed up her life every time he got near her?

A deep voice spoke behind him. "Hey, you slacker. Enjoying lying around getting waited on hand and foot?"

Mac turned his head to look at Colonel Folly. "Hey."

"How are you feeling?"

Mac shrugged. He didn't want to talk about himself. "Any luck IDing Ruala's body?"

Colonel Folly grinned. "Yeah, we got the DNA report back today. That was Ramon Ruala you took out, all right."

Profound relief swept through him. Now Susan would be safe. "Thank God," he said aloud. He shifted his weight in the bed and flinched as his arm protested. His boss made a sympathetic grimace. Mac recalled that the colonel had broken his left forearm on his last mission, too.

Folly asked, "How's the arm? I heard the surgery went well."

"The docs say only time will tell if I'll be able to go out in the field again."

Colonel Folly sat down on the edge of the bed beside him. "If anybody can make it back, it's you. But don't sweat it either way. You know there's a standing offer for you to teach demolitions at the Special Forces schoolhouse."

Mac nodded. He'd been trying to prepare himself for the last two weeks to be put out to pasture like a broken-down old racehorse. Colonel Folly had made the transition all right after his leg got nuked, but the colonel had his new wife, Annie, to comfort him, too.

He had nobody.

If he really loved Susan, he'd walk away from her. Leave her the hell alone and quit wrecking her life every time he came into contact with her. God, it hurt, though.

The colonel's casual voice interrupted his misery. "I hear you've gone off your feed. Been a little out of it, recently. Anything bugging you that I can help with?"

Mac's gaze snapped to his boss's. They were much more than senior officer and subordinate. Much more than teammates. Much more even than friends. They'd been to hell and back together more times than he could count over the past eight years. "Are you asking as a colonel or as a friend?"

"Either. Both."

Mac closed his eyes against the searing pain that swept through him. He managed to grit out, "How's Susan doing?"

She'd been whisked into protective custody straight from

the site of the explosion. Nobody but the guys on Charlie Squad knew she was alive. There'd even been a mock funeral, which thankfully he'd been too laid up from his injuries to attend. In keeping with the story that she'd died in the fire, Tex had even worked out a deal for Frank Riverra to run the ranch permanently.

Colonel Folly shrugged. "She's about like you'd expect. Lonely. Scared. Putting on a brave front."

"Do me a favor," Mac asked abruptly. "Keep an eye out for her, will you? She's not nearly as tough as she tries to be. She could use a friend."

Colonel Folly answered quietly, "She doesn't need *me,* buddy. She needs *you.*"

Mac jolted. "Excuse me?"

Colonel Folly's steady, steel blue gaze met his. "You heard me."

Mac shook his head. "It's more complicated that that. I've hurt her too bad too many times. I don't…" He sighed. "I just can't. Let's leave it at that, okay?"

The colonel shrugged. "It's your life. But that reminds me. I've got something for you." He pulled out a flat, dark-blue box about the size of his palm.

Mac recognized the vinyl container. Military medals came in them. With his right hand he caught the box the colonel flipped at him. He opened the lid and looked inside to see a Purple Heart resting on a background of silver velvet.

"How many is that for you?" the colonel asked. "Four?"

"Yeah, I think so," Mac replied. "I don't keep count."

Colonel Folly grinned. "Congratulations and all that stuff."

Mac grinned, his mood momentarily lightened. They both knew they weren't in their profession for the medals. He snapped the lid closed.

"Seriously, that medal isn't just scrap iron," Colonel Folly commented. "It's your country's way of saying thank you. Lord knows we don't get much recognition in our line of work, but Uncle Sam knows you're out there and that you put your butt on the line to protect him." He added lightly, "Too bad I can't award medals to civilians. Lord knows, Susan deserves a couple of those, too."

Mac stared down at the box in his hand. A tiny fire lit in his gut and caught on. It grew and grew until it was a frenzied firestorm whipping through him. He looked up at his boss. "How fast can you get me out of here?"

The colonel didn't miss a beat. Clever bastard had probably pushed his buttons intentionally. "It's nearly midnight, but I expect I can have you out of here in thirty minutes."

"Make it twenty." Mac sat up briskly and swung his feet over the side of the bed. "Where are my damn clothes?" he growled, spurred on by the sudden flames of hope raging inside him.

Colonel Folly laughed. "I'll go pull the appropriate strings while you track down your pants. And, Mac?"

He glanced up at his boss.

"Ferrare sent his reply to our note. We got it today."

"What did it say?" Mac held his breath, tense.

"He said to bring it on. He bought Susan's death. She's safe."

Mac grinned. "Make it ten minutes, sir."

Susan tossed and turned, the bed sheets hot and clingy. And then she heard it. A thump downstairs. *Somebody was in the house.* Darkness enveloped her, and her room was cloaked in menacing shadows, just like the night this whole nightmare started. Her bedside clock said it was a little after 1:00 a.m.

Her pulse jumped and fear choked her. Had Ferrare's men come for her? Had they managed to kill the FBI agents outside and get into her home? She considered creeping into her bathroom, locking the door and hiding in the bath-tub. But something reckless inside her didn't care if she lived or died anymore. Taking risks had ceased to matter. Mac was gone. Her heart was broken for good this time. So what if she ought to call Charlie Squad right now instead of investigating for herself?

She got out of bed and opened the bedroom door. She paused and listened but heard nothing. Easing down the stairs, she didn't see anything unusual. A dull knife of loss stabbed her heart anew. How she wished for Mac's strong, confident presence right now. He'd make short work of an intruder in her house.

She lurched as a shadow rose up in front of the fireplace. "Don't move," she ordered. "I've got a gun and I'll shoot."

"Don't be silly, Suzie. That's your finger pointing at me."

She exhaled sharply. "Mac Conlon, one of these days I'm going to shoot you for real if you keep scaring me like that."

Her heart raced like a runaway horse. Why was he here? *Did she dare hope?*

An awkward silence fell between them.

"Come sit down, Suzie. We need to talk."

She sat gingerly on the edge of the sofa while he added wood to the fire he'd just built. He sat down close enough to look deeply into her eyes in the fledgling firelight.

"How are you holding up?" he asked.

"I'm fine. It's just that—" the words burst out of her in a rush "—I've been so worried about you, Mac. It was so hard being here alone. Nobody knows if Ferrare bought my death or not, and we don't even know for sure that Ruala's dead, and then I lost you again—"

Somehow she ended up in his arms, her face buried

against his chest, while sobs shook her shoulders. His big, capable hands rubbed her back gently while she cried it all out.

"Whoa, there, sweetheart," he murmured into her hair. "I came to tell you the DNA results came back today. Ruala's dead. And, we heard from Ferrare. He bought your fake death. You can go back to your real life now."

She smiled up at him in huge relief. And then burst into tears again.

He rode out the second round of shoulder-heaving sobs with aplomb and then said, "Things can't be all that bad. We both made it through the op, didn't we?"

She nodded, mortified. She couldn't believe she'd fallen apart like that.

"Better?" he murmured.

"Yes. Except I have the hiccups now."

She felt his smile against her temple. "Want me to scare them out of you?"

"No, thank you," she answered shakily.

He set her away from him and she looked up into his eyes, which glowed in the flickering light. Just looking at him nourished her soul. How was she ever going to survive without him?

"I also came to apologize to you, Susan. I never had the guts to do it after the shooting ten years ago. But I'm going to try to get it right this time."

She frowned. She didn't want any apologies from him. She wanted his heart! Her hopes fell, dashed against the rocky, unscalable cliffs of his damned honor.

He said soberly, "There aren't words to describe how bad I feel about what you've had to go through. If I'd done my job right ten years ago, none of this would have happened. I just want you to know that I'm truly sorry. I mean that from the bottom of my heart."

She closed her eyes against the anguish of listening to

him walk away from her again. He might not be doing it with his feet, but he was closing off his heart and shutting down his soul before her very eyes.

"I brought something for you," he said quietly. He held out a flat box that looked black in the yellow firelight.

"What is it?" she asked as she took it.

"Open it up and see."

It was a military medal. In the shape of a heart. She looked up at him questioningly.

"It's the Purple Heart I was awarded for the mission to save you."

She was vaguely familiar with Purple Hearts. They had something to do with getting hurt or shot. "What's it for?"

"Soldiers get one each time they're wounded in combat."

She looked from the medal to him. "Why are you giving it to me?" she asked, confused.

"Because nobody else is going to thank you for the sacrifice you've made for your country. For identifying Ruala and making the call to us. For agreeing to testify against him. For going through the ordeal of the last couple weeks. And for being willing to give up your friends and family for weeks, months or years if Ruala got away from us. I figure after all that, you've earned a medal."

"Why this one?" she asked, still confused.

"Because you were wounded a hell of a lot worse than I was by all of this."

"How can you say that? Carlos nearly beat you to death. I got a limp and a scar out of it. But you—" Her voice broke. "Colonel Folly told me you may not be able to work with Charlie Squad anymore because of your broken arm."

She took a wobbly breath that very nearly broke over into a sob. "God, Mac, it's all my fault."

The words came tumbling out, and she couldn't stop them. "I'm so sorry. I never meant to cost you your career.

I know how much it means to you. I was so stupid to run out of here when I knew Ruala was coming soon...."

His finger pressed gently against her lips.

"Suzie. Stop. I don't blame you for what happened to me. I made my own choices, and this is the price I paid. The important thing is we both got out alive. Ruala's dead and Ferrare believes you're dead. The mission was a success. Except for the part where I broke your heart again."

She heard his words of absolution, his lips granting her forgiveness, but it meant nothing to her. Her own guilt was too overwhelming to be fixed by any simple statement of exoneration.

And then it hit her. "Oh my God," she breathed. She gazed at him in dawning understanding. The revelation that rolled over her took her breath away. *Dear God, let it not have come too late.*

"What?" he asked sharply, instantly on full combat alert. He looked quickly all around the room.

"I get it now," she gasped.

He frowned. "You get what?"

"Why you spent all those years thinking you hadn't taken care of me like you should have." He looked confused but she rushed onward. "Is this how you felt after the surveillance van got shot up? Like nothing I could say would ever make it right?" She probably wasn't making a darn bit of sense. She must sound like she'd lost her mind.

He stared at her closely. And then he nodded slowly. "Yeah. That's exactly how I felt."

"Oh, Mac, when will you ever listen to me about that night?"

He frowned. "I'm listening now."

She grasped his hands in desperation. She spoke slowly, willing him to really *hear* what she had to say. "If you hadn't been outside the van and managed to back off Ruala with your suppression fire as fast as you did, I'd have died for sure. You *saved* my life that night!''

He stared at her hard. Deep in the back of his eyes, she saw the hard wall around his heart dissolve a little.

"Do you hate me for running out of the house because I was upset that you called me a cripple?" she pressed, frantic to make him see the truth.

He jolted. "Hell, no! I never should have said that. I was frustrated. I understand why it upset you. Why would I hate you for that?"

She stared deep into his eyes, searching for comprehension in them. "Don't you see? I never hated you, either."

He frowned. "But—"

She interrupted him. "Am I right that, at some level, part of why you came to the ranch on this mission was to get my forgiveness for whatever wrong you perceived you'd done to me?"

He thought about it for a second. Comprehension broke across his features. He nodded slowly.

"When I saw you tonight," she continued, "my first thought was to hope I could get you to forgive me for wrecking your arm and your career."

She leaned forward, her body thrumming with need for him to understand. "But, Mac. Neither one of us needs to forgive the other. What we both have to do is forgive ourselves."

His hands squeezed hers painfully tight. "Suzie." His voice was hoarse and he paused to clear it roughly. "Suzie, are you telling me that, after everything that's happened, you don't blame me for the things that have happened to you?"

"That's what I've been trying to tell you ever since you got here! I chose to get in that surveillance van ten years ago, and I chose to be bait this time around to lure out

Ruala. What really counts is how *you* feel about you. In here.'' She touched his chest over his heart.

He frowned as if he wasn't quite sure he bought it.

She pressed the point. ''You said it before. We each make our own choices. Life throws us all curve balls we don't expect, and we just have to deal with them and move on as best we can.''

He looked at her a long time. The fire hissed quietly while he considered her words. He ran a hand through his hair, a sure sign that he was struggling with some disturbing thought.

Panic hovered close to the surface, just beneath her skin. Her future, their future, hung on what he was thinking. ''Talk to me, Mac,'' she urged.

''Dammit, Susan. Every time I come into your life I bring you disaster. If I were going to do the right thing by you, to act on that sense of obligation you keep accusing me of being lost in, I'd get up right now and walk out of your life forever.''

''Because you love me,'' she stated flatly.

''Yes. I love you enough to leave, so you'll be safe from any further harm from me.

She whispered past her constricted throat, ''Love is never safe, Mac. It's the biggest risk of all. And whether you like it or not, I love you. I've already taken the risk. Leaving me won't change that. It'll only cause me pain.''

He turned his anguished gaze on her. His words sounded literally torn out of his throat. ''I don't want to leave you, dammit. I want to get down on my knees right now and beg you to marry me. To ask you to spend the rest of your life with me and make babies with me and grow old together.''

He buried his head in his hands.

She waited him out, praying he'd work it through.

Finally he looked up again. ''I can't be noble any more.

I can't do the right thing and walk away again. It's killing me."

A tiny, little warm feeling started way down in her toes and started to grow upward. "You don't have to walk away to be noble, Mac. Sometimes staying is the courageous choice."

He visibly absorbed her words into himself. Something relaxed around his shoulders like a weight was lifting from them. He spoke carefully. "I don't know how to convince you that I want to take care of you because I love you, not because I'm hung up on some twisted sense of duty."

It was her turn to stare in shock.

"Do you really mean that?" she whispered.

"God, yes! I love you. Just for you. No strings attached, just the way you asked me to a couple weeks ago."

Her skin started tingling and a flush heated her cheeks.

"I can't lie to you," he said low, each word ripped from his gut. "I won't ever completely forgive myself for any part I've had in causing you a single second of pain. That's just the way I am. But it's *not* the basis of my feelings for you. Can you accept that?"

The warm feeling in her heart transformed into blinding light, shining like the sun, illuminating her soul from the inside out.

"Mac," she said carefully, "I'll never forget watching you take that beating for me. I'll never forgive myself completely for it. I'll carry that memory around with me till the day I die. But—" she took a deep breath and then plunged ahead "—I believe it's possible for a relationship to have its scars and not only survive but be strong and wonderful and beautiful."

He reached out and touched the scar on her neck lightly. "Just like people," he murmured.

She reached up out of habit to hide her scar.

Mac intercepted her hand and drew it to his mouth, kissing her fingertips. "Baby, I even love your scar and your wrecked knee. I love everything about you."

"I love your scars, too," she answered quietly. She touched the place over his heart lightly. "I especially admire the ones in here. But can *you* live with them?"

A slow smile broke across his face. "Yeah. I think I can."

And then he slid off the couch and took a knee at her feet. "Susan Monroe, I need you worse than life itself. I want to spend the rest of my life healing your heart. Marry me. Please."

Tears filled her eyes as the light overflowed her soul, bursting forth in a brilliant glow of love around them that would never dim. "Only if you'll let me heal your heart, too, Mac."

She flung herself into his arms, toppling them both over onto the floor. He hugged her close, cushioning and absorbing their fall, protecting her the way he always did.

She sprawled on top of him, alarmed. "I didn't hurt your arm, did I?"

"Who the hell cares about my arm?" he growled. "Are you going to marry me or not?"

"Oh, yes, Mac. Yes, I'll marry you!"

And the healing for both of them began.

* * * * *

If you enjoyed what you just read,
then we've got an offer you can't resist!

Take 2 bestselling
love stories FREE!
Plus get a FREE surprise gift!

Clip this page and mail it to Silhouette Reader Service™

IN U.S.A.
3010 Walden Ave.
P.O. Box 1867
Buffalo, N.Y. 14240-1867

IN CANADA
P.O. Box 609
Fort Erie, Ontario
L2A 5X3

YES! Please send me 2 free Silhouette Intimate Moments® novels and my free
surprise gift. After receiving them, if I don't wish to receive anymore, I can return
the shipping statement marked cancel. If I don't cancel, I will receive 6 brand-new
novels every month, before they're available in stores! In the U.S.A., bill me at the
bargain price of $4.24 plus 25¢ shipping and handling per book and applicable
sales tax, if any*. In Canada, bill me at the bargain price of $4.99 plus 25¢ shipping
and handling per book and applicable taxes**. That's the complete price and a
savings of at least 10% off the cover prices—what a great deal! I understand that
accepting the 2 free books and gift places me under no obligation ever to buy any
books. I can always return a shipment and cancel at any time. Even if I never buy
another book from Silhouette, the 2 free books and gift are mine to keep forever.

245 SDN DZ9A
345 SDN DZ9C

Name	(PLEASE PRINT)	
Address	Apt.#	
City	State/Prov.	Zip/Postal Code

* Terms and prices subject to change without notice. Sales tax applicable in N.Y.
** Canadian residents will be charged applicable provincial taxes and GST.
All orders subject to approval. Offer limited to one per household and not valid to
current Silhouette Intimate Moments® subscribers.
® are registered trademarks owned and used by the trademark owner and or its licensee.

INMOM04   ©2004 Harlequin Enterprises Limited

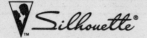